**PLAYERS IN A DEADLY GAME OF
NUCLEAR BLACKMAIL—A GAME
NO ONE CAN WIN!**

THE AFRICAN PRESIDENT—fanatical, ruthless, unpredictable . . . the dream of paradise for his people had become a nightmare of horror and violence. . . .

THE AMERICAN PRESIDENT—he had never learned to lead, only to follow public opinion. . . .

THE SECRETARY OF STATE—chosen because she is a woman, replaced by a man in time of crisis . . . her beauty and brains could be a strong weapon—in the hands of the enemy. . . .

THE SUPER SPY—on a dangerous mission to disarm the missile . . . no one suspects he serves more than one master. . . .

THE GREEK TYCOON—the wealthiest man in the world . . . he'll do anything to get money and power . . . even arm a madman with . . .

THE THOR OPTION

THE THOR OPTION

Mark Benassi

A DELL BOOK

Published by
Dell Publishing Co., Inc.
1 Dag Hammarskjold Plaza
New York, New York 10017

Dell ® TM 681510, Dell Publishing Co., Inc.

ISBN: 0-440-18621-8

Printed in the United States of America

First printing—April 1980

THE
THOR
OPTION

The President of the United States, Wendell P. Henderson, sat down at his desk at ten o'clock in the morning. An English muffin had settled in his stomach and two cups of coffee had him ready for work. He casually picked up a ball-point pen and held it between his thumb and forefinger when his secretary burst through the door.

"Mr. President!"

The secretary held a slip of paper in his hand and fluttered it in an arc that landed squarely in front of Henderson. He placed the pen back on the desk and lightly picked up the canary-yellow telegram. The atmosphere in the room slowly tensed.

"Jesus Christ," Henderson said with the paper still in his hands.

"What do you want me to do?" the secretary said.

Henderson stared at the paper a moment, then closed his eyes. He drew a deep breath and let it out slowly.

"Goddamnit," he said softly.

"Sir?" the secretary said.

Henderson looked up. "Does Marjorie know?"

"I think so," the secretary said.

"I want to see her," he said.

"Yes, sir."

"Macklin?"

"I don't know."

"I want to see him too."

"Yes."

"And get Matulo." Henderson's voice was soft and steady.

"Yes." His secretary turned and hurried out of the office.

"And Simmons," Henderson called out as his secretary reached the door. The secretary stopped, turned, nodded, and let the door swing shut behind him. "And nobody else."

Henderson picked the telegram back up and swiveled in his chair. His right elbow rested on his desk and his eyes bored into the little scrap of paper as though there was something he'd missed, something that should have been there that wasn't, something that wasn't there that should have been. His eyes finally focused on one group of words and lingered there for long moments: "to be launched at an unspecified, heavily populated region of the world at an unspecified time unless conditions are met."

First Day

"Ms. Timkins is here."

Henderson looked up from the cable. His left hand, still grasping the yellow paper, moved up and he glanced at his watch. His right hand moved to the side and touched a button. "Send her in." He swiveled in his chair and faced the door as it began to open. A handsome woman in her early forties wearing a light blue tailored suit was stepping into the office. Her brown eyes looked mystified.

"Wendell," she said in a firm contralto and then seemed lost for words.

"Have a seat," Henderson said.

"Is this really happening?" she said as she approached the President's desk.

"You too?" he said.

A smile broke on her face and faded. "I guess it is," she said, and sat down.

"Maybe it's a joke," Henderson said. "Matulo's crazy enough . . . I think."

"He is," she said.

"Is he crazy enough for it not to be a joke?"

"He's that, too," she said.

"Then," he said, "if I understand you correctly, it might be a hoax, and then again it might not be."

Marjorie gave him a quizzical look. "Are you trying to be funny?"

Henderson pushed himself away from his desk and stood up. He pressed the palms of his hands together and turned to the side. His face had a disgusted look and he shook his head slowly from side to side. "Why?" he said.

Marjorie had the same quizzical look. "I don't understand."

Henderson lifted his hands and stepped away from his desk. "Why?" he said to himself and then turned back to Marjorie. "What's his motivation?"

"Money, power . . ." she said. "I don't understand your thinking."

"Damn it," he said. "This is the stupidest, craziest thing I've ever heard of. How does Matulo expect to get anything out of it? What does he expect to get out of it? I just can't understand it—it's too foreign, too alien, too weird."

"It could happen and it did," she said. "What more do we have to know—really."

"Mr. Simmons is here."

Henderson stepped back to his desk and touched his intercom. "Send him in," he said.

Marjorie turned her head to face the door. In a moment a distinguished-looking man in his fifties stepped into the room. From his meticulously shined black Oxfords to his solid-colored tie and shirt collar that lay just right, he projected the air of a man who liked to pay attention to details.

"That was quick," Henderson said.

"I left before you called," Simmons said in a well-modulated baritone.

"When'd you . . . ?" Henderson said. "Never mind. Who else knows?"

"Not many," Simmons said as he approached Marjorie. "I knew you'd want to see me." He nodded to Marjorie and sat down next to her.

Henderson nodded his head and sat back down behind his desk. "What have you got to tell us?"

"It's very possible he's got the missiles," Simmons said. "We don't have any agents in Toganda, however, so it will probably take a while before I can report anything concrete."

"What do you know for a fact, though?" Henderson said.

"There are nuclear reactors in the country," Simmons said, "and there are people left there who would be able to build a small warhead."

"But what, specifically, do you know about this?" Henderson said.

"As I said, we don't have an agent in Toganda, but I've already taken steps to find the right individual and we should be getting him into the country very shortly," Simmons said.

"Then what you're really saying is that you don't know a damn thing," Henderson said.

Not a single involuntary facial movement disturbed Simmons's facade. "We're proceeding as fast as we can with the resources and requirements necessary to a successful operation," he said. "We should begin to produce tangible results within a very short length of time."

"Before ten o'clock?" Henderson said.

"I don't think we can produce anything significant in that time," Simmons said. "I'm hoping, however, that we will be able to place an experienced agent in the country by that time."

"Excellent," Henderson said, but the sarcasm was lost on the CIA Director.

"What I'd like to know is how he got those missiles in the first place," Marjorie said.

"Isn't that jumping the gun?" Henderson said. "I'd like to know for certain whether he even has them."

"I know you know Matulo better than that," Marjorie said. "We can kid about it as much as we like, but Matulo has never made a threat that he didn't back up. He may be crazy but he isn't stupid."

"He's never done anything this big before," Henderson said.

"Nobody has," Marjorie said. "That's all the more reason why we should believe him."

"Okay," Henderson said. "We assume he has what he says he does. Why is it so important that the first thing we find out is how he got them?"

"A minute ago you asked about his motivations," she said.

"Just talking," Henderson said. "This is too incredible."

"My gut feeling is that if we knew how he got them, we'd be able to understand his strategy," she said.

"Fine," Henderson said. "An excellent thought, but let's concentrate on something we can handle." He looked to Simmons. "We'll find out in due time how he got them." Simmons nodded his head and Henderson turned back to Marjorie. "Meanwhile we're going to have to decide what to do with his demands."

"What's the possibility of the missile being intercepted?" Marjorie said.

"I know it's not good," Henderson said. "Macklin should be showing up here sometime. He'll know more about that, but I know the odds are not going to be in our favor."

"Then there's no question," Marjorie said. "We meet them."

"Just like that," Henderson said.

"What else?" she said.

Henderson pursed his lips, lowered his head, and closed his eyes. "Son of a bitch," he said softly.

"Whatever the demands are," she said, "there's no way we can risk other people's lives. We can play tough all we want and all we're going to do is lose, no matter what Matulo has up his sleeve. This is no Cuban Missile Crisis, and you know it, Wendell."

"General Macklin is here."

Henderson lifted his head and reached for his intercom. "Send him in."

Marjorie and Simmons turned to the door. General Macklin, head of the Joint Chiefs of Staff, strode into the room. Tall and husky, his muscles nearly rippled through the fabric of his custom-tailored uniform. "Gentlemen," he said, and nodded to Marjorie.

Marjorie gave him a polite smile and said, "General."

Macklin briskly made his way toward the desk and shot his body into a straight-backed chair. "I can put fifty thousand men in Toganda within six hours," he said.

Henderson put his right hand to his forehead and leaned way back in his chair. "General, I'm going to forget you said that."

"This is the last straw," Macklin said. "When are we going to stop playing games with these damn . . ." He worked his lips silently. ". . . two-bit countries that think they can control the world. I could have that country so damn saturated with men by twenty-two hundred hours they wouldn't even be able to find that damn button or whatever the hell it is they intend to push or throw or whatever. Damn it, I'm sick of this. The strongest country in the world and some goddamn pipsqueak nigger in a uniform with a bunch of medals he made himself is trying to tell us what to do. Just give me the word and those people are going to learn real fast who they're playing around with."

Henderson stared into Macklin's face. "What the hell is the matter with you?"

Macklin's face deepened a shade of red. "What's the matter with me?" he said. "I am upset and I am mad. I am tired of always having to give in to all these damn little dictators."

"What are you talking about?" Henderson said.

"I'm talking about the status of this country in a world gone crazy."

"General," Marjorie said, "have you found out how those missiles got out of our hands?"

Macklin turned his head to the Secretary of State. "No," he said. "And that's another thing. How the hell is the Army supposed to maintain any kind of security when we can't even recruit the kind of people we need?"

Henderson raised his voice a touch. "Are we missing two S-27's?"

Macklin jerked his head back to Henderson. "No!" he said.

"Then where'd Matulo get them?" Henderson said.

"He stole the plans, damn it," Macklin said. "That's how he got them. That's the only way he could have got them. It's all those damn contractors. They don't know how to handle security worth a good goddamn and that's why we're in the situation we're in now. I knew this was going to happen someday."

"We still don't even know for sure if Matulo really has them," Simmons said calmly.

"That doesn't make a damn bit of difference," Macklin said. "The threat's enough for me."

"General," Henderson said, "can we safely intercept the missile?"

"Not if it's an S-27," Macklin said. "At best we might have a fifty-fifty chance. Why the hell do you think we developed it the way we did?"

"Just checking," Henderson said.

"I've already ordered a general alert," Macklin said. "We'll spot it right away but I wouldn't bet on bringing it down." Macklin's features changed subtly. The tension in his face disappeared and he looked intently toward Henderson. "My idea is to not even attempt intercepting the missile during the test launch. This will prevent revealing our inability to defend against it. After the launch you can make a statement that we have a secret defense against it, but that we didn't want to use it for fear of revealing what that is. That way Matulo, and the rest of the world, won't know if we're bluffing or not."

"Are you serious?" Marjorie said.

Macklin gave her a condescending glance. "Of course I'm serious."

Henderson rubbed his face in his hands. "I would like to know how someone like Matulo could steal the plans from a score of contractors and have the capability of manufacturing two of those missiles. I'm no engineer, but I do know they're loaded with microelectronics."

"Which can be put together from standard parts available from a half-dozen different companies in a score of countries," Macklin said. "The software is everything in that system."

"But why Matulo's, then?" Henderson said. "Why not the Russians, the Chinese—anyone but Matulo."

"Exactly my point," Marjorie said. "How did he get them?"

Henderson nodded his head slowly and thoughtfully. "Maybe you're right," he said. "Maybe that is the place to begin."

"Just because Matulo has the missiles doesn't necessarily mean that he was the one who stole the plans," Simmons said. "The Russians, or the Chinese, could be behind it, or some terrorist group, possibly even one operating from this country."

"But who?" Marjorie said. "And why?"

Simmons carefully draped his right leg over his left knee. "That's a question that will eventually have to be answered, but it will probably take some time. As I said before . . ."

"Yes," Henderson said. "We heard you before." He lifted his head and looked over the three people sitting in front of him. "I think that's enough meeting for now. There aren't enough facts to do anything with and there's probably a hundred people trying to get to talk to me right now and I'm going to have to make some statement to the press. These cables have been sent all over the world, supposed to have been anyway, but all we can do is wait for the test launch."

"What about my idea?" Macklin said.

"What?" Henderson said.

"About not attempting an interception," Macklin said.

"Oh," Henderson said. "I'll tell you later."

"Shall I continue to work on getting an agent into Toganda?" Simmons said.

"Yes," Henderson said. "No, wait. I want a complete report on who you're sending there first. I want to know exactly what's happening and who's doing what."

"Of course," Simmons said, and stood up.

"What about foreign governments?" Marjorie said. "What shall we tell them?"

"I don't know yet," Henderson said. "Do what you think is best for the moment. I'll leave it up to you. I don't want to talk to anyone right now. I have to think this out."

Macklin was already to the door. He left the room and was followed immediately by Simmons. Marjorie lingered behind and waited for the door to close before she turned around. "Wendell," she said.

"What is it?" he said.

"I know this looks like a disaster," she said.

"To say the least," he said.

"But it could turn out to be one terrific break for you," she said.

"How's that?" he said.

"Out of adversity . . ." she said.

"Oh," he said, and smiled for a moment.

She gave him a quick smile that was meant to be reassuring and left the room.

The President of Chile, Dr. Julio Marquez, was home in bed recovering from the flu when an aide notified him of the Togandan missile threat.

"They what?" was Dr. Marquez's first comment. He then pushed himself up in his bed.

"Here," the aide said, and handed the President a cablegram.

Marquez reached to his bedside table and grabbed a tissue with his left hand while he grabbed the cable with his right. As he read he wiped his nose, then handed the cable back to his aide and tossed the tissue into a wastepaper basket. "Does the Foreign Minister know about this?"

"Yes, sir."

"Tell him I want to see him," Marquez said. "Here. Immediately."

"Yes, sir," the aide said, and quickly left the President's bedroom.

When the aide had left, Marquez threw the covers on his bed back and felt his head beginning to clear.

The Foreign Minister, Pedro Anquierro, arrived within the hour, carrying a slim attaché case. Marquez was waiting for him in his study. Anquierro placed his case on the President's desk and opened it. "I brought this material on Toganda," he said.

Marquez nodded. "Good. Do we have any agents there?"

"None inside the country," Anquierro said.

"In the area?"

"Yes."

"Have you heard anything?"

"Not as yet," Anquierro said, "but we're trying to get in touch with him. This has come as a total surprise to everyone as far as I can tell."

Marquez nodded. "We have to find out how he got those missiles, if he really has them—and I'll bet he does—and if *he* can get them, we will too."

"There are two agents on their way there now," Anquierro said.

"Good," Marquez said. He reached for a glass of wine and took a sip. "I want you to contact the United States. Find out what their position is. If they want a statement from us, tell them we're in the process of preparing one."

"Are you going to call a Cabinet meeting?"

Marquez shook his head. "No, not yet. I want to think about this some more, because the more I think about it, the more possibilities reveal themselves to me. There is some great potential here and I intend to grab ahold of it."

"How do you mean?"

"One of the smallest countries in the world is openly and directly challenging the United States, and not just with rhetoric or the threat of cutting off a natural resource. This is something entirely different."

"I agree," Anquierro said, "if he really has the missiles and they're capable of doing what he says."

"Yes, yes, of course," Marquez said. "Of course what he's threatening has to be real, but somehow I know it is, and yet we can't go on that alone. That's why I've called Dr. Cavalho. If anyone does, he'll know the capabilities of that missile. When I've talked with him, I should be ready to call that Cabinet meeting. Meanwhile, I want you to get in contact with Matulo."

"I'll do my best," Anquierro said. "It won't be easy."

"Everyone else will probably be having the same problem."

"And when I do?"

"Just tell him I want to talk," Marquez said. "That's all."

"I'll see what I can do." He reached into the case and pulled a folder out of it. "I'll leave this with you," he said as he handed the folder to Marquez.

Marquez had a tissue in his hands. "Just leave it on the desk," he said. "And let me know the minute you contact Matulo."

Clarence Bishop, thirty-seven years old, male, Caucasian, degree in engineering, Navy veteran, and president of the Sons of Patrick Henry was running a lathe in his model-making shop when he realized that the music he'd been listening to through an overhead speaker had stopped. He strained to catch what was being said, couldn't, and switched his machine off.

". . . in Antarctica. The remaining missile will be launched at an unspecified target at an unspecified time unless the United States meets the Togandan demands, which will be announced sometime shortly after the demonstration launch. We repeat this special news bulletin. President Amdida Matulo of the Republic of Toganda earlier today announced that he has in his possession two Thor S-27 Multi-Purpose Cruise Missiles. These missiles are capable of being launched from any point on the planet and being dropped on any point within a radius of fifty meters. President Matulo has announced that at ten o'clock tonight, Eastern Standard Time, the first of his two missiles will be launched at a specified target in Antarctica to prove that he has them and that they are indeed what he claims they are. The other missile will be launched at an unspecified, heavily populated area of the world at an unspecified time unless certain demands are met. Those demands have not yet been announced. Stay tuned for further details."

Clarence walked solemnly to his workbench and turned off the radio just as the first bars of "Day By Day" began. He felt a thrill run through his body. The familiar tools of his meticulously clean and organized shop suddenly stood out in sharp tones of metallic gray and oily yellow. For years he'd waited for an opportunity to present itself, an opportunity to demonstrate to his country, the country he loved so dearly, that it was being run by a bunch of jackasses. He sat down on a stool in front of his workbench, looked wistfully at his machine tools, and began to dream and plan. He was fully aware of what the S-27 was and what it was capable of and that it was, supposedly, the most closely guarded military weapon in the country and now one of the most insignificant countries in the world had two of them. To Clarence the news bulletin he'd just heard had come as an omen, and he spent the better part of an hour just sitting and dreaming of what it could mean to him. When he was finished dreaming, he turned the radio back on and caught the tail end of Henderson's press conference.

Henderson drummed his fingers on his desk. His tie was pulled open and his top button undone, revealing a tuft of black hair with a touch of gray. "I shouldn't have given that press conference," he said.

"That's your strong point," Marjorie Timkins said.

"Maybe."

"Don't start second-guessing," she said. "It doesn't fit you."

"No," he said. "It doesn't." He stopped drumming and looked up at Marjorie.

"Your image was as good as ever," she said.

"You think so?" He drummed his fingers once—*ta-tarump*. "I can hardly believe the way I'm talking. I can't remember ever feeling this unsettled about anything in my life and I don't even know for a fact if there's anything there."

"I feel the same way," she said. "It's like I've known this was coming for a long time."

"Exactly," he said. "I just know he's got those missiles and I don't know what the hell to do about it."

"I know," she said.

"I have to see beyond this moment and I don't see anything."

"I understand," she said.

"Blaine and some others are going to be here any time and I'm going to have to say something."

"Talk generalities."

"If I only weren't so sure he had them," he said absently.

"As I see it," Marjorie said, "the important thing is not to get tough. I had a short conversation with Guidy-Livron and that's the general impression I left with him and he seemed to be satisfied. People are afraid of that missile."

Henderson chuckled. "That idiot Macklin and his

secret defense. I'd like to take that damn missile and shove it . . ."

"Just keep Blaine on your side," she said. "He can keep the House in line."

Henderson nodded his head. "What do you think of Simmons's 'man from Chicago'?"

"He's got the credentials . . ." she said.

"But?"

"You know what I think of Simmons," she said.

"He knows how to stay out of trouble," he said.

"Except for this," she said.

"Except for this." He shuffled through some papers. "Any thoughts about how Matulo got the missiles?"

"Only that I'm convinced that he couldn't have done it on his own," she said. "I just can't believe he'd have the money or the people to do it."

"What do you think, then?" he said. "The Russians? The Chinese?"

"I can't see the advantage," she said.

"How about making us look like asses?" he said.

"Unrealistic," she said. "Let's face it—eventually we're going to find out, and who's going to want to be known as the country that put a weapon like that in the hands of someone like Matulo?"

"Again assuming it's not a hoax."

"What's the advantage to Matulo then?" she said.

"Recognition," he said. "We already know the man's as crazy as they come."

"Flying a pink-and-green jet is one thing," she said. "Terrifying the world is another."

"It's getting him a lot of attention," Henderson said. "Think of this. Ten o'clock goes by and nothing happens. Matulo releases a statement to the effect that, while this was all a hoax, if it had been real, he would have been able to control the strongest country in the world."

"And give a lot of other people a hell of an idea," she said.

"Which one of them will try to make a reality."

"And it's the same situation all over again, but someone else has the limelight and Matulo is forgotten."

"And in the meantime we get the pressure to get rid of all our S-27's."

"Which makes no difference anyway, because someone else will just build the same thing," she said.

"Which leaves us where?" he said.

"Back with Matulo," she said. "I think the point is that, no matter what happens at ten o'clock, we have to assume he has the missiles until we know for an absolute fact that he doesn't. If it were someone else, I might think differently, but not with Matulo."

Henderson cracked a smile. "I agree," he said. "I agree. No matter how many incomplete circles of logic we go through, that's where we have to end."

"Plus the repercussions of the S-27 itself," she said.

"What's that?"

"Just that," she said. "There's more to this than handling some little African country."

"The big break you mentioned earlier?" he said.

"It could be," she said.

"Like SALT?" he said.

"Partly," she said. "I was thinking of the developing countries in general."

"Possibly," he said. "It's crossed my mind."

"There's a possibility for an initiative, I think," she said.

"Maybe," he said. "Only, how do we get from here to there?"

"I don't know," she said.

Henderson nodded his head and glanced at his watch. "Blaine should be here any minute. Want to stay?"

"Yes," she said and nodded her head. She put her hand to her cheek and ran a finger along her lower lip. "Wendell."

"What?" he said.

"Thanks," she said.

"What do you mean?" he said.

"For talking to me this way," she said.

"I don't understand," he said and shook his head.

"I always thought you gave me this job for the votes," she said, "but you're really listening to me."

"You mean about this?" he said. "Nothing's happened yet."

"I know," she said, "but it's a crisis and here we are talking. I mean, I know I haven't determined any decisions, but that's not the point. See what I mean?"

"I guess so," he said, looking slightly confused.

"I know it must sound silly," she said, "but I appreciate it and I won't let you down."

"I never thought you would," he said.

There was a brief, awkward silence broken by the intercom. "Congressman Blaine is here."

Henderson reached to his side and touched a button. "Send him in."

Marjorie shifted in her chair so she could see the door. Representative Milton Blaine (R. Illinois), a tall, heavyset man with an artfully molded patch of transplanted brown hair on his head, walked into the room and was followed by an aide with a couple of chairs in his hands.

"Wendell," Blaine said in a gravelly voice as he approached the President's desk. "How you feeling?"

Henderson was busily buttoning his collar and adjusting his tie. "As well as can be expected," he said.

"Ms. Timkins," Blaine said, nodding to Marjorie.

"Congressman," Marjorie said with a friendly smile.

Blaine shifted a chair in front of Henderson's desk and sat down. "The others should be here shortly," he said. "I wanted to be a little early in case you wanted to tell me something in particular."

"There really isn't anything," Henderson said. "You saw my performance, I imagine. That's all I know."

"What are your feelings about it, though?" Blaine said.

"All I can say is that I was starting to get used to this job and was getting ready for another four years of it," Henderson said.

Blaine chuckled. "That sounds a little premature."

"What do you think?" Henderson said.

Blaine settled into his seat. "I think you looked as good as you ever have—honest, sincere, concerned. You told the truth and my guess is the people liked it. Nobody but Matulo knows what he has and that's all you really said. Don't forget—you're riding the crest of the biggest economic recovery in the last half-century and people don't want to be bullshitted. Personally, I think you should just relax and things are going to take care of themselves. Don't you think so, Ms. Timkins?"

"I don't think it's that simple," she said.

"Oh, of course not," Blaine said. "Things are never that simple, but let's face it, Matulo's making an ass of himself. Nobody in their right mind is going to put up with that sort of threat, even his own people. Personally, I'm betting this test launch is going to be a dud and Matulo is going to become an even bigger laughingstock than he already is."

"I wish I had your confidence," Marjorie said.

"Don't get me wrong," Blaine said. "This threat is a serious matter, even if it is a hoax. We're going to get a lot of flak about the S-27. We've had a lot already, and it's going to get worse. Obviously something is going to have to be done about it. People are scared, more scared than they've ever been, especially now since the energy crisis seems to be over, but it's just another one of those things that'll have to be handled. Delicately, I admit, but it'll be handled." He gave Henderson a reassuring look. "And I know you can handle it."

"Thanks," Henderson said.

"I mean it," Blaine said. "You've got what it takes

in foreign policy, Wendell, and that's the name of the game these days. You've proved it."

"Then why are my knees shaking?" Henderson said.

"I don't know," Blaine said, and chuckled. "Maybe you're drinking too much coffee."

Henderson smiled politely. "Maybe."

"Believe me, Wendell, you're doing the right things," Blaine said. "You're not overreacting, in public anyway. You're presenting an excellent image to the world, like you always do, and you're going to come out of this in great shape. Just keep your confidence up and everything'll be fine."

"Thanks for the pep talk," Henderson said without conviction.

"Don't mention it," Blaine said and chuckled again.

Henderson looked up past his guests to the door that was opening, while Marjorie and Blaine turned to the side. The first into the office was the House Minority Leader, Fred Seitz (D. Maine), a short, slender man who moved in quick strides. He was followed by Senator Arlan Westbrook (D. California) and Senator Frank Eastland (R. Virginia), head of the Senate Foreign Relations Committee. They exchanged short hellos with the people present and set to arranging chairs quickly and silently till they were all in a rough semicircle in front of Henderson's desk.

"Could I see the cable?" Seitz said as he arranged himself in his chair.

"Of course," Henderson said and slid the yellow paper across his desk. Seitz picked it up and began to read it silently while Henderson kept his attention on the congressman. In a few moments, Seitz put the cable down in his lap.

"I still think it's a hoax," Seitz said, and passed the paper to his right to Westbrook.

"What makes you so sure?" Henderson said.

"Why would you think it wasn't?" Seitz said.

"What's the sense in it?" Henderson said.

"When has Matulo ever made sense?" Seitz said.

"He's ruled eight million people for seven years," Henderson said. "That takes some sense."

Seitz shrugged his shoulders. "The man's a lunatic and this just goes to prove it."

"And you don't think there's any possibility he could have an S-27?" Henderson said.

"Anything's possible," Seitz said. "That's not the point. I assumed you wanted us here to discuss handling this situation and I take that to mean we have to deal with realistic possibilities. There are no missiles missing, there are no records of any missiles being built in Toganda, no records of missiles being transported into Toganda, at least as far as I know, so what am I supposed to assume?"

"I have to agree," Eastland said. "Unless the CIA, USIA, and everyone else involved in gathering intelligence have completely fallen down on the job, there's no other conclusion I can make, either."

"Don't you think Matulo realizes that?" Henderson said.

"He probably does," Westbrook said while handing the cable to Eastland, "but the average person doesn't know that."

"That doesn't make sense," Henderson said.

"Why not?" Seitz said. "He's obviously got a lot of people upset, including you."

Henderson gave Seitz a brief glance and turned to Blaine. "You agree?"

Blaine nodded his head. "But even so, something has to be done about it."

"Naturally," Eastland said. "He's creating a big problem for us, even though he's creating a bigger problem for himself."

"What if he does have them, though," Marjorie said.

There was a short silence.

"I think Fred's made the point already," Westbrook

said. "We have to be realistic about this. If we start acting like he's got the missiles, we're probably going to make things worse than they already are. Funding the development of the S-27 was tough, and there's no way we're going to scrap them now. That would be ridiculous, but Matulo's giving us a black eye. He's getting people worked up over a figment of his warped imagination and he's already started them thinking in crazy directions and that's the problem we're going to have to address ourselves to. That's bad enough, but that's it."

"I agree," Seitz said.

Blaine leaned forward and placed the cable back on Henderson's desk. "I'm afraid I have to agree, too," he said as he settled back into his chair. "I know, for some reason, you're convinced Matulo really has those missiles, and I suppose there's an outside chance he really does, but I don't see how we can get anything accomplished right now going on that assumption. I think, if we want to be constructive, we should try to arrive at some objectives that can be accomplished at this time."

"That's right," Eastland said. "In fact, I'm surprised no statement has been issued from the Army as yet."

"I told them I didn't want any," Henderson said.

"Why?" Seitz said.

"What do you want them to say?" Henderson said.

"Why," Westbrook said with a humph, "how about simply stating that there's no possibility that a missile could have been stolen and that there haven't been any security leaks surrounding it."

"And if that isn't borne out?" Henderson said.

Westbrook turned his head to the side and back to Henderson. "I can't believe you said that."

"Well, I did," Henderson said, "and I meant it. If it's a hoax, I was cautious; if it isn't, I was smart—and right."

"And meanwhile everyone is wondering how much

security we've kept around the damn thing and who's going to be the next maniac to walk away with one," Seitz said.

"There's still time to make a statement," Blaine said, looking squarely at Henderson. "In fact, I think it'll probably work out better his way. It shows some coolheaded thinking rather than shooting from the hip."

"Good point," Eastland said, also looking squarely at Henderson.

"And what if I say I don't think it is a good point," Henderson said.

"All right," Seitz said. "What is your proposal?"

"I don't have one yet," Henderson said. "At least not a definitive one."

"Then why are we here?" Westbrook said.

"I'm just trying to get a feel for what's going on," Henderson said.

"We've told you how we feel," Seitz said.

"Can we at least have some public assurances that the missiles weren't stolen?" Eastland said.

Henderson nodded his head wearily. "Yes, yes," he said. "That I can do. I'll tell Macklin to make a statement, but I'm going to have him make no comment on the security and no conjectures. People will just have to draw their own conclusions till we know more about it."

"Fair enough," Blaine said.

"I guess that's what we'll have to settle for," Seitz said. "But I know one thing. If this isn't a hoax, there's going to be a hell of an investigation into this whole matter."

"If this isn't a hoax," Henderson said, "you're going to have a lot more to worry about than who let what secret out of what bag."

"No question," Eastland said. "If that launch does come off tonight, we're going to be in for a hell of a mess."

"Just because he had one, doesn't mean he'll have another," Westbrook said.

"It doesn't mean he couldn't either," Marjorie said.

"Okay," Henderson said. "I think that's about as much as we're going to get out of this meeting. I was hoping for more, but . . ."

Blaine pulled a fat cigar and a silver clipper out of his jacket. "It's too soon," he said and neatly clipped off a chunk of tobacco.

"Yes, I suppose," Henderson said. "Well, I guess that about does it. Blaine, I would like you back here about ten thirty, though. At least we'll know a little more then."

"Good idea," Blaine said. He stuck his cigar in his mouth and stood up. "See you later, Wendell." He turned and headed for the door. The others made their short good-byes and Marjorie followed them to the door. She overheard Seitz say something about leadership and then Henderson called her name.

She turned around. "Did you want me?"

He motioned for her to come back. "Come here a second."

She slowly walked back toward the desk and stopped just in front of it.

"Do I really sound as bad as I think I do?" he said.

She hesitated. "I'm afraid so," she said.

"I thought so," he said. He leaned back in his chair and ran his fingers through his hair. "I don't know what the hell's the matter with me. I just can't think straight about this thing. I can't be decisive, and I don't know why."

"I don't know," she said. "I don't know what it is. I've never seen you this way."

He shrugged his shoulders and leaned forward to prop his elbows on the desk. "I'll see you later. Say about nine o'clock. Meanwhile I'm going to see if I can get a few things done."

"Such as?"

"I should talk to Tippitz," he said, "and a few gen-

erals, Andreikov, Guidy-Livron. A few things like
that. I'll keep you posted. I'd like to work very closely
with you on this."

"Okay," she said, and waited. Henderson's attention seemed elsewhere. "Anything else?"

"No," he said. "No, that's it. I'll see you at nine."

"All right," she said, turned around, and left the
office.

Herbert Reynolds was jangling a knife in a nearly
empty jar of mayonnaise when he heard a knock on
the door. He cleaned the knife off on a piece of
whole wheat bread and then headed through his living room.

"Coming," he said and pulled the door open a
crack.

An unfamiliar face with an earnest look on it was
staring at him.

"Mr. Reynolds?" the face said.

Reynolds nodded his head.

"Winston sent us," the face said.

Reynolds let the door swing open and noticed the
second man, shorter than the first, and with a pockmarked face. "Come on in," Reynolds said, turned
around, and headed back to his kitchen. "I'll just be
a minute."

"We don't have much time," the earnest one said.
"We were told you'd be ready."

"I'm hungry," Reynolds said from the kitchen. He
calmly laid a half-dozen slices of mortadello on the
clean slice of bread.

"Your plane is scheduled to leave in half an hour,"
the same voice said.

"No problem," Reynolds said as he slapped the
sandwich together. "I'll eat on the way." He
crumpled up the brown delicatessen wrapping and
lobbed it into an empty waste can. When he walked
back into the living room, both his visitors were nervously looking about Reynolds's spartan home, anx-

iously waiting to leave. Reynolds held his sandwich in his left hand, took a bite, grabbed a small grip off his coffee table with his right hand, and said with his mouth stuffed, "Let's go."

His visitors, waiting by the still open door, stepped out, and Reynolds followed. He fumbled for the doorknob with his right hand and slammed the door shut. By the time he reached the waiting Lincoln, his visitors were sitting in the front seat, the one with the pockmarked face in the driver's seat. Reynolds tossed his grip in the backseat and slid in with his sandwich still in his hand. As the car pulled away from the curb, Reynolds went back to finishing his lunch.

At ten o'clock P.M. Eastern Standard Time, a missile was launched from a point in the Indian Ocean, later identified as General Matulo's yacht. It was spotted and tracked by satellite and various earth-bound radar installations. By the time an ABM was launched, the S-27 was halfway to its target. The MPCM detected the ABM and began evasive maneuvers, just as it had been programmed to. In all, six ABM's were launched to intercept the S-27 but it successfully evaded them all and exploded within the predicted fifty-meter radius of its target with the force of a five-kiloton warhead. It was the first complete test of the S-27 in an actual combat situation and it was a complete success.

Before Henderson put down the receiver, Marjorie knew what he was going to say.

"It's a success," he said softly.

Marjorie nodded her head. "What now?" she said.

"Was that rhetorical?" he said.

"Partly," she said.

"Well," he said, and leaned back in his chair. "I guess everyone's going to have to get committed now."

She nodded and stretched long and gracefully. "I'm glad," she said.

"Glad?" he said.

Her body relaxed into her chair. "Yes," she said. "I think we've just seen the end of an era."

"What's that?" he said.

"The era of nonconfront," she said.

"I don't understand," he said.

"I think you do," she said. "Let's face it, Wendell, the world's been falling asleep because people have a few more coins in their pockets. In the last twelve hours only one country, just one, has put the onus of this entire incident on Matulo—Britain. You'd think the rest were trying to act as though they weren't even involved. It's sickening."

"But logical," he said.

"Maybe," she said.

"Well, they'll have to take sides now," he said.

"Of course," she said. "Everything's so simple now—get Matulo and get that other missile if it's there. But then what?"

"We'll have to see," he said. "We don't even have the demands yet."

"You can guess what they'll be," she said. "Money mostly, probably, and maybe a few political exiles he'll want returned."

"Probably," he said.

"At least some of which we'll pay," she said.

"Depending on what happens," he said.

"Okay," she said. "And then what happens?"

Henderson showed a hint of impatience and anger. "We have conferences and we have meetings and we talk about what to do with the S-27," he said. "What the hell do you mean, what happens then?"

"I'm not here to fight, Wendell," she said, "but don't you think we ought to be discussing some initiatives? Don't you think we ought to be talking, now, about what happens when this is over?"

"Who's got the time?" he said. "I don't expect to

even go to bed tonight and you should be arranging meetings right now."

"What am I going to say?" she said.

Henderson's voice rose. "Tell them we're taking care of it, tell them we're looking for cooperation and support but that it has to be coordinated. Isn't that taking an initiative?" He leaned forward to rest his elbows on the desk and lowered his voice. "I don't understand you at all right now," he said. "We've got a crisis that has to be handled as quickly as possible. It's complex, it's embarrassing, and it's frightening. Matulo has the most advanced weapon in our arsenal and he's shoving it up our collective ass. The point is simple—we have to find out if he's got the second one, and if he does, get it out of his hands one way or another, just in case he decides to drop it on a few million unsuspecting people. I realize the long-range consequences of this are complex, incredibly complex, so let's try to keep it as simple as possible so we can do something about it, one step at a time."

"I agree," she said. "I'm not trying to solve the problems of the world in a day. Believe it or not, I'm trying to keep things in perspective, too, but I know how hard it's going to be to keep your attention on the total problem this incident is presenting while you have to deal with it minute by minute. And the same is true for me. That's why these questions have to be brought up now, and have to keep being brought up."

"Fine," Henderson said. "Theoretically, that's beautiful. Just show me what to do with it."

Marjorie was about to speak when the President's red phone began ringing. Henderson picked it up and said, "Hello."

Marjorie kept her eyes glued on Henderson's face. Henderson's eyes were cast down at the desk and there were a few moments of silence before he spoke again. "We haven't decided," he said. "We haven't heard . . . Yes, of course that's our intention. . . .

I don't know. . . . Yes, we will. . . . I understand and I'm in complete agreement. . . . I won't be able to leave Washington, but the Secretary of State will be able to. . . . Yes, of course. . . . As soon as we know what the demands are and have had time to consider them. . . . Yes. . . . Thank you." He put the receiver down slowly and looked up at Marjorie. He seemed relieved.

"Andreikov?" she said.

"Yes," he said, and hesitated.

"And?" she said.

"I'm not sure," he said.

"What do you mean?" she said.

"He wants to talk," he said. "I said you'd go there as soon as we've heard the demands and had time to consider them."

"Okay," she said. "How'd he sound, though?"

"I'm not sure," he said. "He sympathized with our dilemma but he made sure to remind me that it was our own missile."

"Naturally," she said.

"Naturally," he said and began rubbing his hands together. "Well, when do you think we'll hear the demands?"

"Your guess is as good as mine," she said.

"Yes," he said and looked thoughtfully down at his desk. "Hungry?"

"A little," she said. "I haven't had any dinner."

"You too," he said. "Well, maybe that wouldn't be a bad idea and then we can discuss some things."

"Don't you think we should include Macklin and Simmons along with Blaine?" she said.

Henderson thought a moment. "Yes," he said. He nodded his head and reached for his intercom while Marjorie retreated into herself and shut out the sound of the President's voice.

A destroyer was sent to intercept General Matulo's yacht. The six-man Togandan crew offered no resistance to being boarded. They were quickly and quietly transferred to the destroyer and put in the brig while the newly manned yacht accompanied the American destroyer to a port in India.

Three hours after the missile had landed on target, General Matulo called a press conference at the Presidential Palace just outside Balingo, the capital of Toganda, There were three reporters present, the same three he always allowed to be present and the only three that he ever called. Since Matulo's press conferences only amounted to the recitation of a prepared speech, which was supplied to the reporters before the conference, it was all merely a formality Matulo felt necessary to show that he was still alive, well, and in control. The reporters sat on three chairs arranged in a straight line in front of Matulo's desk. Each of them had been trying to contact the President of Toganda for hours ever since learning about the missile threat, and their nerves were on edge. It was a noticeable effort for them to keep the silence that was expected of them. Matulo sat behind his desk holding the paper in front of him which contained the official announcement of the Toganda demands. Around the perimeter of the office were six guards. Two flanked Matulo and the other four were set in pairs on opposite walls flanking the reporters.

In soft, well-modulated tones, Matulo began his monologue. "Earlier today, I launched a Thor S-27 Multi-Purpose Cruise Missile at Antarctica. It was successfully exploded on target despite the best efforts of the United States and its allies to intercept it. As I announced yesterday, I have one more of these missiles in my possession. It will be launched at a heavily populated area of the world which I will not specify at this time, nor will I specify the time at which the missile will be launched, unless the United States of America accedes to the following demands:

"One, the United States will give the Togandan

people unlimited funds to purchase any items we may choose either there or in any other country in the world.

"Two, the United States will release the six crewmen who were manning my yacht. My yacht will be returned to them and they will be allowed to return it to Toganda.

"These demands must be agreed to within eleven hours from now. If they are not agreed to by that time, I will launch my remaining missile as I have already stated. If the United States or any other country attempts to use any type of force, either overt or covert, to occupy the sovereign state of Toganda or to remove, disarm, or in any other way attempt to disrupt my plans, I will launch my remaining missile as I have stated.

"God has ordered me to do this to help the people of Toganda and all the people of the world, and I am therefore compelled to take this action. If I must launch my remaining missile to teach the world a lesson, I will. The worst that can happen to me is that I will be hunted down and killed and I have no fear of dying. I pray that all the people of the world will help me to make it clear to the Government of the United States of America that I mean what I say."

Matulo's words were repeated verbatim over a speaker in Henderson's office approximately twenty minutes after the General himself had uttered them. As Henderson switched off the speaker, General Macklin said, "I could have Balingo secured within twenty-four hours."

Henderson drew a deep breath.

"While we watch a major portion of Hong Kong or Tokyo or New York or London disintegrate," Marjorie said.

"Hell," Macklin said, "we don't even know if he has the damn thing and besides, what good will it do him to launch it? Once he sends it off, he's a dead man anyway. That's the trouble with blackmailers."

"Except that we're dealing with Matulo," Marjorie said.

"What's the difference?" Macklin said. "He's still human and he has a lot to lose."

"Can't you tell a martyr when you see one?" Marjorie said.

"Aren't you jumping to conclusions?" Simmons said.

Marjorie jerked her head to the side. "I don't think so. He just said God told him to do it and I think his religious background speaks for itself."

Simmons calmly nodded his head. "You've got a point, but we still can't be sure."

"He's already gone too far," Marjorie said. "He's got nothing to lose."

"Possibly," Simmons said.

"I have to agree with Marjorie," Henderson said. "There's an outside chance he might not want to launch it, but I would never bet on it, and that's the way the rest of the world is going to see it. We'll agree to the demands and go from there."

"What about our image?" Macklin said.

"What about it?" Henderson said. "Isn't it bad enough already?"

Macklin reached inside his jacket and pulled out a pack of cigarettes.

"Our man is on his way to Toganda," Simmons said, "and he's good. He knows the country and he knows how to handle himself. My guess is that we'll know whether or not the missile is really there within forty-eight hours, and if it is, he's capable of disarming it."

"What makes you so confident he can do all this?" Marjorie said.

"He's always come through before," Simmons said, "and Toganda is a small country and not very tightly controlled."

"Doesn't it bother you that it's been almost seven years since this man Reynolds did a mission?" Marjorie said.

"No," Simmons said and shook his head. "Not at all. Just because he hasn't been working in the field doesn't mean he's lost his ability. I personally think the man is a natural. He has a feel for this sort of thing, and besides, he's the only capable agent we have who's black enough to go unnoticed there."

"But he hasn't even been working for the CIA," Marjorie said.

"Are you questioning his loyalty?" Simmons said.

"No," Marjorie said.

"Marjorie," Henderson said, "I'm satisfied that Reynolds knows how to handle himself, if that's what you're worried about. There's always the chance he might do something wrong, but I think we have to at least take that risk. We can't continue in the dark. We have to know if that missile is there."

"I suppose," she said.

"You don't think we do?" Henderson said.

"It's possible it doesn't even make any difference," she said.

"I can't imagine how you could even consider dealing with something like this without enough intelligence," Simmons said.

"Have you even considered the possibility that it might be irrelevant in this situation?" Marjorie said.

"No," Simmons said.

"Reynolds is going and that's it," Henderson said and turned to Macklin. "General, was anything learned from the demonstration launch?"

"About the missile?" Macklin said.

"Yes," Henderson said.

"Not really," Macklin said. "Except that it's every bit what we hoped it would be. The tapes of the flight are being studied and there is a possibility that there could be a defense against it. The most promising theory is that we could use a special pattern of

ABM's which would be capable of accounting for the missile's evasive maneuvers, assuming the missile Matulo has is programmed the same as the S-27."

"How will you know that?" Henderson said.

"Hopefully, from observing the tapes of the demonstration," Macklin said.

"What do you think are the chances that it might work?" Henderson said.

"I don't know," Macklin said. "It's too early to tell. We'll do a few simulations and see what they look like, but then there's always the chance that the other missile might be programmed differently."

Blaine, having sat quietly through the discussion, cleared his throat and put his dead cigar butt down. "Wendell, I think you're right in taking a conciliatory approach to this matter and I know Congress will back you up on it," he said, "for a while."

Henderson moved his attention, along with the other three people in the room, to Blaine. "How long, do you think?"

"A few days," Blaine said. "Not long enough to really give anything away. After that . . ." He stopped and rubbed his nose.

"What?" Marjorie said.

Blaine turned to Marjorie. "After that they're going to want to get tough."

"That's not enough time," Henderson said.

"I could be wrong," Blaine said, "but I think that's the way you're going to have to look at it. Get some concret results within the next couple of days, something to show you've got control of it, or there's going to be some trouble."

"Such as?" Marjorie said.

"Such as deciding that we can't play games with a lunatic," Macklin said.

"I was asking the Congressman," Marjorie said.

"That's about it," Blaine said. "Like I said, I could be wrong. It's just my opinion, but I think it's usually pretty accurate. The President will be able to do pretty much what he wants for a couple of days and both houses are going to go along with him, no matter what's happening. After that it better look like this threat is on the way to getting wrapped up or the majority is going to want to get tough. That's the way I read it."

"Even at the risk of innocent people's lives, citizens of other countries?" Marjorie said.

"Yes," Blaine said.

"How can you say that?" Marjorie said.

"It's just the way I read it," Blaine said. "It's the mood I sense. Read the papers, talk to the people."

"That was before the demonstration, though," she said.

"That's true," Blaine said, "but I don't really think it makes any difference. There's too much of a feeling that this country has to hold on to what it has."

"Exactly," Macklin said.

"I'm afraid he may be right," Henderson said.

"How long do you think this incident is going to last, Ms. Timkins?" Simmons said.

She turned her head around in a fast, tight arc. "A long time," she said.

"Could you be more specific?" Simmons said.

"Years," she said.

Simmons chuckled. "I don't think this is the time to be making jokes."

"I'm not," she said.

Simmons's smile disappeared. "Do you seriously think that we, or the rest of the world, are about to put up with this sort of thing for very long?"

"I'm not just talking about this missile," she said.

"Aren't you getting ahead of yourself, Ms. Timkins?" Blaine said. "We're talking about one incident, not the future of a new form of international blackmail."

Marjorie jerked her head back around. "Why aren't we?"

"That's exactly my point," Macklin said, sitting up

in his chair, "and exactly why we have to act quickly and decisively right now."

"You mean, that's why we have to act in exactly the opposite way that you want to," Marjorie said.

"All right!" Henderson said. "This isn't getting us anywhere. What we need are facts and that's why we're putting this man Reynolds into Toganda. Hopefully, he'll find out if the missile is there and whether it's operable and then we can go from there. Until then, we're going to be nice to General Matulo and try to make everybody feel as comfortable as possible, so this discussion is over for now." He turned to Blaine. "Milton, I want you to stay and talk to me." He turned to Marjorie. "You know what you have to do." She nodded her head. "Don't disappoint me."

"I won't," she said.

"I know," he said, and gave her a reassuring smile.

Marjorie, Macklin, and Simmons bade their quick good-byes while Blaine pulled a fresh cigar out of his jacket and neatly clipped the end off.

Second Day

Henderson woke up at seven o'clock. He turned off his alarm before it had a chance to ring and sat up on the side of his bed. His wife, Elizabeth, was next to him, still asleep. It was a gray morning—thunderstorms had been forecast. Vaguely, he remembered lying down about four o'clock and then he started going over, in his head, the conversations that he would have that day, the same conversations he'd already gone over a hundred times while he should have been resting. He got to his feet and headed for the bathroom.

Stuart Davis, Henderson's press secretary, was waiting at the President's office. Davis broke into an aggressively encouraging smile as soon as Henderson approached him.

"Good morning, Wendell," Davis said.

"Good morning," Henderson said dully and without returning the smile.

"How are you feeling?"

"Tired," Henderson said and opened the door to his office.

Davis followed him in. "Everything's ready," he said.

"Nine o'clock?" Henderson said as he made his way around the desk.

"You can still change your mind," Davis said as he approached the desk.

"Why should I?" Henderson said as he sat down.

"Something might develop," Davis said.

"Have you heard something?" Henderson said without anticipation.

"No," Davis said. Henderson's mood had taken away his smile.

"Have a seat," Henderson said, and the press secretary quickly sat down. "What's the public reaction?"

"Have you seen any papers yet?"

"No," Henderson said. "I've been too busy trying to put this appropriation together. Why?"

"The consensus is that the S-27 should have been killed a long time ago,"

"Wonderful," Henderson said. "And I signed it."

"That's the way they see it."

"It figures," Henderson said with a scowl.

"There's a plus side, too," Davis said.

"What's that?" Henderson said.

"They like the way you're handling it."

"That's good," Henderson said. "I wonder how they'll feel tomorrow."

Davis waited while Henderson shuffled through some papers. "I've got your speech."

Henderson looked up and reached his hand out. Davis pulled a batch of papers folded in thirds out of his light blue jacket and handed him the speech. Henderson opened them up and began reading. His pupils moved in jerks and his head and hands moved in rapid, short movements that revealed the tremendous tension he felt. "It's good," he said. "Short and to the point." He looked up. "I want to read it over some more and I have to make a few calls. Let me know when you're ready to set up."

Davis recognized his cue and stood up. "I'll be back in about an hour."

"Tell Craig to get me some coffee," Henderson said.

"Okay," Davis said and turned to go. As the door closed behind him, he felt a wave of relief wash over his body.

Reynolds stepped off his plane wearing a dark brown suit, tie to match, and a light blue shirt. He was carrying an attaché case as the man with the pockmarked face walked before him into the customs line and his taller partner walked behind. Their credentials identified the trio as buyers for a multinational corporation. They were in a country adjoining Toganda. Once outside the terminal building, they hailed a cab and were driven to a downtown high rise. They left the cab, got into a small European car, and were driven to a residence outside the city limits. There, Reynolds changed into a red, white, and blue striped sport shirt, khaki pants, and boots, and exchanged his attaché case for a small grip. He left his traveling companions behind and was driven in a Jeep toward the Togandan border. Approximately ten kilometers from the border, the Jeep stopped and Reynolds stepped out. He turned around to face the driver, lifted his hand, smiled, and said, "Have a good trip back."

"Thanks," the driver said, returning the smile. "Good luck." He shifted gears, swung the Jeep around in a dusty U, and took off back down the road. Reynolds watched the Jeep disappear in the dust of the gravel road, kept smiling, and chuckled to himself. The driver of the Jeep, just like the others Reynolds had met briefly in his journey, had taken an almost instant liking to the black agent. That was the kind of person Reynolds was, when he wanted to be. It was the result of the same combination of infectious enthusiasm and relaxed familiarity that had assured him of this assignment in the first place, even though he hadn't done a mission for Simmons in so many years. Reynolds knew Simmons, and he knew how to handle him, and he didn't want Simmons having second thoughts about Reynolds's idealistic motives in jumping at the chance for this mission. He realized that much of the decision to send him in was intuitive and coincidental. It had only been a week since Reynolds had let Simmons know that he would be interested in working with the CIA again, that his bitterness over the South African incident was forgotten, that Reynolds had matured and wanted to do something for his country, that Reynolds felt that there were signs of more trouble in Africa and Simmons agreed. Reynolds was glad that the same idealism he'd shown before, the same idealism that had alienated him once, was serving him so well this time, and that he was going to accomplish something that was his and his alone.

Reynolds was determined to succeed. He whistled and hummed to himself as he walked along the rutted road. He'd never felt so totally self-confident.

Henderson fretted for an unusually long time about his makeup for the telecast and wouldn't say he was ready until he was convinced it was just right even though he sensed that his concern was having a negative effect on the people present, but he was ready on time. At precisely ten o'clock Eastern Standard Time, Henderson began his address.

"Good morning," he said. "By this time, the majority of the people of this world are aware of the threat that has been leveled against this country by the President of the Republic of Toganda, General Amdida Matulo. General Matulo has successfully launched and exploded what we believe to be the equivalent of our Thor S-27 Multi-Purpose Cruise Missile. It is not one of our own missiles. All S-27's built in this country have been accounted for. The missile which exploded over Antarctica was built without our knowledge. It is especially for this reason that I believe General Matulo is telling the truth when he says that he has a second missile, equivalent to the first and also equipped with a five-kiloton nuclear warhead. General Matulo has said that he will launch his second missile at an unspecified, heavily populated area of this planet at an unspecified time unless we meet his demands by twelve o'clock noon Eastern Standard Time. His demands are that we give

the Togandan people as much money as they request
to buy whatever they want either here or in any other
country in the world and that General Matulo's
yacht, which is currently in our custody, be returned
to him.

"I find it very repugnant to see this country forced
to comply with such demands under such a threat, yet
at the same time I do not feel that I can take it upon
myself, nor do I think the people of this country
would want to take it upon themselves, to be responsible for the possible deaths of what could potentially
be hundreds of thousands of lives because we were
unwilling to part with a sum of money. I fully realize
that there are serious questions of honor, dignity,
prestige, and precedent involved in this situation as
well as many other questions, but I find it impossible
to put a price on a human life, even though there
may be a possibility that General Matulo would never
launch the missile we believe is in his possession in
the manner he has threatened.

"I have, therefore, been in contact with leaders in
both the House and Senate as well as other business
and political leaders to see that sufficient funds will
be made available to the Republic of Toganda until
this problem can be settled in a more satisfactory
manner. I am now asking you, the people, to support
me and my decision. I cannot say for certain that
General Matulo has the missile he says he does, nor
can I know for certain that he would do anything as
abhorrent as killing and maiming thousands of innocent people, but I can't say for certain that he doesn't
have the missile or that he will not launch it. I do
not feel that I can take a chance. I can only hope
that General Matulo will come to his senses and realize that what he is doing can only harm him and his
people in the long run. In the meantime I intend on
doing my utmost to see that nothing happens that
might provoke General Matulo into doing something that can only horrify the world, because I am

convinced that that is the only sensible course of action at this time. Thank you."

Henderson waited for a signal to indicate they were off the air and took a deep breath. He felt a bead of sweat slowly working its way down his right side and turned to Davis. "Get the office cleared out as soon as possible, Stu. I'll be having a meeting here at ten thirty."

Reynolds affected the indifference of a native as he sipped a Coke at a small bus station less than a kilometer inside the Togandan border. He had crossed the border through a hole in a Cyclone fence out of sight of the road and its border station, a hole big enough to walk through without breaking his stride. Leaning against a two-by-four that was keeping a corner of the overhanging roof of the station from collapsing, he would occasionally glance toward the mountain Entike that dominated the horizon to the north. Out of that mountain's perpetually white peak flowed the river Ulalu and along the western bank of that almost totally polluted river, midway between the mountain and the station he was resting against, lay Reynold's first destination, the capital, Balingo.

Reynolds threw his empty can into a large wire wastebasket that had at one time been painted green but was now mostly rusty brown. He caught sight of a cloud of dust slowly growing toward the north and assumed that it was his bus. He shifted the grip he was still carrying to his right hand and glanced at the two Togandan soldiers who were the only other people waiting with him. They broke into tight, restrained laughter but Reynolds hadn't heard the joke. He looked back up the road to where the cloud of dust was growing larger and then evaporated as the bus reached the short stretch of pavement that ran into the village.

In a few minutes the bus was stopped in front of the station. The door swung open smoothly and a

Togandan soldier stepped out. Reynolds recognized
his insignia for that of a lieutenant. The lieutenant
walked past Reynolds and the soldiers without saying
anything and entered the station. The driver followed
him. A few moments later Reynolds heard a clank,
then a pause, then another clank as two Cokes were
dispensed from a machine and then the lieutenant
reappeared in the doorway.

The bus station was distinctly the work of General
Matulo. It was a small, wood frame building that
housed a small ticket booth along with the Coke
machine. One man, wearing a neat, clean, blue uniform, ran the station. He dispensed one or two tickets
a day, occasionally a few more, for the one bus that
came there every day to turn around. For handling
this responsibility, the man received fifty Togandan
pounds a week, almost double the average working-
man's wage.

The lieutenant took a long swallow and lowered
his can. He wiped his mouth with the back of his
hand and said, "Papers," in a disinterested tone.

The two soldiers reached into their pockets while
Reynolds already had his in his hand. He stepped up
to the lieutenant and handed the papers to him. The
lieutenant casually took them and looked them over,
occasionally taking another swallow from his can
while Reynolds patiently waited for him to finish.

"Okay," the lieutenant said, and handed the travel
permit and identity card back to Reynolds.

Reynolds took them, carefully refolded them,
slipped them into his wallet, and returned his wallet
to his back pocket. He stepped aside for one of the
Togandan privates to get by and headed for the bus.
He found a seat with a fair amount of padding still
left in it and sat down to watch the lieutenant finish
with the second private.

The driver reappeared from the station and started
talking with the lieutenant while the lieutenant kept
glancing at the bus in Reynolds's general direction.

Suddenly they burst out laughing and the lieutenant tossed his empty can toward the wire wastebasket and missed. The driver followed suit with a lob of his can that hit the edge and fell in.

The lieutenant walked back into the bus followed by the privates and looked directly at Reynolds. Reynolds calmly looked back at him and the lieutenant smiled faintly and sat down. The driver dropped his bulk into his seat and turned the ignition. The bus started vibrating, jerked, and moved forward. Reynolds was pushed to the side as the bus swung into a U-turn that took it off the pavement, around, and back up the road, headed north. Reynolds looked out the window at the nearly deserted street of the village, the few rickety shops, the shacks at the fringe, and then the grassland that surrounded it. He started thinking about the small talk he'd had with the ticket agent and how no mention had been made of Matulo's threat to the world and then, before he realized the window to the seat in front of him was open, he was breathing dust.

Clarence Bishop had stayed up all night, first waiting for more word on the missile demonstration launch and then, after word of its successful launch was broadcast, pacing through his home, keeping his wife awake with his raving about what a sorry state his country was in and what its incompetent leaders were doing with it. When at last he heard the announcement of the Togandan demands over the radio, he went into an even greater frenzy about how the President and the fools in Congress were going to pay through the nose with his money. When his wife began dozing, he became even more infuriated and left the house to visit a friend, where he listened to the President's address to the nation.

"That fool," Clarence shouted at the TV set before the President was even done. "That stupid, cowardly jackass. What does he think he's doing? He's trying to hand this country away on a silver platter, but he's not going to get away with it. This time the Sons are going to do something."

His friend raised an empty beer can in salute. "Right on."

General Matulo awoke promptly at five thirty each day, not from a sense of having to get the day started early, but from chronic insomnia. He would take a shower, get dressed in one of his uniforms—one of a set of twelve that he had had personally designed for him—and then have coffee and English cigarettes for breakfast in his office. Waiting for him on his desk would be the previous day's copy of *The New York Times* and the London *Times*. He would spend several hours looking through both papers as well as translations of five other major daily papers. The translations were in the form of neatly typed sheets and represented the indiscriminate translation of the bulk of a newspaper. He firmly believed that locked inside these papers, in articles that most people would consider of little or no significance, lay bits of information of great importance that only a certain type of person, a person such as himself, could detect and put to effective use; and, thus, he could not allow the services of an editor, and, thus, he kept a team of fifteen translators working full time in the Presidential Palace.

The morning of the day after giving his demands to the United States, he went through his same routine with a touch of added anticipation and, as he had expected, found several bits of information he considered highly significant: shipments of Chilean copper were down, Honda had just introduced a new motorcycle into the American market, and unemployment in Berlin had just dropped for the second month in a row. Having made a mental note of these facts, as well as several others of lesser significance, he gathered all the papers on his desk into a neat pile

and placed them into an Out basket. The only reports in the papers that referred to Matulo were
about his original threat before the demonstration
and these the General considered trivial. Having completed that part of his daily routine, he called his
Foreign Minister, Litotho Amamelu.

Amamelu was one of the few permanent residents
of the Presidential Palace. This allowed him to appear in Matulo's office within a few minutes of being
called. In many ways, as well as formal position, Amamelu's relationship to Matulo was very much like
Marjorie Timkins's relationship to Henderson. Since
Matulo prided himself on being constantly informed
about what was really going on in the world outside
the tiny borders of Toganda, and since Matulo based
his most important decisions on inspiration, only a
figurehead was needed to occupy the Foreign Minister's position; and since the Togandan treasury had
limited resources, Amamelu spent most of his time in
Toganda agreeing with the General's opinions and
serving as a prestigious messenger, even though he
had a degree from Oxford and had done graduate
work at Harvard.

Matulo was speaking on the phone as Amamelu
swung open one of the heavy wooden double doors
that separated Matulo's office from the rest of the
palace. "That's right, Kantho," the General said. "I
want you to include several oil-drilling rigs in the first
order. . . . I think there may be oil in the Lake
Kolana area. . . . I don't care. A similar situation
occurred in Kenya and they're now producing a thousand barrels a day. . . . Fine. I'll talk to you
later. Good-bye, now."

Amamelu took a seat in front of the General's desk
and Matulo trained his eyes on the minister. "These
foreign oil companies," Matulo said contemptuously.
"What do they know? They say one thing one day
and another the next, whatever suits their fancy."

Amamelu nodded his head. "What did you want to see me about?"

Matulo's eyes lost their focus and he was silent for a few moments. Then, just as abruptly, they refocused on Amamelu. "I want you to get in touch with our public relations people," Matulo said. He gestured toward the pile of papers in his Out basket. "There should have been more about the threat. I didn't like it."

Amamelu nodded his head.

"Great Power indifference to our problems must be stressed and communicated," Matulo said. "People have to understand that this is the only way we can get the United States to respond to our problems."

"I'll talk to them," Amamelu said.

"I want them to emphasize the United States' responsibility," he said in a tight, penetrating voice. "I want no question in the world's mind of that. I want it emphasized that I could launch the other missile anywhere. There must be no implication that my only real target would be the United States. That opinion can't be allowed. That uncertainty is the key to my strategy."

"I'll see to it," he said. "Is there anything else?"

"That's all," Matulo said. He relaxed a bit and leaned back into his chair.

By the time Amamelu had made his way through the double doors, Matulo was reaching for another cigarette. By the time one of the doors began to swing open again, he was lighting it. Sithele Mulele, Togandan Ambassador to the United Nations, made his way to Matulo's desk and was greeted with a trickle of smoke from the General's mouth.

"You wanted to see me?" the unprepossessing ambassador said as he sat down in the chair before Matulo's desk.

"Have you been in touch with Cletho?" Matulo said.

"Yes," Mulele said. He tried not to show how worried he was. He knew now why he had been called back to Toganda the day before the demonstration launch, leaving his one assistant behind in New York. Up to the moment Matulo had made his threat, Mulele had known nothing about it and had not even suspected that something of that magnitude was in the offing, but he knew better than to offer any objections now. He was one of the few diplomatic links Toganda had with the rest of the world and he took that responsibility willingly but heavily. At one time there had been an ambassador to the United States as well as an American consulate in Toganda, but Matulo had broken off formal diplomatic relations with the U.S. because of the criticism he'd received concerning the methods he'd used in consolidating his political power. Henderson's predecessor had accused Matulo of "destroying democracy in Toganda," and Matulo didn't feel that any country that would have a leader who would say such a thing deserved his formal friendship. Using the same type of reasoning he'd also broken diplomatic relations with a number of other countries as well. For this reason there were only six Togandan ambassadors besides Mulele remaining in foreign countries, one each in Japan, China, Russia, Brazil, Egypt, and Colombia.

"Had he discussed the threat with anyone?" Matulo said, his attention totally fixed on Mulele.

"He said the U.S. Ambassador tried to bring it up with the Security Council but it was too late in the day, and besides, the other members wanted to wait for further developments. He expects the U.S. Ambassador to address the General Assembly today."

"Is that all?"

"Yes," Mulele said. "There's really nothing he can say. He doesn't know anything. Nor do I."

"Yes," Matulo said. He drew on his cigarette and his eyes lost their focus.

Mulele waited. "What am I supposed to do?"

"I've prepared a speech," the General said. "You'll

leave here as soon as we're done. As soon as you arrive in New York, you'll go to deliver it. I only wanted you to come here first to remind you that it's your duty to impress on that body that we are fighting for the rights of every economically oppressed nation in the world."

"I understand," he said.

Matulo's eyes again focused on the ambassador. "You can do it. I have confidence in you."

"Once I've delivered the speech, do I remain in New York?" Mulele said.

"Yes," Matulo said. "Yes, stay there. I'll be in touch with you daily."

"Is there anything else?"

Matulo shook his head and ground his cigarette out in a massive glass ashtray that was already half-filled with butts from that morning. Mulele left without saying anything more and Matulo started leafing through a stack of military reports.

Only six of the ten bank presidents and chairmen of the board Henderson wanted for his ten thirty meeting were able to make it in time. They sat in a semicircle around the President's desk and, having made their hellos on the way to their seats, were perfectly silent.

"I'm glad you could make it in time," Henderson said. "There are a few people missing I would have liked to have seen here but I think we can get started without them." He cleared his throat and adjusted himself in his chair. "The problem is very simple. Congress is not going to appropriate the money for Toganda fast enough."

"It's only ten thirty," one of the men said.

"I know," Henderson said, "but I've been working on this most of the night and most of this morning and what I thought might happen has happened. Some legislators have left town, figuring Washington could be a prime target for Matulo's remaining missile if all didn't go right, and of the rest, not everyone is convinced we should pay."

"I can understand that," another one said.

"The point is that there's less than an hour and a half left," Henderson said. "The money will be appropriated. That I'm sure of."

"How much?" Clark, president of Chase Manhattan, asked.

"Two hundred million," Henderson said.

Several eyebrows rose.

"Why that much?" Clark asked.

Henderson concentrated his attention on Clark, sensing that he was the key. "To make it look legitimate. A couple of million isn't going to buy Matulo off."

"But you're not even sure he has the missile," Clark said.

"Are you ready to take that chance?" Henderson said.

"I don't know that it is taking a chance," Clark said. "My understanding is that none of these missiles are missing."

"That's right," Henderson said.

"Then where did this demonstration missile come from?" Clark said.

"We don't know," Henderson said.

"Could it have been the Russians?" Clark said. "The Chinese?"

"I don't think so," Henderson said. "I really don't think they would have done something like that, but I don't know. Only Matulo knows and that isn't going to do us a damn bit of good. The point is that this is not a hijacking or even a Cuban Missile Crisis. This is something new and unique."

"I don't know . . ." Clark said.

"We need time," Henderson said.

"What about the precedent, though?" Clark said. "You're getting ready to ask us to advance, or in some way to commit ourselves, to giving Toganda two hundred million dollars."

"Which Congress will cover," Henderson said. "I've talked to Westbrook and even he is willing to go along with this initial appropriation."

Clark nodded his head thoughtfully. "And after this?"

"What do you mean?" Henderson said.

"This can't go on indefinitely," Clark said. "You must be doing something to retake that missile, or disarm it, or something. Or at least find out for sure if it's there."

"Of course," Henderson said. "We're working on it, but this is a delicate matter. I can't say how long it'll continue, but I believe we're only talking about a matter of days. Look at it this way—how fast can Matulo spend your money even if Congress can't make the appropriation immediately?"

Clark again nodded his head thoughtfully. Henderson leaned back in his chair and noticed that all the attention was now on Clark. "When you look at it that way, the risk doesn't really seem all that great, even if Congress doesn't make the appropriation. After all, it would simply be another loan to Toganda, an exceptionally poor risk, but then once this is over, there will be a new government."

"There has to be," Henderson said.

"I think we could handle a portion of it," Clark said, then raised his eyebrows. "Without a guarantee?"

"I'm afraid not," Henderson said. "Except my intentions."

"We'll go along," another one of the bankers said.

"We will, too," another said.

Henderson felt himself relax and felt the wetness of his palms on the arms of his chair.

Clark adjusted his heavyset frame. "How do you want the money channeled to the Togandans?"

Henderson leaned forward and allowed himself a

modest smile. Nearly an hour was spent reaching a method of apportioning the potential debt, paying suppliers, and arranging short-term credits for suppliers, as well as explaining to the latecomers what was going on. The last of the bank officials left Henderson's office shortly before eleven thirty. Henderson checked his watch and reached for his intercom.

"Craig," Henderson said. "It's time to get in touch with Matulo."

"Yes, sir," his secretary said.

"And get Blaine," Henderson said. "Even if someone has to take him off the floor. I want to talk to him before I talk to Matulo."

"Yes, sir," his secretary said. "Anything else?"

"No, that's it," Henderson said and turned the intercom off. He absently picked up a pencil lying on his desk and started pushing it between his thumb and middle fingers against the surface of the desk, up and over and back again while he pictured some aide feverishly hunting down Blaine and giving him the message. He kept that image and held on to it, semiconsciously keeping out anything else. He jerked his head at the sound of his name over the intercom and reached out his hand. "Yes?"

"Congressman Blaine," his secretary said.

"Okay," Henderson said and pressed the button to his telephone speaker. "Milton?"

"Hello," Blaine said.

"What's happening there?" Henderson said.

"A little resistance," Blaine said, "but I'm not worried."

"Will there be a vote before noon?" Henderson said.

"I could force it," he said. "We'd probably win."

"Don't," Henderson said. "I've got the money."

"The entire two hundred?" Blaine said.

"Yes," Henderson said. "Direct bank loans, unguaranteed."

"Excellent," Blaine said. "I'll shift the issue to

guaranteeing that portion actually dispersed. Good job. Good job."

"It should keep Matulo happy," Henderson said. "I'm going to talk to him as soon as I finish talking to you. You want to wait there?"

"Yes," Blaine said, "of course."

"I'll put you on hold." Henderson pressed another button. "Craig, put the Congressman on hold. Have you got Matulo yet?"

"Yes," his secretary said.

Henderson felt a point at the base of his stomach start to rise. He took a deep breath and let it out slowly. "Put him on," he said.

"Mr. President," came a tenor voice with a touch of British accent.

"General Matulo?" Henderson said.

"Yes, it's me," Matulo said. "What is your decision?"

"You didn't give us much time," Henderson said.

"This is an age of fast decision," Matulo said. "This is the way it has to be."

"I haven't been able to get Congress to authorize unlimited funding," Henderson said. "There just wasn't enough time, but I have authorized the Navy to release your yacht and its crew."

"Does this mean you're not going to agree to the rest of the demands?" Matulo said without changing his tone of voice.

"No," Henderson said. "What I've done is to arrange for a number of banks to advance you a certain amount of money, two hundred million dollars, which I trust will be enough for the present time."

"Then you are agreeing to the demands," Matulo said.

There was a short pause while Henderson mulled over the next word in the face of Matulo's galling self-confidence. "Yes," he said.

"Excellent," Matulo said. "I want to congratulate you on having made the right decision, as unpleasant to you as I'm sure it is. I cannot be less than perfectly honest in telling you that I regret very deeply the necessity of having had to act in this manner, but I have been given no choice. All I'm really asking for is what rightfully belongs to my people in the first place, and I sincerely hope you understand that. There is nothing malicious in my actions. I want, I hope, you understand that. All that I am doing is in the interests of justice and what is right. Do you understand that?"

Henderson hesitated. "No," he said. "No, I don't understand that."

"That's unfortunate," Matulo said. "I sincerely thought that you of all people would truly understand my position. Hopefully, in the next few months, you'll begin to. Meanwhile, my people will begin arriving in your country tomorrow. They have their instructions, which I won't go into at this time. They're much too lengthy and detailed. I'm sure you'll show them every courtesy and give them all the assistance possible."

"We'll do our best," Henderson said.

"I'm sure you will," Matulo said. "Now, if there's nothing else, I have quite a number of things to do."

"There is one thing," Henderson said. "I would like to request a personal meeting between us at the earliest possible opportunity."

"I'm afraid that's out of the question at this time," Matulo said.

"Then could you arrange a meeting between your Foreign Minister and myself, or possibly between my Secretary of State and yourself."

"No," Matulo said. "That is also out of the question at this time. I can understand your wanting to discuss what is happening in more detail and I'm sure you would find a meeting with me most enlightening. Let me assure you, I have every intention of permitting such a meeting in the near future but before that there are many, many things that I will have to look

after. I will also have to see your good intentions
expressed in the way you treat my representatives in
your country as well as the way you help my representatives in other countries. I hope you understand."

"Yes," Henderson said. "I think I do."

"If that is all," Matulo said, "then I'll say good day
and will be back in touch with you in the near
future."

"Yes, that's all," Henderson said. "Good day."

"Good day," Matulo said.

Henderson reached for the intercom. "Put Blaine
on."

"Just a second," his secretary said.

There was a short pause. "Wendell?"

"Yes," Henderson said.

"What did he say?" Blaine said.

"He accepted it," Henderson said.

"And?" Blaine said.

"That's it," Henderson said. "I tried to arrange a
meeting of some sort but he wouldn't go for it. He
wants to see if we're really going to come through
with the money."

"Did you get any impressions, though?" Blaine
said.

"Just one," Henderson said. "I'd say the man is one
hundred percent confident of what he's doing, the
way we're reacting, everything."

"What makes you say that?" Blaine said.

"Just a feeling," Henderson said. "Nothing
specific."

"You know, Wendell," Blaine said, "I would never
have dreamed that someone like Matulo would have
had the guts or the brains to even try something like
this."

"Why do you say that?" Henderson said. "What do
you really know about Matulo, anyway?"

"Not much, I agree," Blaine said. "But still . . ."

"I know what you're saying," Henderson said, "but
the fact is, he's done it."

There was a short pause. "I have to get back on the floor," Blaine said. "I'll talk to you later."

"Later," Henderson said and again reached his hand to the intercom. "Craig, is Stu still out there?"

"Yes," his secretary said.

"Send him in." Henderson once again reached for the intercom and this time turned it off. Almost instantly, Davis was walking through the office door with an attempt at an encouraging smile on his face.

"How's it going?" Davis said.

Henderson shrugged his shoulders. "As well as can be expected, I guess," he said and massaged his eyes with his fingertips.

"What did you want me to do?" Davis said as he approached the President's desk.

Henderson let his hands fall away from his eyes to rest on the desk. "I've talked to Matulo. The ten largest banks in the country have agreed to lend two hundred million dollars to Toganda. Congress is being asked to guarantee the amount actually dispersed."

"Then you don't think this will last very long," he said, standing in front of the desk.

"I have no idea," Henderson said. "This is only the beginning and I don't want people getting the wrong impression. I have no idea how long this threat is going to hang over us and I don't want anyone getting the impression that we have something up our sleeve that's going to settle everything in the next few days or whatever."

"I understand," Davis said.

"And I also want it clearly understood that I do not suspect the Russians or the Chinese or anyone else of being involved in this except Matulo."

"That's going to be a hard one to accept," Davis said.

"It shouldn't be," Henderson said. "Every phase of security on that project is being checked at this very minute and I can tell you right now what they're going to find. Security has been weak, very weak, and I don't care what anyone says, that's the reality of it."

"Is that what you want me to say?" Davis said.

"No," Henderson said. "Just say there's probably been some lax security. You know what to do. If I can't count on you now, what the hell good are you, anyway."

"You've told me enough," Davis said. "I know what to say. The only other thing I'd like to know is whether you're planning to give any sort of address."

"Not for a while," he said. "I want to wait and talk to Marjorie, find out what Andreikov has to say, see what the Togandans do— It's too soon."

"Okay," Davis said. "I'll put a statement together and have it back for you to look at within a half hour."

"Fine," Henderson said. "I'll be here."

Marjorie Timkins arrived in Moscow for her meeting with Andreikov with an open mind and an intense desire to uncover every fact she could. The meeting had been arranged by Marjorie directly and was to include only Marjorie, Andreikov, and a couple of translators. Marjorie went directly from the airport to the Kremlin, briefed on the way by the U.S. Ambassador on the latest developments in Washington.

"I want you to realize how much we deplore General Matulo's tactics," Andreikov, a short, stocky man with a pudgy face said.

Marjorie nodded her head. "As does everyone."

"Yes," he said. "No other attitude is imaginable, but yet we cannot ignore the fact that the S-27 was developed and built by the United States, and this makes it very difficult for us to be sympathetic."

"Yes," she said. "I understand that."

"Of course, we will be willing to do whatever we can to help end this crisis," he said. "People all over the world are understandably concerned that a nu-

clear warhead could land on their city because of the
whim of a madman."

"Of course," she said.

"Of course, the chances of this missile being direct-
ed against my country are very slim," he said. "Very,
very slim, yet a chance exists, in a theoretical sense,
anyway."

"But not in a real sense?" she said.

"How else could we realistically look at it?" he
said.

"How can you say that?" she said. "Isn't Matulo in
reality challenging all the wealthier countries of the
world? Haven't you also been trying to develop a
cruise missile comparable to the S-27?"

"Yes, we have," he said. "There's no question that
we still feel a need to maintain technological parity
with the United States in all areas of military technology, even though it is a necessity that we find distaste-
ful and fundamentally opposed to the basic peaceful
goals of our society. Unfortunately we have no choice,
and I sincerely believe that the world's leaders, even
one as unstable as General Matulo, recognize that
fact. This is actually the fundamental reason why the
United States finds itself in its current difficulty. It,
along with its allies, has attempted for too long to
dominate countries such as Toganda and this is simply an expression of suppressed desire to become free
of that domination, as misguided as that expression
may be. Fortunately, my country has not developed
this type of hatred toward itself and, therefore, what
is happening with Toganda is simply the expression
of an historical development which has been in
process for many years."

"But we are looking at the very probable, imminent proliferation of the S-27 and Russia cannot be
isolated from the effects of that proliferation," she
said.

"I'm afraid I can't agree," he said. "I do not see
where the existence of one missile, possibly two, in

the hands of General Matulo automatically indicates
any imminent proliferation of the S-27 or the threat
you're referring to. Ultimately, yes, there will be a
proliferation and that is something that we've been
afraid of for some time. That is exactly the reason
why we have been working so hard on a defense
against the Thor-type cruise missile."

"Are you saying that you aren't worried about the
remaining missile because you have an effective defense against it?" she said.

"No," he said quickly. "Of course not. You know
quite well that the defense I'm speaking of has not
been tested in an actual combat situation, but that is
not really the point. General Matulo is a symbol of
something that cannot be denied. The United States
must understand and accept what its true position is.
It has managed to extricate itself from the strictures
of material-resource scarcity and in the process has in-
tensified its stranglehold over the economies of the
world, and I'm not just referring to the United States
alone. Other countries—Federal Germany, France,
Japan, and others—have been involved in the same
process. Capital has become more powerful than ever
and this is the consequence of that process."

"And you don't include yourself in this category?"
she said.

"Of course not," he said. "These demands for capital that we're referring to are being met by us in a
fundamentally different way, just as they always have
been."

"I'm afraid I can't see that," she said.

"It is the manner in which capital is applied," he
said. "A joint venture or a turnkey contract or a li-
cense is something entirely different with us than it is
with you. The entire political and economic thrust
and goal of our capital supply is oriented in a different direction from yours."

"And you think Matulo recognizes that?" she said.
"You think that will protect you?"

"Yes," he said. "I believe he recognizes this distinction. Why has he made his demands of the United States and not us? This is not to say that we can excuse his methodology, but what is happening is a symptom, not the disease. It is a natural manifestation of a problem which refuses to be solved by other means. General Matulo's actions, therefore, while they cannot be condoned, neither can they unequivocally be condemned."

"Are you ready, then, to face the instability that this is going to create?" she said.

"Certainly," he said. "Fundamentally, this is something that has been developing ever since the first terrorist conceived of building a nuclear device. The problem is that the world, including, I will admit, ourselves, has chosen to ignore this possibility as a viable reality, but now it is upon us and the inevitability of the historical process will determine what happens from now on. In that sense we're prepared. Getting down to more concrete and immediate matters, I will agree that this may, if continued for a sufficiently long enough period of time and given the proliferation you mentioned developing in a very short space of time, seriously disrupt world capital flows which will affect this country, possibly seriously. There is no way for me to predict at this point how serious that disruption may be but I do not believe that it will affect us, the other CMEA countries, and the underdeveloped countries as much as it will hurt the developed capitalist economies."

"Then what are you prepared to actually do?" she said.

"I have already begun to attempt a meeting between myself and General Matulo, the purpose of which will be to persuade him to act in a more reasonable manner, differentiating the real problems from the spurious. And again, this is really, and has been, the entire thrust of our foreign policy all along. Remember, there is right now in Moscow a permanent representative of the Republic of Toganda."

"But don't you see that as in effect approving of what he's doing?" she said.

"No," he said and shook his head vigorously. "In no way do we approve of General Matulo's tactics."

"Would you attempt taking the missile out of his hands?" she said.

When the translator finished, a smile grew on Andreikov's face. "No," he said. "To attempt taking the missile out of General Matulo's hands would serve no useful purpose. It would merely be an empty political maneuver. What is required is an understanding, an understanding among all the countries of the world, something which is long overdue. I would also like to say that if I am able to arrange this meeting with General Matulo, that one of my prime objectives will be to arrange a second meeting which would also include yourself and President Henderson in the interests of promoting a true and ultimate world peace."

"Thank you," Marjorie said and thoughtfully examined Andreikov's face. "I appreciate your thoughts on the matter but I feel that already the majority of what I wanted to accomplish at this meeting has been accomplished. More facts are needed, obviously, but I do want to assure you that we do not think that General Matulo received his missiles from the Soviet Union or from any other country and that our intentions are to do whatever is necessary to keep General Matulo from being provoked into launching his second missile, assuming, of course, that he has it. We would also like to keep in very close contact with you in this matter and hope that you will reciprocate."

"Let me assure you that we will," he said.

The meeting was over. Marjorie had what she wanted, Andreikov seemed pleased, and there was really nothing more to be said.

Reynolds arrived in Balingo with the taste of dirt in his mouth and feeling that his spine was a centimeter shorter. The bus was filled as it entered the new bus terminal, one of the accomplishments of Matulo's administration. Reynolds took his time getting off, patiently waiting for the women on their way to shop and the soldiers back from leave to get off ahead of him. As he walked through the terminal, he noticed the cracks appearing in the bare concrete walls and columns and the crumbling of the steps that lead to the street, visibly worse than the last time he'd walked through the station. Little more than three years old, the terminal was solid testimony to the way Matulo made his country work; yet, at the same time, there were buses going to places that hadn't had any access to regular, modern transportation before Matulo took office, and building the facilities had brought much needed employment both to the people who had built them and the people who worked in them. The contractors had also done quite well.

Reynolds walked the three blocks to his hotel with the same nativistic indifference he'd affected since entering the country, a relatively easy matter for Reynolds, since he was thoroughly familiar with this section of the city, although Simmons wasn't aware of that fact. The hotel Reynolds headed for had been built during Toganda's colonial days, and even though outwardly it cried out for a major face-lift, it had been built solidly and was still very functional. Once the residence of colonial administrators and foreign businessmen, it was now principally the home of single workingmen employed in the factories not far from it.

Reynolds stopped in the lobby to use a public telephone and had to dial his number three times before a connection was made. When he at last heard a voice at the other end, he said, "Is Senghor there?"

"No," the voice said. "Who wants him?"

"Tell him Reynolds is in town and I'll call him back in four hours."

"All right."

Reynolds hung up the phone, stepped out of the booth, and walked up to the desk. He produced his identity card and travel permit. The clerk casually looked them over, turned around, and looked for a key to an empty room.

"Seven-fourteen," the clerk said as he turned around and reached his hand toward Reynolds.

Reynolds finished signing the register and took the key. He handed the clerk a week's rent, then bent down, picked up his grip, and headed for the elevator. It jolted and groaned, but got him safely to the seventh floor. Reynolds walked down the dark, silent, musty hall to his room, unlocked it, stepped inside, locked the door behind him, and sat down on the bed. He opened his grip, pulled out an alarm clock, set it to wake him in three hours, placed it on the stand next to the bed, and lay down on top of the covers with his clothes still on. In a few seconds his body jerked and he was asleep.

Sithele Mulele arrived in New York shortly after noon and was driven directly to the U.N. The Togandan situation was being discussed in the General Assembly when he arrived, but as Mulele's presence was noticed, the discussion ceased. The Togandan Ambassador and his assistant calmly took their assigned seats and the assistant placed a sheaf of papers in front of Mulele. The ambassador leaned forward slightly toward his microphone and softly spoke into it, asking for the floor. The Nigerian who was presiding recognized him.

Mulele rose, his short, slight body barely supporting his over-large head. He cleared his throat, gazed directly ahead at the Nigerian on his temporary throne, and spoke hesitantly.

"The people of Toganda, under the guidance of President Amdida Matulo, wish at this time to announce to the world that a new era in international relations is being born, and that the first step in this birth is the first truly independent expression of international independence by one of the formerly most internationally oppressed countries of the world. While the wealthy nations of the world, those that control a vast, disproportionate majority of the world's wealth, view the recent actions of the Togandan people with horror and heap acrimony on our leader, the oppressed people of the world, the vast majority of mankind, can only applaud us.

"What we are doing is bold, courageous, and fraught with danger, danger that we are perfectly and completely aware of. We are risking everything, but then again, what are we really risking? We have little enough as it is. The average Togandan lives at a standard of living that existed in the United States half a century ago, with every indication that this same inequality in wealth will continue into the indefinite future.

"President Matulo has announced that the remaining cruise missile in our possession will be launched at an unspecified location anywhere in the world unless certain conditions are met. On the surface, this may be interpreted to mean that Toganda has set itself against the entire world, but it should be obvious to anyone that this would be a foolhardy, stupid, senseless act, if that were the case. The real object of this threat is to change the indifference of the wealthy industrialized powers of the world who have chosen to align themselves against the disadvantaged people of the world. To accomplish this objective, the Togandan people have chosen to act on their own, in a manner which allows them complete freedom to act on their own, to direct themselves to any part of the world independently, but yet which allows them to draw on the resources of the most advantaged country of the world, the United States of America. This is the true intent of our act and it is the responsibility of the United States to see that this threat does not have to be carried to its ultimate conclusion. Nobody

wants to see the destruction of thousands of innocent
lives. We certainly do not. Yet it must be clearly and
unequivocally understood that if necessary the ultimate step will be taken. No assumptions can be made
that it will not be. The Togandan people have too
little to lose and President Matulo has said many
times that he would gladly give his life not just for
the welfare of his country, but for the well-being of
humanity. If it is necessary to sacrifice thousands of
lives for this goal, if it is necessary to take this ultimate step to prove to the world that now is the time
to change, to share the wealth, to take the destinies of
our lives out of the hands of a few powerful people,
it will be done.

"There is only one more point that I wish to make
at this time. The Togandan threat is not simply the
act of one man. Amdida Matulo is the democratically
elected leader of Toganda and as such has the complete trust and devotion of his people. He has given
them more political and social stability than they
have ever known and he has done everything in his
power to bring them the economic prosperity that is
their right, but in this he has been consistently
blocked from achieving his goals, just as every other
underdeveloped country in the world has been
blocked by the industrialized wealthy powers of the
world with their technological superiority and
economic power. It is this indifference to the plight
of the majority of the world's people that has forced
us to take the action we have taken. We cannot fail
because we are right and God is with us. Thank you."

Mulele sat down to an immense silence. Several
moments passed before the U.S. Ambassador, Clyde
Tippitz, asked to speak. He was exactly the opposite
of Mulele, tall, heavyset, with a square face and a
crisp voice filled with self-confidence.

"My country agrees completely that there are serious problems in the world today, one of the principal
ones being the distribution of wealth, and we have

tried to do all we could to help alter that situation. The fundamental problems, however, have to do with lack of resources—natural, human, and financial— which the current actions of President Matulo can do nothing to alleviate. It is true that Toganda, as many other countries, does not enjoy the same standard of living that exists in this country, or western Europe, or Japan, or the Soviet Union, but there is no hunger in Toganda and virtually no major health problems, unless one wishes to count the increasing problem of heart disease, something which is really an indicator of beginning affluence, and the same can be said for virtually every other so-called underdeveloped country in the world. That is why the issue today is not really the distribution of wealth but the manner in which one individual country has taken upon itself the right to demand something for nothing. It is the worst form of international blackmail and one which my country intends to do everything in its power to stop, without at the same time doing anything that might incite President Matulo to press his button."

The Chilean Ambassador rose. "Was it not the United States that developed the S-27 in the first place? What was the reason for developing that missile in the first place if not to ensure the domination by the United States and its allies, either directly or indirectly, of countries such as Toganda? While we are all apprehensive at President Matulo's tactics in achieving his legitimate goals for this country, we can't entirely deny the logic behind his actions."

"Are you condoning the Togandan acts, then?" Tippitz said.

"No," the Chilean Ambassador said. "I'm only saying that the Togandan Ambassador has explained the justification for President Matulo's act in valid terms. I'm not saying that theirs is necessarily the most effective method of attacking that problem, but I think that the implications of his act must be much more thoroughly discussed before any sort of resolution is adopted concerning it."

"I would like to know how long President Matulo intends to exact his ransom from the United States or how much he intends on taking?" Tippitz said.

"As long and as much as necessary," Mulele said.

"Necessary for what?" Tippitz said.

"For the standard of living of the average Togandan to meet that of the average citizen of the United States," Mulele said.

"That's impossible," Tippitz said. "There is no way the United States could afford to send that kind of money to Toganda or to any other country of the world."

"The process will be gradual," Mulele said.

"Maybe in a hundred years," Tippitz said.

"That would be too long," Mulele said.

The Nigerian filled the room with the banging of his gavel. "Enough," he said. "This discussion will continue in an orderly manner."

Tippitz looked about the room, exasperated, while Mulele looked about calmly, in his introverted way, taking in the attitudes of the delegates as though by osmosis for future reference, as he always did. It was one of the features of Mulele's personality which brought him respect out of all proportion to the strength of the country he represented.

Marjorie tried for several hours to contact Henderson from the embassy, spending her time reading translations of newspapers and asking questions, trying to get a feel for the way the Russian people were really thinking.

"Marjorie," Henderson said over the phone at last. "How did it go?"

"Not well," she said.

"What do you mean?" he said.

"Andreikov is having his own internal problems,"

she said. "It looks to me that he's going to use this incident to help himself out."

"In what way?" he said.

"He's trying to dissociate himself from us as much as possible," she said. "He can throw the increasing ties between the two countries that so many of his party opponents have been supporting right back in their faces. In other words, it couldn't have come at a better time for him and his political future."

"He's acting as crazy as Matulo," he said.

"I know," she said, "but there's nothing we can do."

"Maybe we can turn it to our advantage," he said.

"How's that?" she said.

"I don't know," he said, "but we have to start turning something to our advantage."

"To turn something to our advantage," she said, "we first have to know what we want to turn it to."

"I thought we decided that," he said.

"We did?" she said. "When?"

"When we discussed your trip," he said.

"Really?" she said. "Tell me what we decided."

"We're trying to eliminate the threat," he said. "Show Matulo he can't get away with it, people won't stand for what he's doing."

"That's not a decision," she said. "That's an evasion."

"Don't give me that semantic crap," he said.

"It's not crap," she said and noticed her hands starting to quaver. "What do we gain by turning the world against Matulo? Where does that get us in the long run?"

"I don't understand what you're trying to get at, but I don't think this is the time to go into it," he said. "You're supposed to get facts, impressions, whatever, and do some persuading if you can. Just stick to that. Mulele gave an address at the U.N."

"I heard it," she said.

"What does Andreikov think of that?" he said.

"I don't need to ask him," she said. "It doesn't change anything."

There was a short silence. "We need a strategy, but we're not ready for it yet," he said. "Can you accept that for now?"

"Yes," she said.

"Good," he said. "I'll expect to hear from you tomorrow."

"Okay," she said. "Good-bye now."

"Good-bye," he said.

She put the receiver down and ran her fingers through her chestnut hair.

The majority of the world's population spent their day just as they normally would. A few psychologists predicted a mini baby boom in nine months, school attendance was off slightly, and a few of the inhabitants of every large city asked for early vacations so they could take their families out of town, but their numbers were infinitesimally small.

Almost three hours to the second after Reynolds had set his alarm clock, he woke to its buzzing. His mouth felt gummy, but his head was clear. He hopped off the bed and went to the bathroom with his grip. He quenched his thirst, washed his face, shaved, brushed his teeth, and feeling refreshed and ready for work, he went back downstairs to get something to eat before calling Senghor.

He pulled a newspaper out of a dispenser in the lobby and carried it into the cafeteria. He took a cup of coffee and a hard roll to one of the tables and spread the paper out. The front page was filled with the news of President Matulo's victory against the United States. There was also a lengthy explanation of how the buying delegation, which had already left for the United States, was going to operate and how the merchandise would be distributed. In the lower right-hand corner there was a picture of a Russian agent whom Reynolds recognized. The story explained how he'd been picked up while trying to find the remaining missile and had been killed in the attempt. Reynolds chuckled softly to himself when he finished reading the story. The Russian agent's body had actually been found over a week ago, stabbed to death by a petty thief.

Reynolds quickly leafed through the rest of the paper. Almost the entirety of it was articles relating to the missile threat, recapitulations of how secretly Matulo had arranged everything and taken the entire world by surprise, how the distribution of new goods would be handled, and projections of how fast the standard of living of the average Togandan would soar in the next five years. Reynolds found himself mildly amused at the total production, but it didn't affect his admiration for the righteous dictator. Matulo knew how to run his own country and Reynolds couldn't find it in himself to refuse to admit that. At the same time, Reynolds was still convinced that he understood Matulo, not completely, but enough to predict his actions under certain conditions, and under the present conditions, Matulo was still acting predictably and that made Reynolds feel relaxed and good.

Reynolds glanced at his watch. It was time to make his call. He slipped the paper under his arm and left the cafeteria for one of the public telephones in the lobby. After several attempts he was connected. "Senghor, please," he said.

A few moments passed. "This is Senghor."

"Reynolds," he said. "I'm at the Zimcoro Hotel. I'll be waiting in the lobby."

"It'll be about half an hour," Senghor said.

"I'll be waiting," Reynolds said. He hung up the phone and took a padded seat in the lobby.

The minutes passed quickly. The newspaper was read more minutely. He concentrated on his breathing. He let his eyes follow a couple of hookers as they jiggled through the lobby, too heavy for his taste.

"Reynolds."

Reynolds looked up at the sound of his name being called and recognized Senghor's smooth, boyish face. "It's been a while," he said, and smiled.

Senghor looked ill at ease. "Where do you want to talk?"

"Let's take a walk," Reynolds said, and dropped his refolded paper onto the seat at his side. Senghor followed him out of the hotel onto the street.

The soft streetlight made Reynolds feel more comfortable. "I'll be joining the army first thing in the morning," he said.

Senghor stopped and looked up, surprised, to Reynold's face. "What?"

Reynolds stopped. He loomed a good ten centimeters over Senghor and spoke down to him in a relaxed manner. "I won't be in long," he said. "I'll get back in touch with you in a few days. I just wanted to let you know I was in the country."

"Make sense," Senghor said. "You didn't need to meet me in person to tell me that."

Reynolds pursed his lips. "Let's keep walking." He started down the street again with Senghor keeping pace. "How are things going?"

"You mean the party?" Senghor said.

"Yes," Reynolds said.

"Well enough . . . better if we had the money and the help you promised."

"That's good," Reynolds said. "I'll have the money next time I see you. How fast can you be in action?"

"Fast enough," Senghor said.

"How fast?" Reynolds said.

"You want it in hours and minutes?" Senghor said.

"That sounds good," Reynolds said.

They walked along in silence past a whistling drunk weaving down the sidewalk close to the buildings.

"Will you be serious?" Senghor said when the

drunk had passed. "How could I possibly know how fast I can have my people ready? And ready for what?"

They kept on walking around a corner, past glaring neon bar signs and washed-up hookers.

"I have to see Matulo," Reynolds said. "I have to know what condition he's in."

"Isn't it obvious?" Senghor said. "He's gone completely berserk with his missile."

"I don't see anyone complaining," Reynolds said, gesturing toward a clot of young men lighting up their cigarettes.

"What does that mean?" Senghor said.

"Just what I said," Reynolds said.

They kept walking.

"Okay," Senghor said. "I see what you're getting at, but they don't know what's really happening, or what's going to happen."

"That's a problem," Reynolds said.

"Damn it, I know what you're trying to do," Senghor said, "and I don't appreciate it."

They kept walking.

"I said I'd be back with the money and the help and that's what I'm going to do," Reynolds said. "I'm trusting you to be ready."

"I'll do what I can," Senghor said, "but this missile thing has me baffled. I don't know what it's going to do and now you show up just as it starts. It has me confused."

"Don't be," Reynolds said. "Just be ready. I'll be back in a few days and that's when you'll have to be ready."

"After you've seen Matulo," Senghor said.

"Right," Reynolds said.

They kept walking, across a street and alongside a park, past a homosexual being picked up.

"Why do you have to see Matulo?" Senghor said.

"I told you," Reynolds said. "To see what condition he's in."

"I don't believe you," Senghor said.

"Why not?" Reynolds said.

They kept walking.

"It doesn't make sense," Senghor said.

"You're getting smarter, Julius," Reynolds said.

"What is it?" Senghor said. "Have you got something going with him?"

"In a way," Reynolds said.

"It has to do with the missile, doesn't it?" Senghor said.

"Yes," Reynolds said.

They kept walking, around another corner and along another edge of the park.

"Everytime I see you I trust you a little bit less," Senghor said.

"Why's that?" Reynolds said with a slight change in his voice.

"It should be obvious," Senghor said.

"It isn't," Reynolds said. "Everything I've ever told you was the truth. If I said I'd see you at a certain time, I was there. If I said I'd do something, I did it." He looked genuinely hurt.

"It's what you don't say," Senghor said.

They kept walking.

"Maybe I should tell you more," Reynolds said. "I don't know. Some things are just too important to take a chance on."

"Like what?" Senghor said.

"Like what I'm doing right now," Reynolds said.

"Which is what?" Senghor said.

"Helping you," Reynolds said.

"Stop it, damn it!" Senghor burst out angrily. "You're doing it again."

"Julius, I said I'd get you the money and the help and I'm going to do it," Reynolds said. "That's all I'm going to say."

"Then fuck it," Senghor said. "As far as I'm concerned, I'm on my own."

Reynolds stopped and grabbed Senghor's arm at

the elbow. Anger shot from his eyes and soft voice. "Julius, you've always been on your own. Ever since we met, you've been on your own. You have your own mind, you go your own direction. That's all I look for and that's all I want. I'm in the midst of something big right now and part of it is helping you beat Matulo. I'm going to see that you're a winner. You're going to rule this country and whether you reject me or not doesn't really matter. I'm going to do what I said because it's for me and it's what I want for me and you'll be a part of it, but for yourself because it's what you want for yourself."

Senghor was silent, taken by the sincerity in Reynold's voice yet disturbed by his vague meanings. He pulled his elbow in to his side and Reynolds let go. "Let's walk," Senghor said, and they continued walking uneasily.

"I'll be waiting," Senghor said. "And I'll be ready."

"Good," Reynolds said.

Their conversation descended into small talk about the weather, movies, books, and casual affairs till Reynolds said he had to return to his hotel and they parted.

Third Day

Kunthile Kantho arrived in Chicago with the twenty
members of his buying delegation. They were greeted
formally by the mayor as they stepped off their plane
and, in the midst of a cloud of Secret Service men,
were guided to waiting limousines. They ignored the
peaceful band of demonstrators waving signs reading:
YOU CAN'T BLACKMAIL THE U.S.A. and MA-
TULO BELONGS BEHIND BARS (this accompanied by a picture of a monkey hanging onto the bars
of a cage) and YOU'LL BE SORRY.

The Togandans were taken to the Sheraton Black-
stone, where the two top floors had already been
cleared to accommodate them. The floor below was
occupied by more Secret Service men. One suite had
already been arranged into an office for Kantho complete with a small reception area with a steel desk
and a switchboard, and an inner office with an impos-
ing wooden desk supporting six telephones and ten
file cabinets along one wall, five of which were already filled with brochures and price lists. A State Department official patiently guided them through what
had taken fifty people working through the night to
put together.

Kantho was pleased. "This will do," he said, turning to the official.

"If there's anything else," the official said, "just dial
six and you'll get my office on the floor below."

"Thank you," Kantho said.

In the lobby of the hotel were seventeen vice-
presidents representing seventeen of the largest U.S.
industrial corporations. They were awaiting word of

when they would be allowed to meet with one of the Togandan buyers.

Marjorie Timkins was in Paris for her meeting with the French President, Guidy-Livron, a tough, handsome leader with a distinctive Eurocommunist philosophy that played a major role in his popularity. He had met Marjorie before and liked her, but he surprised her by starting the meeting questioning her about where Matulo got his missiles.

"For all we really know," he said, "no such missile exists in their hands."

"That's right," she said in fluent French. "We don't know."

"Then what makes you so certain they have it?" he said.

"The demonstration missile he launched had to be equivalent to the S-27," she said. "No other missile could have functioned the way that one did. They had one, they could certainly have another. We simply don't feel that we can take a chance, plus our psychological analysis of Matulo suggests that he's not bluffing."

Guidy-Livron pulled at his mustache. "Then how do you think he got them?" he said. "Off the record."

"I don't know," she said.

"Do you think Matulo could have built them in Toganda?" he said.

"Possibly," she said.

"And the plans?" he said.

"They could have been stolen," she said.

Guidy-Livron showed a row of even, white teeth. "Matulo must have some outstanding spies."

"They might have been purchased from a third party," she said.

"Such as whom?" he said.

"I don't really know," she said.

"Russia? China?" he said. "Off the record, of course."

"No," she said. "I really don't think so. What would the advantage be?"

"It's hard to say," he said. "Then you have no theory at all."

"No," she said. "We're hoping to discover within the next few days where this other missile is or whether it doesn't even exist, but before we get some more facts, I would personally rather not speculate."

Guidy-Livron pulled at his mustache again. "Perhaps you might like to hear a theory I've heard."

"What's that?" she said. Her curiosity was aroused and she showed it.

"That the United States has engineered the entire incident," he said.

For a second, she wasn't sure that she'd understood the French correctly. She ran the words over again through her head, translating into English. "Are you serious?"

"Interesting, isn't it?" he said.

"Fantastic," she said.

"Perhaps," he said, "but the logic behind it is interesting. You say you have no idea where he could have obtained the missiles. None are missing, yet I find it very difficult to understand how Matulo could manage to steal all the necessary plans, or even purchase them from a third party, let alone build an entire missile in his country undetected."

"I agree," she said. "We've discussed that problem over and over and it is possible. Most of the work could have been done in any of a million machine shops anywhere in the world, and the electronics could be put together with standard parts."

"It's possible," he said. "but the United States has had its share of difficulties with Matulo over certain multinationals operating in that country."

"As France has also," she interjected.

"Yes," he said, "but, continuing with the theory, one question keeps bothering me. How does Matulo plan to escape from this act of terrorism?"

"He's a religious fanatic," she said.

"Maybe," he said, "but let's assume that he is not that idealistically motivated or, rather, suicidally motivated. After all, he occupies a position of power traditional terrorists do not. But let's say he has an agreement with the United States, an agreement which will allow him to personally escape his inevitable destruction in exchange for participating in the production of a dramatic confrontation between a rich and a poor country, a confrontation that could possibly lead to justifying using a certain measure of force, military force, in that country."

"To what end?" she said.

"Capturing the Togandan market," he said.

"There isn't enough there," she said.

"It's developing," he said. "American banks are holding the majority of Togandan debt, debt which might have to be written off as a total loss if Matulo stays in office."

"And the debt is getting higher," she said.

"And so you have your opportunity to foreclose," he said.

"But you've got loans in that country," she said. "And so does England, West Germany, Japan, Russia. Besides, why would we possibly want to do something as insane as what you're suggesting?"

"It could be justified where rigging an election through the CIA or something such as that couldn't be," he said.

"I think I've heard enough," she said.

"It's just a theory, he said, "but one which is getting some attention. I only brought it up in light of the mystery surrounding how Matulo acquired his missiles and the fact that you're so certain he has the other one."

"Mr. President," she said and fixed her deep brown eyes on him, "all I can say is that that theory is absurd, and I'm genuinely surprised that you would even consider such a thing. We're not involved in any type of global game even remotely resembling what you've proposed. How Matulo got his missiles is a mystery, that's all, and we would appreciate any help you could give us in resolving that mystery,"

"What we can do, we will," he said.

"Thank you," she said. She felt discouraged. She felt like she was walking in mud, mud that went to her knees and sucked at her feet while she tried to get someplace but was too tired to remember where.

At one time General Amdida Matulo had been just another member of the Togandan Legislative Assembly at a time when the Assembly actually had some power independent of the president of the country. Matulo's constituency covered an unusual portion of Balingo. One part of it contained some of the wealthiest people in the country and they were the ones who provided his greatest support at election time. This part was as modern as any modern city in the developed world. It contained luxury high rises, expensive and exclusive jewelry and clothing shops, and the offices of wealthy and influential lawyers and doctors. The other part of his constituency contained some of the poorest members of the urban population who were crowded into one small sector of the area he represented. The crisis that catapulted him into power occurred in this latter area.

A cannery on the outskirts of his district invested in some newly developed automatic machinery from Germany. Once it was installed and operational, about one hundred workers were laid off, the majority of whom lived in the slum portion of Matulo's district. For one of the workers, it was the fifth time he'd been laid off as the result of automation in three years. He became so despondent over his inability to keep a job that he committed suicide, leaving his wife and four children with nothing but the small proceeds from his government life insurance. A reporter for the major daily newspaper in the country heard of the incident through an acquaintance and looked into it. The reporter considered it a fitting symbol of the problems that were confronting the average Togandan's aspirations and persuaded the editor to run it on the front page.

The night after the story appeared, the new machinery in the cannery was destroyed. The owners of the cannery blamed the editor of the paper, a man who had shown increasingly liberal tendencies, for causing the incident. The editor was fired by the owner of the paper, a good friend of the cannery owner. The editor refused to leave his office and three policemen were sent to forcibly remove him. The editor still refused to leave, so the police grabbed him and tried to drag him out of the building. The people in the newsroom came to his aid and attacked the police and threw them out of the building. Several hours later a hundred police were surrounding the building and demanding that everyone inside come out. The people inside refused, and the police proceeded to lob tear gas grenades into the building. The timing of the police action was a crucial factor in enlarging the scope of the incident, since it began shortly before the majority of workers left work to go home. As a result, thousands of workers were in the streets at the same time the tear gas grenades were being lobbed into the newspaper building. A spontaneous riot erupted which eventually involved several thousand people, although the exact figures were never known. The army was called in to restore order. Thirteen people were killed, including two policemen, and over four hundred were injured.

The following day there was a call for a general strike from certain leftist leaders. Only a handful of people refused to go to work in response to the request, and they were promptly fired. Those who called in sick were investigated to make sure that they actually were sick and not simply staying away from their jobs in protest. Word of what was happening spread through the country, and a wave of arrests began, starting with the leaders who had called for the strike. This then triggered another series of incidents. Several policemen were attacked and seriously injured while on routine patrol, the cannery was burned to the ground (the owner collected his insurance and left the country with his family), and sporadic rioting broke out from demonstrations against lack of employment due to automation, high prices, and poor housing. The President asked for, and received, additional powers from the Legislative Assembly to restore peace and order and to save property. The Assembly, in a close vote, gave him total authority over the police and the army until order was restored. With that authority, the President recessed the Legislative Assembly, declared martial law in Balingo, and ordered all workers to continue at their jobs under penalty of prosecution under the laws against treasonable acts.

At the time of the crisis Matulo was part of the majority party which supported giving the President unlimited power in restoring order. As the situation worsened, with more and more workers refusing to go to work, the newspaper closed, and even occasional desertions from the army, Matulo decided it was time for him to act. He met secretly with one of the major leaders in the principal minority party of the Assembly to offer him his support for the presidency in a new government which Matulo would help him form. Matulo, even though his public image was as a conservative supporter of business interests, had also managed to maintain contacts with certain underground opposition leaders. He persuaded two of the wealthiest and most politically powerful men in his district to announce their support of a moratorium on new technology and the support of more labor-intensive industry to create jobs if he could persuade the major dissident leaders to agree to a temporary halt in their activities. The dissident leaders agreed, in turn, to a temporary cessation of their more militant activities if the President would resign and new elections be held.

Matulo then contacted the President and convinced him that a group of officers in the army were planning to assassinate him, and that it would be next to impossible to get rid of them without turning the entire army against the Government. Matulo assured the President that he could arrange safe passage out of the country for the President and his family. In return Matulo wanted access to secret documents containing information about a number of the Legislative Assemblymen and other political and business leaders in the country which had been compiled by the intelligence branch of the Togandan National Police. Matulo convinced the President that with that information he would help restore order in the country so that the President could return at a later date. Since Matulo had carefully cultivated the President's friendship and trust over a period of several years, the President agreed to leave the country.

Matulo arranged for a plane, a pilot, and a briefcase full of gold. Shortly after takeoff, however, the plane developed engine trouble and crashed, killing all on board. When the news of the President's death reached Balingo, the Legislative Assembly reconvened and the Vice-President, who owed Matulo the equivalent of nearly a hundred thousand American dollars, asked Matulo to be his special assistant in forming a new government. New elections were announced, two major business leaders announced their support of a moratorium on new technology, and the strikes and demonstrations stopped. The minority party leader who Matulo had agreed to support announced his candidacy for the presidency, and Matulo began to actively campaign for his election, explaining to the acting President that he was too tainted by his prior association with the late President to be able to win enough popular support.

This earned Matulo the loss of his position as special assistant to the President, an action which he had anticipated.

The minority leader was popular with the agricultural workers and the unemployed, and appeared to be the likely winner. Two weeks before the elections, he died in an automobile accident. Matulo called the death "murder" and blamed it on the two wealthy industrialists who had announced their support of a moratorium on new technology. Matulo charged that the conciliatory promises of the industrialists had merely been made to obtain future favorable treatment from the Government and that they had no intention of actually sticking to their promises. Matulo then obtained a special mandate from the acting President to organize a quick trial. Two witnesses, whose reliability went unquestioned, swore that they had been paid by the accused to tamper with the minority leader's car. During the trial, Matulo announced his own candidacy for the presidency, having been drafted by an unlikely coalition of members of both major parties who saw him as both having the current popularity necessary to win an election and as being controllable once in office. Three days before the election, the two industrialists were executed for murder; Matulo won the election easily.

Matulo's first act as President was to call for new legislative elections. The proposal passed easily, a date was set, and active campaigning began. In the interim the Legislative Assembly was virtually powerless, because two-thirds of the members had to be present to vote on any legislation and more than half the assemblymen were out of the capital campaigning. During that time, the wife of a wealthy lawyer was killed. Matulo demanded that the murderer be found and quickly brought to trial, so that peace could be maintained among all elements of society by seeing that there was equal and swift justice for all.

The alleged murderers were found and brought to
trial. Allegations were made that the three men on
trial were not the actual murderers and that they
were being unjustly accused because of their prior in-
volvement in leading demonstrations against the government. Demonstrations were held, the National
Police and later the army were called in and rioting
began once again. Matulo announced that he had to
claim the powers that the former President had been
given by the Legislative Assembly even though there
hadn't been a proper vote because too many of the assemblymen were outside the capital. He then accused
the head of the National Police of purposely arresting
the wrong people to instigate the rioting and use the
resulting confusion to further his own political ends.
The head of the National Police was arrested and
thrown in prison. With the army firmly on his side,
Matulo began to reveal plot after plot designed to
overthrow the government and impose a dictatorship
financed by moneyed interests. Arrests and rapid tri-
als followed the revelations, and before the new elections were held for the Legislative Assembly, Matulo
was certain of solid backing from the majority of assemblymen, who would win their seats on the basis of
Matulo's new popularity.

It took another six months before Matulo was able
to eliminate enough of his opposition to no longer
feel any constraints from the Legislative Assembly
and to take total, direct control of the army and assume the title of General. The Legislative Assembly
became a rubber stamp and Matulo spent virtually
all his time in the Presidential Palace. In all, it had
taken five years for Matulo to rise from his first elec-
toral victory to his present position.

Having read the previous day's newspapers, Matulo
called his press aide and instructed him to arrange
for a worldwide satellite broadcast. The press aide
went to work, and later that same day the double

doors to General Matulo's office swung open and a
man carrying a minicam walked in with the press
aide. The General was studying some documents,
principally requests from the heads of state of countries, both small and large, asking for personal audi-
ences with the General to discuss his new era in
international relations. There were also reports from
his secret police concerning the activities of foreign
agents within Toganda. He paid no attention to the
technicians as they set up the lighting and positioned
a microphone on his desk. When everything was arranged, the press aide addressed the General.

"General Matulo, we're ready," he said.

The General put the papers he'd been studying to
one side and picked up the papers containing the
speech he'd personally prepared. The camera was
aimed at his face. The director pointed to him and
Matulo looked intently into the camera with his dark
brown eyes that protruded ever so slightly.

"People of the world," he began, "I regret very
deeply the necessity for this broadcast, but your leaders have made it necessary. I have tried to make it
clear that if I must I will launch the remaining missile in my possession at a heavily populated area of
the world, *not necessarily in the United States of
America*. I don't know what I have to do to make my
position any clearer. I have stated it very simply a
number of times already. Still, when I read what some
of the newspapers around the world are saying about
my threat, I can only conclude that I have not been
understood. I have therefore decided to make this
broadcast in hopes that any further doubts will be
erased.

"Only yesterday I had to have two agents of the
U.S. Government shot as spies." (Simmons was sitting
next to Henderson in the President's office, watching
the broadcast. "He's lying," Simmons burst out. "He's
done no such thing." "Quiet," Henderson said impa-
tiently.) "They were trying to find the location of my

missile. I also know that there are agents in Toganda from many different countries who hope to be the first to find that missile. I want the people of the world to tell their leaders that if this spying continues, I will have no choice but to launch that missile. Now, I know that many of you have been asking yourselves, 'What can he really hope to gain by this?' and 'Has he stopped to consider what will happen to him and his country once that missile has been launched?' The answer to these questions is quite simple. The Togandan people can only end with more than they have now as a result of what I am doing, no matter what happens.

"Let me explain this in very simple terms. I am perfectly aware that many people consider me an irresponsible leader, even insane, but I am perfectly aware of the fact that if I launch the cruise missile in my possession, I will be a dead man. I know that I will be hunted to the farthest corners of the world by the secret agents of certain countries and that many of my closest associates will also be hunted for the same reason, and they are fully aware of this also. At the same time I know that the people of Toganda will *not* be hunted down and killed. They *will* have things that they would not have been able to get otherwise and once they have them, they will not be willing to let them go. I would defy any country in the world to attempt to forcibly take those things away from them once they have them in their possession. I am willing to give my life for that and I am willing to launch the missile in my possession to prove that no matter how powerful a country is, it cannot force the Togandan people to do whatever it wants them to do. If each one of you were to tell your leaders that you are not willing to die to support their desire to control another nation's right to independence and freedom, there would be nothing to fear. Thank you."

General Matulo returned to examining the

documents he'd put down and the camera crew began removing their equipment. They turned off the extra lights, removed the microphone from the General's desk, and quietly left.

Simmons turned to the President. "Why the hell doesn't he just come out and say the United States? One minute he acts like he's fighting the world and the next it's developed versus underdeveloped. What the hell is the matter with the man? What does he want?"

Henderson was concentrating on the blank television screen in front of him.

"And this crap about him being willing to sacrifice his life for his people," Simmons continued contemptuously. "Who does he think he's kidding?"

"What makes you think he's kidding?" Henderson said quietly.

"What?"

"Maybe it's the truth," Henderson said. "Maybe he really is selflessly seeking the best for his people and is willing to sacrifice himself in the process if necessary."

"I'd never buy that," Simmons said. "All you have to do is look at the way he came to power, his psychological profile. . . . I'm surprised you'd even consider that possibility."

"Well, I do," Henderson said, and turned to face Simmons. "In fact, I'm convinced that's the truth."

"Now you must be kidding me," Simmons said.

"Don't you think it's time you admitted that Matulo's smarter than you're willing to give him credit for?" Henderson said.

"Smart, yes," Simmons said. "Idealistic, no. His motivation is simpler than that."

"I didn't think there was any motivation that came simpler than that," Henderson said.

"Maybe I used the wrong word." Simmons said. "Maybe 'basic' is better, like getting out of that country alive and wealthy."

"And you really think that's all Matulo wants?" Henderson said.

"Yes," Simmons said.

"Don't you think he could have found an easier way of doing that?" Henderson said.

Simmons adjusted his neatly groomed figure in his chair. "Maybe not. Matulo was ruthless in consolidating his power. Since then, conditions haven't really changed much. Now, let's say that Matulo is afraid that he's about to be overthrown. If he stays in the country it's a virtual certainty he'll die; if he leaves, he had better have some money stashed away somewhere to fall back on and a place to go. Now, let's say he doesn't have that money stashed away. What does he do?"

Henderson gave Simmons a withering look. "He gets two S-27's and threatens the world."

Simmons shrugged.

"Don't you think that's going a little far, especially considering the fact that your own reports indicate no organized opposition to Matulo within the country?" Henderson said.

"None that we're aware of," Simmons said.

"All right," Henderson said. "I'll assume the opposition is there. Then what?"

"We take the cue," Simmons said. "We offer him his life."

Henderson turned his head to the side and thought a moment. "Have you heard anything from Reynolds?"

"Nothing," Simmons said.

"Isn't he supposed to be giving you some kind of reports?" Henderson said.

"Only if he finds something," Simmons said.

Henderson shook his head slowly.

Clarence Bishop pulled the tab off a can of beer in the paneled basement rec room of his friend Marty's house. Marty's father had been a leading American

Nazi, but Marty had found the Nazis a little too extreme for his taste, so he had joined the Sons of Patrick Henry. Clarence considered him his right-hand man. Clarence, as president, was the organizational and ideological backbone of the organization, while Marty handled the hardware and desert training. Clarence walked over to the fireplace and stood beneath a gunrack. He rested his elbow on the mantel and turned to his friend. "I still think the best approach would be to hit part of that buying delegation."

Marty was lounging on an overstuffed sofa. "It's easier than going to Toganda, but not much. Those people are surrounded by Secret Service agents constantly."

Clarence shrugged. "They let the Togandans walk off with that missile," he said. "As far as security in this country goes, I think that should speak for itself."

Marty nodded his head. "Well, I'd say we'd definitely have to get them away from their headquarters in Chicago. They're going to be too hard to get to there. That leaves their traveling and I'd say that's our best chance, but it also means we're going to need some intelligence work."

Clarence's eyes lit up. "In a car being driven someplace, like by a salesman taking some of them for a demonstration or something like that."

"Something like that," Marty said. "We could have a couple sharpshooters get it, but we'd have to know where they were going, when they were going . . . the works."

"Yes," Clarence said thoughtfully. "In a car."

"The problem is where to get the information. All that traveling information is top secret. We're not the only ones who'd like to see those monkeys get what's coming to them."

Clarence took a long draft on his beer. "We'll find a way."

* * *

Westbrook focused on Henderson. "What I would really like to know is why we had absolutely no information, no indication whatsoever, that this situation was developing." He turned to Simmons. "And you can't imagine how shocked I was to discover that we didn't even have someone in the country."

"We did," Simmons said, "up until a few years ago."

"And what happened to him?" Westbrook said.

"I pulled him out and didn't replace him," Simmons said.

"You pulled him out and didn't replace him," Westbrook said. He turned around and looked knowingly toward the other congressmen in the President's office.

"That's right," Simmons said defensively. "I had to. It was shortly after Matulo took over. He was too involved in local politics, Matulo knew about it, DuPont and some other company were about to have their assets appropriated over it, so I took him out and nothing came of it."

"But you didn't think he was worth replacing," Westbrook said.

"It's a small country," Simmons said. "We run on a tight budget and there's only so much we can do. And if my management is going to be the subject of this discussion, I want it known, for the record, that the CIA under my administration has had less unfavorable publicity and the tightest budgetary control in the history of the agency."

"We're very aware of your record," Seitz said. "What bothers us is the almost total lack of any facts concerning Matulo and his missiles."

"There are other intelligence-gathering organizations," Simmons said. "Why don't they know anything either?"

"We're not talking to them right now," Westbrook said, "but believe me, there's going to be a full-scale investigation into this entire incident. I intend to see to that."

"Senator, I think you've made your point," Blaine said, accompanied by a bluish puff of smoke. "I think the question at this point should be what's being done. That's what I'm worried about."

Simmons relaxed visibly. "We have a man in the country who's competent, very competent, and I expect to hear from him at any time."

"You're sure that's not the one Matulo referred to in his speech?" Westbrook said.

"That was just a lie," Simmons said. "If he were really dead, we would know about it."

"Just like the missile," Westbrook said.

Simmons struggled to control himself. "Senator, I have been in the intelligence-gathering business for over twenty years and when I say I'd know if our man was dead or not, you can count on it. Check my record. This is the first disaster I've ever been a part of. Nobody batted an eye when I took over this post. They welcomed me. They couldn't approve me fast enough." He shook his finger in the air. "One incident. Just one, and I will guarantee you right now that I'm going to come out of it smelling like a rose."

"How long before we can expect some word from this man?" Senator Eastland said.

The redness started to bleed out of Simmons's face as he turned to the other senator. "A few days, maybe. I can't say for sure, but that was his estimate and his reputation leads me to believe it. Maybe it'll be less, maybe more. If we could make a reasonable guess as to where the missile might be, I could be more specific, but we really don't have a clue. For all we know, it might not even be in Toganda. The first one was launched from sea."

"Damn," Westbrook said and slapped his hand on his leg. "Don't you people know anything? What the hell do we have a CIA for?"

Simmons pressed his lips together as Eastland

turned to the President. "Have you heard anything more about how Matulo could have obtained the missiles?"

Henderson leaned forward. "I got a report from the FBI that they have discovered some very poor security at the company that was making the onboard computer. They think it's likely that someone could have stolen the design for it, hardware and software, without much trouble, but nobody's been picked up in connection with anything."

"Then Matulo really could have simply stolen the information and built it himself," Seitz said.

Henderson nodded his head. "I'm afraid so."

Westbrook's pudgy face turned red. "My God, do you realize what you're saying? That's the most advanced missile in existence. It was supposed to be the best-kept secret in the whole damn country. We weren't even considering selling it and that pint-sized, pop-eyed General Matulo stole the damn thing right out from under our noses and we didn't know a damn thing about it."

"Senator," Henderson said, "I can understand why you're upset, but what is it going to accomplish? You'll get your investigation, but right now we have to deal with the possibility of one of those missiles being dropped on some major city, and that means appropriating the money for the Togandans. That's the first order of business."

"All right," Westbrook said, "let's talk about that."

"I personally think," Seitz said, "that appropriating those funds is a mistake. As soon as we do that, Matulo is going to know he's got us. As it stands, he's got to be on edge."

"I can agree with that in principle," Henderson said, "but that two hundred million is going to be spent pretty quickly, faster than I thought, and we're going to need more than vague loan guarantees. I think it's apparent that all indications are that this is going to continue longer than we originally expected.

We need direct appropriations and Matulo isn't going to give us the time to debate fine points. The man's a religious fanatic. He talks to God and God told him to do this. Now, are you prepared to take a chance on that? Are you prepared to watch a five-kiloton warhead drop on New York, or Chicago, or some other city? That's the whole issue, right there."

"There's another way of looking at this, however," Seitz said calmly. "First, we're assuming he has the other missile, but we don't know if he does or not. Secondly, we're assuming that that second missile can't be intercepted. I find it hard to believe that the Army didn't learn anything from the first launch. In fact, I would assume they would have a much better chance of intercepting a second launch, if there is one. But then, let's assume the missile is launched successfully. What happens? We move into the damn country and take over with every justification in the book and get indemnification as well as Matulo himself."

"When the country isn't worth enough to pay for a few square blocks of downtown New York?" Henderson said.

"What makes you so damn sure he's ready to die?" Westbrook said.

"Exactly," Simmons said.

"Damn it," Henderson said. He looked over his audience and his voice rose. "That is not the point. Maybe he's bluffing, maybe he's not. Maybe he's got the missile, and maybe he doesn't. The point right now is that it won't be long before ten banks will be out two hundred million dollars with nothing but my word and a vague resolution in the House that they'll ever get it back." He focused on Seitz. "Fred, you're on the Banking Committee. You know what kind of shape the banks are in. Are they ready to write off that kind of a loss?"

Seitz hesitated. "You're right," he said reluctantly. "A loss like that, at this time, could be serious. In fact, that kind of a commitment for some of those banks is going to put them in violation of reserve requirements."

"Then do I tell Matulo we're reneging on the deal?" Henderson said. "What the hell am I supposed to do?"

"You had no authority . . ." Seitz said.

"What the hell am I supposed to do?" Henderson said a little louder. "Damn!" He settled back into his chair. "I'm getting sick of going in circles. I want that money and I want it now. We can keep on debating in the dark like this forever but I'm getting tired of it right now. We need some action and we need some time and I'm not ready to see a financial crisis erupt in the middle of this missile crisis. I've been doing my best to work with all of you, to keep you informed of my thinking. I've been hoping that we could work together, but maybe I've been wrong."

"I'm behind you a hundred percent," Blaine said.

"Me too," Eastland said.

"Thank you," Henderson said quietly and paused to collect his thoughts. "If we can't work together, I'll work alone. I'll work in secret and I'll do what I can. I'll bring every bit of pressure to bear that I can to get what I want, even though I really don't want to do that because I'm trying to think in longer range terms as much as possible. But right now it's got to be one thing at a time until we get more facts, until we get more reactions."

Westbrook nervously rubbed his hands together. "I'll support the two hundred million, but that's as far as I'll commit myself at this time."

"Okay," Henderson said and looked to Seitz.

Seitz nodded his head.

"Good," Henderson said and felt a burning point of pain in his stomach. "Let's leave it at that for now."

In a few minutes the office was cleared and Henderson was left alone with his thoughts.

*   *   *

Dr. Julio Marquez was back on his feet and putting in his normal sixteen-hour days. He wired his approval to the Chilean Ambassador to the United Nations of the way he had been handling himself but cautioned him against appearing too much in favor of Matulo's actions. He was disturbed at the fact that he hadn't received any more information on what exactly was happening inside Toganda from his intelligence sources and let the proper people know how he felt. The Chileans did have a source inside the Presidential Palace—one of Matulo's translators had been receiving payments in a Swiss bank account from the Chileans—but even she didn't know where the second missile was or even if the second missile actually existed. All she could report was that it appeared that only a very few people besides Matulo knew anything at all about the entire strategy and only Matulo knew all the details. Marquez also continued attempting to contact General Matulo directly, but without success.

"Then you're convinced the Togandans could have the resources to build the missile," Marquez said.

Dr. Martin Cavalho, physicist and adviser to President Marquez, hesitated a moment, considering his answer so as not to give the wrong impression. "They could afford it," he said, "and I would guess that they might have enough technicians to do the work. But—and this is a big 'but'—I find it difficult to imagine them building all the components in that country without attracting attention. Theoretically, it could be done—although I doubt that it was—for maybe thirty million U.S. dollars, but that would be a major undertaking in that small a country, and some of the advanced electronics, the miniaturization particularly . . ." He shook his head. "That would have to be stolen."

Marquez was getting impatient. "But it could have been built outside the U.S. I mean, building that missile wouldn't necessarily require their resources."

"Yes, of course," he said.

"Do we have the resources?" Marquez said.

"If we had the plans," Cavalho said, "certainly. I think we would even be capable of duplicating the electronics here."

Marquez nodded and leaned back in his chair. He was sitting there thoughtfully when the phone rang. "Excuse me," he said and leaned forward to his desk to pick up the receiver. "Hello?" After a moment his mouth started moving in anticipation. "Yes, yes, of course, arrange a meeting as soon as possible. What did you say his name was? . . . Somerville, Somerville. That name sounds familiar. . . . ITT. Well, find out what you can about him, but I'll be willing to see him if you think he's telling the truth. . . . I'll talk to you later, Pedro." He looked up to Dr. Cavalho. There was a thoughtful half smile on the President's face. "Well, we may have the source of Matulo's missile."

"What?" Cavalho said.

"We've been contacted by someone who says he can help us get one of those missiles," Marquez said. "He wants a meeting with me, and I want you to be there. It'll be arranged for sometime tomorrow if all goes well."

Cavalho pursed his lips and put his finger to his goatee.

Iti Mlulo stepped through the front door of his modest but modern one-bedroom fourth-floor apartment in Balingo.

"Iti, is that you?" his wife said.

Iti's muscular arms, bare past his shoulders, glistened with a light patina of sweat, his jeans had a light coat of tan sawdust, and his leather work shoes were stretched from use to conform to his feet. He let the front door close behind him and dropped onto the worn sofa that dominated the center of their living room. His brother Anti was sitting on a plain steel chair reading a newspaper.

"What's the latest?" Iti said.

His brother looked up from the paper. "It looks like the United States is going to start paying."

"Good," Iti said. "Maybe I'll get a raise."

Anti had been trained to be an engineer in Toganda's one university. He graduated near the top of his class shortly before Matulo was elected president. He went to work for a company that made structural steel, but he made no secret of his feelings about Matulo's rise to power, and during the short recession that followed Matulo's election he was laid off and hadn't been able to get a regular job since. Fortunately, the Mlulos had always been a close family and, with both their mother and father dead, Iti had agreed to let his brother move in with his wife and himself when they got their new apartment, and the arrangement had worked out surprisingly well.

"If you're smart," Anti said, "you won't count on getting a damn thing."

"How do you know so much about it?" Iti said.

"I don't have to know very much," Anti said. "Anyone with any sense would know the United States is just buying time. Nobody is going to let the General get by with something like this."

"Except that he is," Iti said. "He pulled those missiles right away from the Americans. Nobody else did."

Anti shrugged his shoulders. "How do you know what the General really did?"

"Are you going to tell me black is white?" Iti said.

"I'm saying someone helped him," Anti said.

"Like who?" Iti said.

"I don't know," Anti said, "but that fool in the palace didn't do it. I know that."

"That fool in the palace keeps me working," Iti said, "and you eating."

"He keeps you working and someone else from

working," Anti said. "One of these days you're going to see what kind of a great leader this country really has."

Iti shrugged his shoulders and turned his head to the side. "Lesi, is dinner ready?"

"Just about," she said.

"Good," Iti said. "I'm hungry." He turned back to Anti. "I think I've had enough politics for today."

Anti shrugged. "Okay," he said, and returned to reading the paper.

Herbert Thomas Reynolds grew up in a suburb of Chicago. His friends called him Tom. His father was a sales representative for a construction-equipment company. His mother was a registered nurse. He liked all types of sports but in his freshman year at high school he decided that there were too many others who were better at athletics than he was. Team sports only interested him to the extent that he could gain personal recognition. He never could appreciate the team spirit that would grip his friends. He had to be *the* star, not just one of the members of a starring team, and when he realized that he wasn't going to achieve that recognition on the football field or the basketball court, he quit and looked for another area to excel in. He kept his mind open and in his junior year decided to run for Senior Class president. He lost the election by a narrow margin, but even though the school he was attending was predominantly white he didn't consider his loss in racial terms.

That small taste of a political defeat was enough to send his mind searching for another area to excel in. He went to Harvard on an academic scholarship and majored in political science with the idea of success in a political context still in the forefront of his mind. He didn't run in any elections, but bided his time, waiting for the proper area to express his ambitions to present itself. Still not having formed a defi-

nite goal, he went on to do graduate work at
Northwestern University in comparative foreign policy. His doctoral dissertation was entitled "Quantitative Analysis of Multinational Corporations in
Foreign Policy Initiatives." During his postgraduate
work he was approached by the Central Intelligence
Agency with the offer of a job. Reynolds found the
prospects they offered, and the possibilities of finding
the proper outlet for his personal ambitions there, intriguing. Upon graduation he accepted a job with
them as a foreign policy analyst. It was there that the
details of his ultimate goal began to form and become
more concrete. Shortly after going to work at Lang-
ley he let it be known that he was interested in working as an agent. An opportunity arose during the South
African Civil War and he jumped at the chance.

The United States was attempting to remain neutral in spite of the strong economic vested interests in
the white ruling government by a number of U.S.
multinationals and the realization that there was no
way of escaping the inevitability of a black victory.
The goal was, therefore, to save as much American
private investment as possible without antagonizing
either party. To accomplish this, the United States attempted to serve as a mediator, and the CIA was authorized to conduct clandestine operations within the
country for the purpose of gathering information
which could be useful in attempting to guide the negotiations. Reynolds's job was to infiltrate the strongest of the black liberation armies. He saw the U.S.
policy as a proper one, considering the circumstances,
and felt that contributing to the success of that role
might give him the opportunity to achieve that personal victory he had waited for so patiently. His infil-
tration was successful and he was able to relay
important information to the CIA on the location of
arms and troop movements.

Reynolds was convinced that the information he
was gathering would be used only to facilitate U.S.

diplomatic strategy in the form of helping negotiations. When his cover was blown he barely escaped the country with his life and in the process showed a resourcefulness any agent would have been proud of. When he returned to the United States he learned that the army he'd infiltrated had nearly been annihilated with the loss of over fifty thousand lives. He suspected that the rout could only have been the result of certain information he had gathered having been given to the white South African government. He attempted to confirm his suspicions but only received repeated assurances that the information he'd gathered had not been released to any other government. He became convinced of his suspicions when the United States gained a major diplomatic victory by getting both parties to agree to a temporary ceasefire, an agreement that could only have occurred at that time as the result of the destruction of the black army. Reynolds pretended to be satisfied with the CIA's assurances, but three months later he left, explaining that he had lost interest in doing undercover work and wanted to pursue the writing of scholarly texts on foreign affairs. Simmons, the recently appointed CIA Director, expressed his disappointment at seeing Reynolds leave and let him know what an excellent job he thought Reynolds had done in South Africa, and Reynolds parted on friendly terms.

He began doing research on the quantitative analysis of foreign policy implementation in underdeveloped countries. Shortly after beginning his research he was contacted by Andros Stavropoulos, the wealthiest man in the world. Reynolds was asked to be a foreign policy consultant to the Greek magnate at a salary of $200,000 per year, payments to be made in any manner Reynolds chose. Reynolds upped the price to $300,000, $50,000 to be paid in the open and the remainder secretly. Within two years Stavropoulos had made back considerably more than what he had paid Reynolds for his highly accurate predictions of foreign policy decisions that affected Stavropoulos's various business enterprises.

It was during this period that Reynolds was asked to do another job for the CIA. Stavropoulos was attempting to gain a concession to build a major aluminum-manufacturing complex along the Red Sea using cheap geothermal power. Alcoa was his principal competitor for the concession and it seemed that Stravropoulos was about to win. Alcoa was convinced that Stavropoulos had special influence with the Saudi Arabians that the U.S. was not aware of and that the influence might be detrimental to the welfare of U.S. interests in the area. An appropriate comment was made to the President, and the CIA was asked to look into the matter. The CIA, in turn, being fully aware of Reynolds's relationship with Stavropoulos, appealed to Reynolds's patriotic feelings and asked him if he knew what it was that Stavropoulos had. Reynolds said he didn't know, but would be willing to find out.

Reynolds then had a meeting with Stavropoulos on the Greek's yacht in the Mediterranean and when he returned to the United States a few days later he contacted the CIA and explained that Stavropoulos had certain documents, which Reynolds had managed to copy. These documents contained information about the Saudi President's background which, if revealed, would be certain to force him out of office, if not get him executed. Simmons thanked Reynolds for his quick work, took the copies of the documents, and that was the last Reynolds saw of the CIA for several months.

The information Reynolds had produced was leaked in Arabia several days later. There was a scandal, the Saudi President was forced to resign, and the Vice-President took his place. Alcoa feted the new President who, it seemed at first, was about to give the concession to the American company. Stavropoulos, in turn, raised his offer slightly, and the concession was his. For his part, Reynolds received a bonus of $200,000.

At their next meeting on Stavropoulos's yacht, the Greek calmly sipped a Scotch and soda as the two men warmed themselves in the sun.

"I'm still not really sure how you put it all together," Stavropoulos said. "You said I'd get the concession for the price I was willing to pay, and I did, but I still think the ex-President would have given it to me anyway."

Reynolds shook his black head in short, quick motions. "Believe me, Andros, he was only trying to force Alcoa to raise their price, and doing it in an incompetent manner. You never would have gotten it with him in office."

"But how did you know the new President would be so disgusted with the way the CIA leaked the information on the ex-President?"

"That's what I get paid for," Reynolds said with a bemused smile.

Reynolds had no trouble enlisting in the Togandan Army. Any able-bodied man with the correct identification could do it. To Matulo the Togandan Army was primarily a means of alleviating the unemployment which persistently hovered between the forty and fifty percent marks, but at the same time it was one of Matulo's most prized possessions. Matulo himself had never risen above the rank of Sergeant-Major. The title "General" had been bestowed upon him shortly after his election by an appreciative Commander-in-Chief, General Mgombwe, who was grateful for Matulo's promoting him after the unfortunate death of the obstinate General Imkoto, who had been standing in the way. Matulo had asked Imkoto to take an early retirement, but the competent, disciplined General had refused. His refusal became moot when his body and that of his driver were found at the bottom of a ravine, the result of an accident.

Mgombwe had studied military science in several countries abroad, but had really missed his calling as a contractor. His chief interest was in construction, and in that capacity he was noted for outstanding efficiency and foresight. The results were barracks that were some of the most modern and well-built structures in the country, food that was well above the average Togandan fare, pay that was good but not exorbitant, and an opportunity for any reasonably healthy man or woman to join without any trouble. Matulo only interfered with the commander in the promotion of certain generals and left the details, which he so scrupulously monitored in the civilian sector, to Mgombwe. Mgombwe, in turn, spent hours poring over blueprints for barracks, mess halls, and administrative centers and most of his days consulting with subcontractors, personally making sure that the best materials were used, that the best tradesmen available were on the job, and that they were paid the best wages.

To the complaints of some junior officers who questioned the real effectiveness of Toganda's fighting capability, Mgombwe rejoined that he didn't have time to examine all the methods of training (that was to be handled by the drill sergeants and was to be done by the book), or the conditions of any weapon (that was to be handled by ordnance), or the qualifications of every officer (that was the responsibility of the Togandan Military Academy). He explained that an army needed a chain of command to take care of details and his duty was to see that the proper people were put in charge and that they had the proper facilities in which to work. Any officer who persisted in criticizing the lack of real training that the troops were receiving, or the inability of artillerymen to aim their guns, or the inability of the infantrymen to hit a bull's eye, or the absurdity of maneuvers which made a good spectacle but didn't teach anything, was retired early. The only good fighting unit in the country was the Palace Guards, since Matulo personally saw to it that they were led by a qualified general whose loyalty Matulo could trust.

Reynolds was taken to a training camp outside Balingo the same day he enlisted, and after dinner he approached a corporal who had a scar where his right ear should have been. The corporal was standing outside the mess hall by himself, lighting a cigarette.

"Corporal."

The one-eared corporal turned to his side and threw his match away. "Don't you know how to salute?"

Reynolds gave him a sharp Togandan salute.

"That's better," the corporal said gruffly. "What is it?"

"I understand you can tell me where there's a game tonight," Reynolds said.

"What?" the corporal burst out. He stared intently at Reynolds. "What are you talking about?"

"A game," Reynolds said, unintimidated. "Dice. Gambling. I'd like to play."

"I don't know what the hell you're talking about." The corporal turned aside and started to walk away.

"I've got a thousand," Reynolds said.

The corporal turned around and gave Reynolds a closer look. "Where'd you get a thousand?"

"My parents," Reynolds said. "To start me off."

The corporal eyed him suspiciously. "You look a little old to be starting on your own."

"I worked on a farm," Reynolds said, "but prices are down and it was either me or my brother who had to leave. They gave me what they could."

"A thousand's a lot for a poor farmer," he said.

"I found a game in the city and got lucky," Reynolds said quickly.

"Lucky, huh?" The corporal kept looking Reynolds over. "What makes you think I know about a game?"

"My cousin," Reynolds said. "He told me to find a corporal with one ear if I wanted to play."

The corporal reached a hand to the side of his face self-consciously. "What's your name?"

"Umlika."

The corporal nodded his head slowly. "I remember an Umlika. Is that your cousin?"

Reynolds nodded. The corporal walked up next to him and blew smoke in his face. "If you want to play, meet me behind the mess hall at midnight and have your money. We play for cash only."

"I'll be there," Reynolds said.

Marjorie Timkins wasn't sure if she was already feeling the effects of jet lag or whether her mind was simply clouding with doubts about the value of her trip, when she arrived for her meeting with the British Prime Minister, Anthony Elsworth, the soft-spoken heir to a toy fortune. She was expecting the same basic position that had confronted her in her last two talks and she was feeling that the world was going to let the United States handle this incident entirely on its own. What bothered her was that she was beginning to feel that that might really be the proper attitude for the rest of the world to take. Why she felt that way, she wasn't quite sure, but she couldn't help it. Elsworth surprised her.

"I'm ready to back the United States in whatever decision it makes," he said, "and I stated that very explicitly in Parliament earlier today."

She was surprised to hear herself say, "Why?"

He chuckled in a way that put her at ease. "Because Matulo's threat is just as much a threat to us as it is to you, of course."

"But," she said, "don't you think that's exposing you to risks that don't necessarily have to be yours?"

"I think Matulo has made it very clear already that he'll launch the missile anywhere," he said. "Don't you believe him?"

"Yes," she said. "I do, but that doesn't seem to be the way the rest of the world sees it."

"Of course not," he said. "I'd be surprised if they did, the majority anyway. You weren't, were you?"

"Frankly, yes," she said. "I was."

"But why?" he said.

"I'm not really sure," she said.

"It seems obvious to me that Matulo has voiced his threat the way he has to accomplish just the thing that has you so surprised," he said. "You know, what really surprises me is how little credit Matulo has ever been given for his intelligence. The man is no fool. He wants everyone to concentrate on the United States as the villain until the plot thickens, so to speak, to further his own ends, and he's succeeding."

"But doesn't it bother you at all that it's our missile?" she said.

"But it's not, is it?" he said.

"No," she said. "It's true they didn't actually physically take one of our missiles, but we did develop it."

He chuckled again. "Miss Timkins, don't take this wrong, but I find your questions somewhat odd. What difference does it make who developed that missile? The point is that Matulo has it now, and before very long, someone else will have it, and before much longer, someone else will also have it, and so on. If other countries want to concern themselves for the moment with keeping Matulo's missile off their own heads, that's fine. Personally, I would rather concern myself with where we go from here and I think that when President Henderson starts getting his wits about him and stops letting himself get buried in momentary trivia, he'll point a direction, and when that happens, you can let him know that I'll stand behind him—I have that much confidence in the man."

She relaxed and smiled. "You can't imagine how that makes me feel," she said. "But does Parliament agree with you?"

"Some do, some don't," he said. "But then, I don't need this job to make a living, do I?"

She started laughing in a release of nervous tension. "No," she said. "I guess you don't."

"And I would imagine you don't either," he said quite seriously.

She thoughtfully shook her head. "No, I guess not."

"So, you see, there you have it," he said. "You can either act like a rational human being or not."

She smiled and nodded her head. "I'd like to get back to something you said a moment ago. You were talking about Matulo's intelligence and a plot. What is his strategy, really, do you think?"

Elsworth leaned back in his chair and thought about the question. "Matulo is one of my favorites. By that I mean he's fascinated me ever since he took over that country and I've spent a lot of time trying to study the man. He's smart in a sickening kind of way. He keeps his people off balance. They never really know exactly what to expect, but at the same time, there's just enough order that everything doesn't all collapse. He maintains a delicate balance. He's religious, very, but like a prophet. He's direct, he's inspired, and he's unpredictable. How he got the missiles—and I'm convinced he has the second one—is hard to guess. I don't think he could have done it by himself, with his own people, but I could be wrong. He has people who are intensely loyal to him. They almost worship him, and some of them are brilliant. There aren't many, but there are a few. It's even possible that a few of them could have stolen the plans and seen to the building. I don't know. He has ideals, he's intensely puritanical about sex, and he'll launch that second missile if he feels he's being thwarted. That I'm convinced of. He'll do it just to prove he wasn't bluffing."

"What makes you so convinced of that?" she said.

"Have you ever met the man?" he said.

"No," she said.

"I have," he said. "I've seen him, here in England, in the middle of winter, walk out in sub-zero weather in his shirtsleeves and act like it's the middle of summer, and then the next day refuse to go out because it's too cold. I saw him once walk into the middle of a firing range because he thought he saw something, and was oblivious to the shells exploding around him." He leaned forward. "If there is anyone on this planet who could do what Matulo is doing right now, it's Matulo. He's the only person I can imagine who has the right position and the right psychology. He's irrational in just the right proportions and I believe everything he says. The man never lies. He just states the truth in a distorted way. That's why I'm so convinced that Henderson is doing the right thing."

"But what's he really after?" she said.

"Exactly what he says," he said.

"Do you think he's going to succeed?" she said. "Is he about to win?"

"It all depends on what you mean by winning," he said. "In a way, he's already won. He's done exactly what his Ambassador to the U.N. said. He's made a totally free and independent action. He's done it. It may be stupid, it may end up being pointless, but he's done it."

"But where does it end?" she said.

"Why," he said with a soft chuckle and leaned back in his chair, "when he says it will end."

"What?" she said.

"When the standard of living of the average Togandan equals the standard of living of the average American," he said.

"I'm afraid you're getting a little too philosophical for me now," she said. "I'm talking about an incident, not the future history of the world."

"Miss Timkins," he said, "all I can see quite clearly right now is that the entire international scene is about to change, and change rapidly. Traditional methods of applying power and influence are about to change. It's been coming, but the idiot genius, Amdida Matulo, is making it happen now. Justifica-

tions and accusations aren't going to change a thing.
I don't know where this Togandan incident is head-
ing exactly, but I intend to see that Britain makes the
best of it."

"Which is why you're so solidly behind President
Henderson," she said.

"Precisely," he said. "Henderson is a very capable
man, I admire him very much and I believe he's going to take the lead, he's going to take the initiative,
which is the way it should be. The United States
should take the lead. After all, it's in his hands. Matulo put it in his hands and I know Matulo looks at it
that way."

Marjorie looked to the side and crossed her legs.

"Have I answered your question?" he said.

"I don't know," she said. She thought a moment
and turned back to him. "I think so."

Reynolds had no trouble getting out of his barracks
to meet the one-eared corporal behind the mess hall.

"The money," the corporal said with outstretched
hand as Reynolds approached him.

Reynolds reached into a back pocket and produced
the thousand Togandan pounds he'd promised.

The corporal quickly leafed through the bills,
nodded that he was satisfied, and turned around to
open the door behind him. The game was already in
progress. Reynolds was quickly introduced to the
half-dozen players, and the sergeant-major, whose
turn it was to shoot, turned back to roll the dice. Reynolds took a few moments to size up the two brawny
privates who were there to maintain order and then
kneeled down to watch the dice. The sergeant-major
had rolled a seven, let out a shout and added another
stack of bills to the pile he had sitting on the floor in
front of him. Reynolds took fifty of the next roll and
lost it. In less than an hour Reynolds had a little over
two hundred pounds left and the sergeant-major had
nearly all of everyone else's money.

The dice passed to the sergeant-major again, but just as he was about to shoot, a hand reached for his wrist. "Let me see those," a scar-faced corporal said.

The sergeant-major clenched his fist tighter around the dice and turned his head to the side. "You think I'm cheating?"

"Let me see the dice," the corporal persisted.

"No," the sergeant-major said.

Suddenly a knife appeared in the corporal's free hand. Reynolds had been watching and was ready. He grabbed the corporal's wrist, pulled it toward himself, and twisted at the same time. The corporal fell forward on his face and dropped the knife. One of the guards threw his arm around Reynold's head and started to twist when the one-eared corporal shouted, "Hold it!"

The guard loosened his grip.

"That's it for tonight," the one-eared corporal said.

The losers sullenly began to put their money away and trail out of the kitchen. The scar-faced corporal gave Reynolds a venomous glance. Reynolds left with the sergeant-major, who was elated to get out of the game with his money, and his face uncut.

"That corporal is a killer," the sergean-major said when they were outside. "Thanks."

"It's okay," Reynolds said. "I don't like sore losers."

The sergeant-major laughed and slapped Reynolds on the back. "You're all right—what was it—Umlika?"

"That's right," Reynolds said.

"Come on," the sergeant-major said turning to his left, "let's have a drink. It's still early."

Reynolds turned to follow him, somewhat stunned at how his luck was going. The sergeant-major led Reynolds into his apartment, which was set at one end of a barracks. Reynolds took a seat while the sergeant-major went to a cabinet and produced a bottle and two glasses. "Vodka?"

"Fine," Reynolds said.

"I got a taste for it while some Russian advisers

were in the camp," he said as he poured the drinks. "That was before Matulo. Since then, we haven't had any advisers." The sergeant-major sat down on the edge of his bed with the glass in his hand. He took a long swallow. "You know, there was a time when we didn't have games like that. It would have been unthinkable. We had to wait for the weekends and we really had to watch out. I got busted five times for gambling, but now it's nothing. Just about every night there's a game, and if you're shot in the morning, you just go on sick call." He took another swallow. "That's the new army," he said, and grimaced.

"Doesn't sound too bad," Reynolds said.

"Not bad," he said with a humph. "I'm no saint, that's for sure, and I've broken just about every rule there is, but at least there was a time when I had some pride in my company. Now half the army doesn't even know how to shoot straight. Pitiful." He finished off his glass and headed back to the bottle on his desk.

Reynolds was nursing his drink. "I think I know what you mean," he said. "I was in a gang once, just a bunch of kids, but we were tight, real tight. You know what I mean?"

"Yeah," the sergeant-major said.

"I liked that," Reynolds said.

"You came to the wrong place, then," the sergeant-major said as he refilled his glass.

"What about the Guards?" Reynolds said.

The sergeant-major turned around. "What about them?"

"I've heard stories," Reynolds said.

The sergeant-major nodded his head. "You have to be good if you want to get in there."

"I am," Reynolds said.

"You know how to shoot?"

Reynolds nodded his head confidently. "I'd say so," he said.

The sergeant-major returned to his bed. "Where'd you learn?"

"I worked for a guide once," Reynolds said. "He showed me and I got pretty good."

"Why do you want to get in the Guards, though?" the sergeant-major said. "No gambling there. Strict discipline. It's run the way an army's supposed to be run."

"I hear the pay is better and it has its advantages," Reynolds said, smiling from the side of his mouth. "You know what I mean?"

The sergeant-major laughed and took another swallow. "Impress the girls, huh?" he said. "Well, I guess it does."

Reynolds took a short sip from his glass. "How do you get in?"

"Easy enough," the sergeant-major said. "If you can shoot straight, take orders, and get a good recommendation, there's no problem."

"How do I do that?" Reynolds said. "Get the recommendation, I mean."

"Easy," the sergeant-major said. "You go to the target range and prove you can shoot. Show you can take orders on the drill field and I'll give you the recommendation."

"That's it?" Reynolds said.

The sergeant-major shot what was left in his glass down his throat. "It'll make us even," he said with a distant glazed look in his eyes. "Easy to get in, another thing to stay in."

Reynolds sipped at his drink as the sergeant-major lay back on his bed.

"Never could handle liquor," the sergeant-major said.

Reynolds hesitated with his glass poised on his leg. "Were you in?"

The sergeant-major closed his eyes. "Once," he said.

"What was it like?" Reynolds said.

"Great," the sergeant-major said thickly. "I even met Matulo."

"What did you think?" Reynolds said.

"Great man," the sergeant-major said. "Smart. Tough. I liked him. Still do."

Reynolds finished his drink. "I appreciate the help."

"It's nothing," the sergeant-major said. "Really, nothing."

Reynolds put his glass down on the desk and stood up. "I better get going. I want to be in shape for tomorrow."

"Yes," the sergeant-major said with his eyes still closed. "Get some sleep. I'll see you tomorrow."

Reynolds slipped quietly out of the room. He felt tired and resentful at the way the sergeant-major had sucked at his energy.

Majorie went to her room in the U.S. Embassy. She called Henderson and briefly described her meeting with Elsworth. Henderson was pleased and had little to report in exchange aside from some further FBI reports on security problems at more of the sites where components for the S-27 had been made or designed. Marjorie cut her conversation with the President as short as she could and then ordered a sandwich to be sent to her room. When it arrived, she ate about half of it and realized she didn't have any appetite. She lay back on her bed and closed her eyes but didn't go to sleep. She kept thinking about her conversation with Elsworth and wondered if she were really acting in a rational manner or just moving from one event to another, caught up in the details of reacting to one incident at a time and then, when that reaction was over, moving to another. She thought about a time when she could see the future stretched out for years in front of her and when she could see herself, even though only faintly, at each point in time, moving closer to something she believed in, but somehow, somewhere, that feeling had slipped away. She knew she was in the middle of something important, important to her personally, but she still couldn't quite grasp where things were going.

She pushed herself off the bed and walked over to a full-length mirror on the wall. She looked at herself slowly, her stockinged feet, her rust-colored skirt, her light-yellow blouse. She stopped when she reached her face and concentrated for a moment on each line she saw, then focused on her eyes. She felt tired and she could see the tiredness in her own eyes, but she couldn't tell where the heaviness she felt was coming from. "What the hell am I doing here?" she said out loud.

In a theater in New York, a young man sat casually eating popcorn. He turned to the girl sitting next to him and said, "I heard Matthew is planning to have lunch with Missy." A woman sitting behind him overheard the words and thought he'd said, "I heard Matulo is planning to launch his missile." Since she'd neglected to watch the evening news that day, she turned to her husband and said, "That man just said he heard that Matulo is about to launch his missile." Her husband said, "At New York?" A middle-aged man sitting behind them was convinced they'd said, "Matulo is planning to launch his missile at New York." He also had neglected to watch the evening news or read the evening paper, so he turned to his girl friend and said, "That woman just said Matulo is planning to launch his missile at New York." He, in turn, was overheard by a nervous young woman, lacking in self-control, who said quite loudly, "Matulo is about to launch his missile at New York." She stood up and began bumping knees and kicking feet in her haste to leave the theater. A teen-ager with his date who had just had his feet kicked said, "What's the matter with you?" The nervous woman said, "Matulo is about to launch his missile at New York. I have to get out of here." Within a few minutes two hundred people were trying to claw and elbow their way out of the theater. One person was crushed to death.

Fourth Day

Fred Somerville had been an executive with ITT in Chile. He had also at one time worked part time for the CIA, collecting information, but Simmons had dropped him fast when his name came up in connection with the murder of a young woman. The woman had been Fred's mistress and her body had been found in an alley, beaten to death. Somerville was investigated, but there wasn't enough evidence for a conviction. Instead he lost his job and was asked to leave the country. The incident occurred shortly after Reynolds had gone to work for Stavropoulos, and having come in contact with Somerville's work during his days at the Agency, Reynolds offered him a job with a meat-packing company in Argentina, a subsidiary of one of Stavropoulos's companies. He thus became the first full-time member of Reynolds's organization.

The day after the Chilean Ambassador to the United Nations had delivered his partial defense of Toganda, Somerville received a call. He was asked to arrange a meeting with the Chilean President and to offer him an S-27. Somerville knew the right people to contact and the meeting was set at Marquez's home in the mountains. Present were Marquez, Anquierro, Cavalho, and numerous bodyguards as well as Somerville, who arrived alone. He was searched for weapons and recording devices, but was clean. Marquez eyed him suspiciously as he walked into the library where the three Chileans were waiting for him.

"Good day," Somerville said amiably.

Each of the three responded politely. Anquierro indicated the chair he was to sit in, and Somerville sat down.

"Mr. Somerville," Marquez began, "I'm sure you realize we've checked your background."

Somerville nodded in agreement.

"It is unsavory, to say the least," Marquez said. "I was tempted to refuse to come."

"I can understand that," Somerville said calmly.

"But you have had some important connections in the past," Marquez said, "so I'm willing to listen, but my time is limited. Be convincing if you really have access to the S-27."

"I will," he said. He reached inside his jacket and produced a packet of papers. "Here are the plans for the laser-tracking unit of the S-27."

"May I see those?" Cavalho said, and reached toward him.

"Of course," Somerville said, and handed him the packet. Cavalho got out of his seat and went to a table on the other side of the room where he began to spread the tissue-thin papers out. Somerville turned back to the President.

"Is that what you're offering, then?" Marquez said. "The plans for the missile?"

"Plans and components," Somerville said. "However you want it. We're very flexible."

"How much?" Marquez said.

"Ten million American dollars," Somerville said.

Marquez didn't react. "That's cheap."

"It's our cost," Somerville said.

"Whose cost?" Marquez said.

"Let's just say I'm working for an independent organization," Somerville said.

"What does that mean—an independent organization?" Marquez said. "And what kind of an organization offers to sell plans and components to something like the S-27 for cost?"

"I can't answer that because I don't know," he said sincerely. "I only get paid for doing a job."

"This looks like it could be authentic," Cavalho said, "but I'm not a specialist. I'd have to have someone else take a look at it and even then . . ."

"Your proof isn't thoroughly convincing, Mr. Somerville," Marquez said. "What do you have to say to that?"

"Show it to whatever experts you want," Somerville said, "and if it isn't enough, I'll produce more plans. I'll even start producing components and you can start assembling one. When you're convinced and the missile is built, you can pay us."

Marquez started to laugh. "You sound like you're ready to just give it to us."

Somerville didn't laugh. "We want you to have one."

Marquez turned serious. "You mean you're ready to supply us with this missile with no guarantee of being paid anything?"

"In the form of certain components and plans," he said. "Certain parts you'll have to supply yourselves, like the body. That would be too much trouble for us to handle but I'm sure you already have something in your arsenal that would be compatible."

"I see," Marquez said very thoughtfully. "But you can't tell us what this organization is that you're representing."

"No, I can't," Somerville said. "My job is simply to arrange the necessary machinery for your getting the missile secretly. I have no contact with the head of this organization. I get everything through post office boxes and over the telephone. If you let me know where you want the information delivered and where the components are to be shipped and how, we'll make our arrangements. I've been assured that everything can be handled very flexibly. All I need is your agreement to begin."

"But this is crazy," Marquez said. "Whoever's doing this must want something out of it."

"That's something I couldn't possibly explain," Somerville said.

Marquez took a deep breath and considered the situation. He still couldn't believe that there wasn't some trick involved, but yet he couldn't imagine how either he or his country could be hurt by agreeing to the offer. "Very well," he said, and turned to Anquierro. "You'll leave here with Mr. Somerville. Arrange the necessary details. The faster we get the missile, the better." He turned back to Somerville. "Thank you. That will be all for now. I have to be going." He shifted his attention once again. "Dr. Cavalho."

The doctor looked up from the plans and turned around. Marquez was out of his seat, stepping around his desk while Anquierro had turned to his side and was already discussing plans with Somerville.

Marjorie called Henderson to let him know she was coming home and wanted to cancel, for the time being, the remaining stops on her loosely scheduled trip. Henderson's immediate response was, "Why?"

"Because it's a waste of time," she said.

"Why do you say that?" he said. "What are you going to do back here?"

"Try to find out what's really going on," she said.

"But we're working on it," he said insistently. "The FBI, the CIA, the USIA. I don't even know how many people are trying to figure this thing out."

"I don't care," she said. "I'm just convinced I'm wasting my time with this trip. What we need is more digging right there, where you are. The answer is there, finding out where Matulo got those missiles and deciding what direction we're going to turn our foreign policy from now on."

There was a long silence. "Okay," he said. "Cancel the trip and I'll talk to you when you're back here."

"Thanks, Wendell," she said, and hung up the phone.

*   *   *

Kunthile Kantho was busy placing orders for sewing machines, electric irons, televisions, radios, and automobiles. One of his first orders was for five Rolls-Royce limousines placed through a dealer in Chicago. To begin the immediate delivery of merchandise, he chartered three DC-10's. He encountered a few difficulties but no resistance on the part of the suppliers he dealt with. What he did encounter was an enormous desire to do business. This desire was so great that the small switchboard that had been installed at first had to be expanded to handle the enormous number of calls the buying delegation was receiving from companies all over the country wanting to do business with the Togandans. He even had to hire an American secretary to help with the load.

Clarence Bishop learned through the newspaper that the Togandans were interested in a hydroelectric project being conducted in Arizona. He became inspired with the possibilities that might present themselves and began contacting the members of the small group of people he led. He queried them, looking for a possible contact who could uncover the exact time and route which the Togandans might travel in getting to the project. He uncovered some leads and resigned himself to waiting.

Sithele Mulele patiently sat through the debating in the U.N. on the Togandan situation, declining to become involved. The proposal in the Security Council by the U.S. Ambassador to the U.N. to condemn Toganda didn't even come close to passing. The Chilean Ambassador softened his approach of the preceding day and tried to get a private meeting with the Togandan Ambassador. He was unsuccessful, as were all the others.

Both houses of Congress finally approved by a narrow margin the initial 200 million-dollar appropriation that Henderson had requested. Westbrook called for an investigation into the conduct of U.S. intelligence agencies in the Togandan matter and someone leaked to a Washington columnist that President Henderson was counting on a special agent in Toganda to end the crisis. Henderson refused to comment.

Marjorie went directly to the White House from Dulles. She was met there by a weary Henderson and an aloof Simmons. Tense and unsure of herself, Marjorie wasn't in the mood for a meeting. It was an effort for her to concentrate.

"How do you feel?" Henderson asked after she'd sat down.

"Tired," she said.

Henderson rested his arms on his desk and leaned toward her. "What's the problem?"

Her attention fixed on the heavily embossed bags beneath Henderson's eyes. "No problem," she said. "I just realized I was wasting my time on that trip. That's all."

"You weren't thinking that way when you left," he said. "Why the change?"

She hesitated. "I just wasn't accomplishing very much and I didn't see it leading anywhere."

"You mean you didn't learn anything from it?" Henderson said.

"No," she said quickly. "I don't mean that. I was supposed to get facts and impressions. I did. I was supposed to persuade. I tried. But there are other ways of accomplishing that. We've got an entire State Department full of professionals. Why not put them to work?"

"But none of them are the Secretary of State," Henderson said. "I thought the purpose was to let these countries know we weren't about to deal with this entirely on our own, that we wanted to take their interests into account, work with them."

"Yes," she said, "but I think that can be handled just as well in other ways."

Henderson leaned back in his chair, obviously displeased. "So what are you going to do here?"

"Try to concentrate," she said. "Jet lag doesn't help that."

"On what?" Henderson said.

"Resolving the situation, planning some initiatives," she said, starting to lose her patience. "I just think the answers to how Matulo got his missiles, what his real objectives are, how to end it all, are sitting right in front of us if we would just take the time to look at it the right way."

"Which way is that?" Henderson said.

"I don't know for sure, yet," she said. "I started getting some ideas after talking with Elsworth."

"Let's hear them," Henderson said.

"I need more information," she said.

"Like what?" Henderson said.

She turned to Simmons. "For one, I'd like to know what you've heard from your man Reynolds."

"Nothing as yet," Simmons said calmly.

"How long has it been?" she said. "Two days?"

"About," Simmons said.

"Do you know if he's still alive?" she said.

Simmons nodded his head. "If Matulo had found him, we'd know about it."

"How can you say that?" she said slightly louder.

"It's the way we analyze Matulo," Simmons said.

She gave him a disgusted look and shook her head slowly.

"Marjorie, what are you getting at?" Henderson said.

"I'd just like to know more about this man Reynolds," she said. "He isn't even a regular CIA employee and he's handling about as delicate a mission as there ever could be."

"We've been over this before," Henderson said. "Steve assures me that he's the best available, you've seen his record, I've seen it, and we have to do something to get some more information."

"But he works for Stavropoulos," she said.

"What difference does that make?" Simmons said. "Stavropoulos is Greek, Greece is an ally, and in case you've forgotten, he's just a businessman. The man's loyal and he's good. What else do you have to know?"

"And what does Reynolds's background have to do with anything?" Henderson said. "I thought you were talking about some theory."

"I don't know," she said and looked away from them. "Maybe I'm just tired. I've got too many things going through my head at once. I just don't understand why we didn't have one bit of warning about this whole thing. I don't understand why we don't have any agents in Toganda."

"I think I've explained all that," Simmons said, slightly perturbed.

"I know," she said. "It's still a pretty sad commentary on the way your agency is run."

Simmons thrust his face forward defiantly. "What the hell are you after? You and those damned senators. I've headed the CIA for ten years. I've kept the budget down, I've avoided any hint of scandal, and I've kept the government better informed than any of my predecessors. Now, one incident and everyone acts like I'm a total incompetent." There was a short silence while Simmons leaned back and fixed his eyes on Marjorie like a cornered dog. "I've done my job and I've done it pretty damn well, I think, and I intend to take care of this. You'll see. Reynolds will do his job and he's not going to make Matulo send off his missile, news leak or no news leak. I have this situation just as much under control as anybody, but"—he turned to Henderson—"if you want my resignation, you can have it right now."

"That won't be necessary," Henderson said quietly, and turned to Marjorie. "I wish I knew what you were getting at, but I don't, and I don't think you do

either. You said you wanted information. That's fine,
but I don't think this is the time or place to be attacking Steve."

"Sorry," she said.

"If you've got some new ideas, fine, I'd like to hear
them," Henderson continued. "Otherwise, I've got
too many things to do. I have to act—right now. Who
knows where the missile came from? I haven't got
time to theorize. If you want to go off in a corner and
meditate about it, fine. I'll get along."

"I didn't mean that," she said.

"Whatever," Henderson said. He grabbed a ball-
point pen off his desk and started to play with it.

"I need some sleep," she said, and stood up. "I'll be
in better shape tomorrow." She turned and left the
office in tense silence. A limousine took her to her
home in Virginia where she took a hot shower and
found deep sleep.

General Matulo was informed of the rumor that
Henderson had sent a special agent into Toganda to
get the missile. He wasn't surprised at the news itself,
only that it had leaked so soon. Matulo decided to issue a statement through his press aide that he would
be willing to meet with the Secretary of State of the
United States at her earliest convenience. The
message arrived while Marjorie was still asleep. Her
secretary woke her up. Marjorie got out of bed half-
awake, managed to smile faintly, and told her secretary to tell Henderson that she would get in touch
with Matulo first thing in the morning. She then lay
back on her bed to relax for just another moment
and fell asleep. Having issued his statement, General
Matulo retired for the remainder of the day to his
bedroom to meditate.

Iti Mlulo spent his lunch break discussing the first
shipments from the United States that were due to arrive very shortly and the lottery system that Matulo

had devised to handle the distribution. That evening,
both Iti and his wife were excited at the prospect of
the prosperity that they were convinced would soon
be theirs. Anti wasn't, and persisted in prophesying
that nothing of lasting value could come from Matulo's methodology. This time Iti wasn't disposed to
shrugging off his brother's pessimism. They argued
and Anti left the apartment, something he had
planned to do that evening anyway, since he had to
meet his friend Julius Senghor at Julius's apartment.

Julius Senghor's father was Indonesian, his mother
Togandan. His father had been a well-to-do merchant
before Matulo, but was accused of profiteering during
the somewhat confusing days preceding Matulo's election to the presidency. He'd bought several ware-
houses full of shoes and other apparel cheap during a
temporary panic and resold dearly as order was
restored. His conduct had been brought to Matulo's
attention, and being without any special influence
with the new President, he was brought to trial,
wiped out financially, and left with his life. He died
shortly afterward. His father's fall didn't particularly
disturb Julius, who was a student at the time and
wanted nothing to do with his father's business. The
change in his family's financial status only meant that
Julius had to find work to support himself at the university. He turned to tutoring and found himself
teaching mathematics to the daughter of a Togandan
colonel.

In the second year of Matulo's reign, Julius was
selected to attend a university in the United States,
the result of the Colonel's recommendation. Matulo
wanted to use him as a symbol of the new Togandan
enlightenment where the sins of the fathers were not
to be visited upon the heads of the sons. Julius
showed an aptitude for languages, and even though
the official language of Toganda was English from its
colonial days, Matulo wanted Julius to begin his

studies in the United States and then to go to France,
Germany, and Japan.

Reynolds first met Julius while he was studying in
the United States. Reynolds wanted to discuss the
problems of Toganda with a native Togandan and
Julius was the only Togandan in the country at the
time. Reynolds impressed Julius with the amount of
background research he'd already done on the small
country and Julius found Reynolds a welcome com-
panion in a strange country. Their discussion rapidly
moved from the life of the average Togandan to Matulo's politics, something Reynolds found fascinating
but which Julius found barely tolerable. Reynolds
saw political promise in the young Togandan and, in
the later stages of their political discussions, shifted
the topic to revolutionary methodology. Shortly after
that, Julius was transferred to the Sorbonne and the
discussions came to an end. They were revived six
months later when Reynolds appeared in France and
sought out Julius. Julius became more receptive to
Reynolds's theories on the problems of the aspiring
middle class in countries such as Toganda and
methods of creating a viable opposition party in a
country where none existed. When Reynolds was confident that he'd planted the proper seeds in Julius's
head, he returned to the United States.

After two years of studying abroad, Julius returned
to Toganda to work as a translator in the Presidential
Palace. Six months after beginning his job there, he
was dismissed for making improper remarks about the
arbitrariness of Matulo's politics. The dismissal came
shortly after Julius had met Reynolds for the third
time in Balingo.

Anti Mlulo was one of the first members Julius had
recruited for the Togandan Freedom Party. They'd
met while studying at the university and had managed to stay in contact.

"When do we begin?" Anti said anxiously after a brief hello.

"Not yet," Julius said.

Anti looked shocked. "But I thought you contacted your American friend?"

"I did," Senghor said. He was busily searching a shelf of books.

"And?" Anti asked expectantly.

"We wait."

"For what?" Anti said.

"Until he comes back," Julius said.

"Which is when?" Anti said.

"A few days," Julius said.

"A few days!" Anti said.

"Yes," Julius said.

"Why?" Anti said.

Julius left the bookshelf and went to his desk. "There's something he has to do," he said while pulling open one of the drawers.

"I don't get it," Anti said, and found himself a seat. "Why do we have to wait for him?"

"The money, for one," Julius said and pulled a tobacco pouch out of the drawer.

"He didn't bring it?" Anti said.

"Not yet," Julius said as he unfolded the pouch.

"Why not?" Anti said.

Julius turned around, his mouth taut in anger. "What is this, an interrogation? Who's leading the Freedom Party anyway? I said we'll have to wait a few days and that's all I'm about to say."

"Okay," Anti said, slightly cowed. "I just wanted to know what was happening, that's all. I thought I was number-two man in this."

"You are," Julius said, calming down. "It's just that . . . Damn it." He sat down next to Anti on his dingy green sofa.

Anti patiently waited while Julius reached into the pouch, pulled out a wheat-colored joint, and lit it.

"My brother thinks he's going to become a millionaire," Anti said as he took the joint from Julius.

Julius nodded his head. "It figures."

Anti slowly sucked smoke into his lungs and let it trickle out. "If we don't do something fast, Matulo is going to become a national hero. We'll be dead before we even get started."

"I know," Julius said. "I just hope we're not dead already."

"Why?" Anti said. "You think Matulo's going to get out of this?"

"I don't know," Julius said. "It's possible."

Anti held out the joint to Julius, but his attention was elsewhere. "What's the matter with you?" he said.

Julius took his time. "I'm thinking," he said. "Been thinking."

"About what?" Anti said.

"A lot of things," Julius said. "My friend, the money, the guns, the organization, the missile, Matulo . . ." He paused and stared at the papered wall in front of him. "The timing mostly. The timing. That's what I can't understand. That's what has me worried. I thought we were ready, I thought the country was ready, I thought now was the time, and then Matulo rescues himself like magic. I just don't understand it."

"Maybe there's nothing to understand," Anti said.

Julius turned to him and gave him a quizzical look. "What does that mean?"

Anti pulled on the joint. "Maybe you're thinking too much. Maybe we should just do something."

"Without the guns, without the money?" Julius said. "What are we supposed to do? Charge the Presidential Palace with our fists waving?" He brandished his fist in the air. "Even with the money and the guns, it would take a while to get everything arranged. That's why we've been waiting."

"And look what our waiting has produced," Anti said. "Right now, Matulo is stronger than he's ever been while we're right where we've been for the past two years. If we wait any longer, we'll be in worse shape. I say we act now and to hell with waiting. What if your friend doesn't make it back? What if he doesn't have the money? What if he can't supply the guns? I say let's just do it and hope for the best."

Julius looked at Anti thoughtfully. "We'll have to change our strategy to account for the missile."

"Of course," Anti said, "but all we have to do is expose it as another of Matulo's tricks, which is all it is, just like every other scummy political trick he's used ever since he took over."

"And you think enough people will see it that way?" Julius said.

Anti leaned back and away from Julius and shook his head in bewilderment. "What is the matter with you? Has this one gambit of Matulo's shaken you so much?"

"Yes," Julius said softly.

"Damn it," Anti said, gesturing with his hand. "If enough of the people can see through his other tricks, why can't they see through this one?"

"It's different," Julius said.

"How?" Anti said.

"It's bigger, it's stronger," Julius said. "He's exercising some real power."

"Do you really believe that?" Anti said.

"Yes," Julius said emphatically.

"Then you're a fool," Anti said, and stood up. "You're a fool if you think that and you ought to get out of the party right now."

"No!" Julius said. "I'm not giving up the party. Not now. Matulo is going to lose—eventually. I'm certain of that. The problem is the timing. Matulo is on the crest right now and there are things happening that I don't understand, that I can't quite grasp. The right time will happen, but it's not now. We just have to wait."

Anti tossed the cold joint into an ashtray. "Okay," he said. "You're the leader. We'll wait, but I won't wait long. I've had it with Matulo. I've had enough of his slimy politics. I've watched him play games with my brother and all the others like him long enough and I'm sick of it."

Julius calmly watched Anti's labored breathing for a few moments. "Timing," he said. "Timing is the key. It always is and it always will be. We have to accept that."

"All right," Anti said and turned toward the door. "If we're going to wait, we're going to wait." He opened the door and turned back to Julius. "I think I'll take a walk."

"I'll be in touch," Julius said.

"Right," Anti said, and pulled the door shut behind himself.

Julius picked the joint out of the ashtray, rolled it between his fingers absently for a few moments, and tossed it back. "Damn him!" He slammed his clenched fist down on the coffee table so hard the ashtray fell off onto the carpet.

Fifth Day

Marjorie Timkins arose feeling more rested than she had in days. The thought of talking directly to Matulo started running through her mind even before she had her eyes open. She took her time in the shower, imagining what the upcoming conversation would be like. She pictured the popeyed General Matulo raving at her in lunatic phrases, gloating over her inability to stop him. She pictured herself calm and poised, ready for anything, revealing nothing, but showing Matulo in careful, extemporaneous phrases that it was just a matter of time before his house-of-cards power would come tumbling down on top of him and he'd better come up with a way of escaping before it was too late.

She called the President with a cup of steaming black coffee poised by her left hand.

"What took you so long?" Henderson said.

"I was tired," Marjorie said.

"You were tired," he said. "I'm climbing the wall and you were tired."

"I'm sorry," she said. "That's just the way I am. The same thing happened when I heard you were going to ask me to join your cabinet. It was late, I was tired, so I went to sleep."

"I don't think this is exactly in the same category," he said.

Marjorie sipped at her coffee. "I'll be there about ten."

"Fine," he said.

"And can we talk without Simmons being there?" she said.

"Sure," he said. "I wasn't expecting him, anyway."

"I never could understand why you want him around so much," she said.

"Really?" he said, obviously quite surprised. "I thought you knew."

"No," she said. "I don't."

"Remind me to explain it to you sometime," he said.

"I will," she said.

"Ten, then," he said.

"Ten," she said. "Bye, now."

"Bye."

Marjorie put the receiver down and smiled. She felt good. She felt electric. She felt power. She picked the receiver back up and started dialing.

"Hello," said a strong, masculine voice.

"Henrik?" she said, a trifle reluctantly.

"Marge?" the voice said, surprised.

"Yes," she said.

"What . . . ?" he said.

"How are you?" she said, her confidence building.

"Fine," he said. "How are you? I thought you were in Europe."

"I was," she said. "I returned yesterday."

"How'd it go?" he said. "How's it going? I mean . . . Tell me about it."

"There's not much to tell," she said. "I talked to a few big shots and I came back home."

He chuckled. "Okay," he said. "Say, can you wait a second?"

"Sure," she said and sipped at her coffee.

"Just wanted to get a cigarette," he said after a few moments. "Now, are you going to tell me why you called?"

"I wanted to see you," she said.

"Is this Togandan thing getting to you that much?" he said.

She laughed, lightly, easily. "No," she said. "I'm

not cracking up. I just wanted to see you. I wanted to talk to you."

"About what?" he said.

"Just things," she said.

"Okay," he said. "When?"

"Later today," she said. "I'm not sure when."

"Okay," he said. "Why don't you give me a call whenever you're ready. I'll be in all day."

"Henrik?" she said.

"What?" he said.

She hesitated. "Nothing. . . . I'll see you later."

"Okay."

"Good-bye," she said.

"Good-bye," he said.

The bags under Henderson's eyes were even more pronounced than they had been the day before. He had a harried and nervous look about him. He moved too quickly. When he spoke his voice was either too loud or too soft.

"Have a seat," he said, and started to pour her a cup of coffee.

She sat down feeling confident in a relaxed way.

He pushed the cup across the desk. "Black, right?" he said.

"Thank you," she said.

"Well," he said. "What do you think of Matulo's offer?"

"Could be promising," she said.

"Could be," he said. "I've already been discussing the possibilities."

"With whom?" she said.

"Simmons, a few congressmen, Blaine, Westbrook, even Macklin got in on it," he said. "He's still trying to convince me to land the Marines."

She smiled involuntarily.

"Don't," he said, straight faced. "I haven't totally ruled it out."

"There's no reason to get that desperate," she said.

"If you were in my seat, you wouldn't say that," he said.

"You're not really thinking of . . ."

"No," he said quickly. "It hasn't come to that point yet, but the way things are going, it might."

"Why do you say that?" she said.

"Because," he said, "believe it or not, there are a lot of people who don't like the way I'm handling things."

"What else is new?" she said, and reached for her coffee.

He looked at her intently. "I don't think you realize what's really going on. You don't know what a hell of a time I had getting that appropriation passed."

"I thought Blaine said there wouldn't be any trouble," she said.

"Blaine was wrong," he said and leaned back in his chair. "One of the few times he has been, but wrong nevertheless. The fact is that people are tired of getting pushed around by other countries. We're finally out from under oil, and now this. It just doesn't set well."

"So you're going to let that dictate your decisions on Matulo," she said.

"No," he said and shook his head. "I'm not going to let that dictate what I do, but I can't ignore it. I have to take it into account and satisfy that feeling, otherwise what good am I?"

"Okay," she said and nodded her head slowly. "So, what are you getting at?"

He leaned forward to rest his lanky arms on the desk. "I want to offer Matulo a deal," he said. "He gives us the missile, he leaves Toganda, we guarantee his safety, and we throw in a couple of million to keep him happy."

Marjorie cocked her head and looked at him askance. "Did you say what I think you said?"

"You know damn well what I said!" Henderson said.

She looked straight at him. "That is the craziest thing I've ever heard you say."

"What's so crazy about it?" he said.

"First of all, what possible guarantee could we give him that he could trust," she said. "And secondly, you can't possibly believe that he'd ever accept it."

"The first part is easy," he said. "We get the money to him in gold, secretly, he gets some people he trusts to take him to some neutral country, and it's over with. As for the second objection, what really makes us so sure he's the idealist we think he is."

"He could have put a couple of million together and done what you're saying a long time ago," she said.

"Maybe not," he said.

"This is Simmons's idea, isn't it?" she said.

"He likes it," he said.

"He's stupid," she said.

"He's not the only one who likes it," he said.

"Do you like it?" she said.

"No," he said, "but it'll make a lot of people happy if we do it, and it just might work."

"Not a chance," she said.

"Marjorie, I'm not really interested in what you think of it at this point," he said.

Sitting was an effort. She crossed her legs and shifted her attention to the desk in front of her, to the blueness of her skirt, to the collage of papers in front of Henderson, but she couldn't return to Henderson's face.

"I think you know what I mean," he said. His voice was changed, distant. She nodded, slowly, equivocally. "You asked about Simmons," he said.

She looked up and caught his eyes. "Yes," she said.

"That told me a lot," he said.

"How's that?" she said.

"I never realized it before," he said. He seemed disappointed or disillusioned, she couldn't tell which. "It's really so simple. Simmons is the right man for the job. That's all. He may appear stupid at times, he does appear stupid at times. He could be more thorough, but then what would that bring? A few scandals? Foreign relations debacles like South Africa? He took over right after that, remember? And ever since then, the CIA has been a good boy. It's gathered the information it could, but it never goes too far. It's not out to create history anymore. It does what it's supposed to. It does what a modern intelligence-gathering organization is supposed to do. It does what it can. It doesn't aspire to perfection. It keeps its expenses down. What more could I ask for, and it's Simmons who does it. The man has limitations—God, does he have his limitations—but he has the right mind in the right place and because of that he also has a sense of things which I miss. He has a perspective I can draw on and that's why I like him to be around." He paused, "Can you see what I'm saying?"

"In a way," she said reluctantly. "I can see his political advantages, but I can't see doing what he says."

"Who said I'm doing what he says?" he said and pulled his hand toward his body for emphasis. "I'm doing what I think is right. I don't think it'll work any more than you do, but it's what I want done."

"Okay," she said.

"It's simplistic," he said. "I agree, but it's the kind of thing Simmons can understand and therefore it's in tune with what a lot of other people think. I know that for a fact already."

"Okay," she said.

"And it might even work," he said. "Matulo must have some idea of how he's going to get out of this and this might be it, or he might have had something else in mind which hasn't worked out and he's changed his mind."

"Okay," she said.

"And that's what has me so surprised about you," he said. "I've seen it, but I've never really realized it until now. You're too ambitious." He shook his head.

"No, that's not it. Simmons is ambitious, too, but in a different way." She could tell he was having a hard time finding the right words. "You're trying to grasp things beyond your reach. Your intentions are right and you want to cause the right effects, but you're trying to extend your reach too far. It's always been there, and I admire it, but not now."

"I haven't done anything yet," she said.

"I know," he said. "But I can see it. It couldn't be any plainer. You want Toganda to be your lever."

"Maybe it is," she said. "For you and me."

"Yes," he said and nodded his head briskly. "Yes, I've considered that, but I'm not about to let it dominate me. There are too many other things I have to concern myself with."

"You want to survive," she said.

He looked directly into her deep brown eyes. "Yes, if you want to put it that way. But if you want to put it in those terms, what's the matter with surviving? I have just as many ambitions as you, Marjorie, and you know it, but they won't be worth a damn if I don't have any power."

"They're not worth a damn if you don't exercise the power you've got, either," she said.

He leaned back in his chair, folded his arms across his chest, and looked to the side. "Marjorie . . ." He shook his head. "I never expected this, but I guess things like this happen in a crisis." He hesitated. "You know what I want." He turned his eyes back on her. "Are you going to do it?"

"Yes," she said.

"Good," he said. "Shall we set the appointment?"

"Yes," she said.

Dr. Julio Marquez called for a special conference of developing countries to meet to discuss the Togandan situation and its special implications for the less developed countries of the world. He did not specify any place or time for the meeting.

* * *

The meeting with General Matulo had been arranged and Marjorie was getting up to leave.

Henderson had relaxed a little. The deep-set lines in his face had softened. "What are you going to be doing now?" he said.

She shrugged. "I'm not sure," she said. "Think about some things."

"Call me later," he said with the beginnings of a smile. "Just in case."

"In case of what?" she said.

"Whatever," he said. "Just keep in touch."

"I will," she said, and turned to leave.

As the door to Henderson's office closed behind her, she noticed James Hawkins, a professor from Yale and a recognized foreign affairs authority, sitting in the reception area. She only knew him professionally, had met him only twice before, but instantly recognized his broad squared face and neatly trimmed red mustache.

"Mr. Hawkins?" she said hesitantly.

He stood up and smiled broadly. "Yes," he said. "You recognized me."

"Couldn't miss your mustache," she said.

He pulled at the corner of his mustache. "I guess it has its uses," he said.

"Here to see the President?" Marjorie said.

"Yes," he said. It came out uncomfortably. "You might say I'm representing a different viewpoint than some people feel the President should hear."

She nodded her head slowly, thoughtfully.

"Not that I disagree with what's been done up to now," he said.

"It's nice to hear that you approve," she said.

"But only up to a point," he quickly added.

She nodded her head. "Well, I have to be going." She reached out her hand and he took it. "Nice meeting you again."

"Yes," he said, shaking her hand. "Nice meeting you."

His grip was firm and hard. Her hand relaxed, he let go. "Good-bye, now," she said.

"Good-bye," he said.

She turned. She felt her heart pounding and her blood pressure rising but remained outwardly calm and cordial as she made her way to her car.

Marjorie could tell instantly from Henrik's smile that he was glad she'd come. It was almost noon. She hadn't called ahead. He seemed uneasy, unsure of how to act. His hand moved forward. She thought he was reaching out to her, but his hand went instead to a chair in front of his desk and pulled it out slightly. She smiled and relaxed and the session with Henderson passed out of her mind for the moment.

"It's been a long time," he said softly.

"I know," she said.

"Can I get you something?" he said. "Coffee?"

"No," she said with a small shake of her head. "No, but thanks."

He headed back behind his desk and sat there a moment, silently. He looked at her face and wished he'd kissed it when she'd come through the door, but it was too late now. She was still as beautiful to him as she had been, though her chin was a little too broad, her mouth a little too full, her eyes a little too present to be called that by most men. She had a sexual presence that still fascinated him. She was so serious about it, as earnest as she was about her career. He remembered some playful times because they'd been so rare. Most of the times they'd been together had been almost like a contest to see who could perform the most competently and thus they had brought a curious satisfaction, like coming home after a hard day's work. He wanted to lock the door and make love to her on the floor.

"How have you been?" she said.

The spell was broken. "Not bad," he said. "How about you?"

She cocked her head and shrugged. "Pretty good."

"Glad to hear it," he said. "How's Matulo doing?"

She laughed, he smiled. "Just the man I wanted to talk about," she said.

"Really?" he said. "I was hoping you were here to talk about us."

"That too," she said. "Later. Right now, I want to know about Matulo."

"Okay," he said. "What about him?"

"What can you tell me about him?" she said.

"I don't know," he said and turned aside. "I'm sure no expert on Matulo. I would think the CIA or some-place like that would be the place for you to go, but then I suppose you've already gone there."

"What I'm trying to figure out is what kind of a man he really is," she said.

He thought for a moment. "That's a tough one."

"I know," she said. "I think I have a pretty good idea already, but sometimes you have a different way of looking at things."

"Thanks for the compliment," he said.

"You're welcome," she said and adjusted herself in her chair. She could feel his eyes on her body. "Maybe I should put it this way. Is Matulo really a religiously inspired visionary, idealist, or whatever you want to call it, out to accomplish some holy mission which only he understands, or is he just a cold and calculat-ing politician out to achieve the greatest personal po-litical power he can? Or is that the wrong question to ask?"

"Sounds like you're trying to put it too simply," he said, "which isn't like you."

"Maybe I gave the wrong impression," she said. "What bothers me is that I can't see any possible, logical way for him to get out of the position he's put himself in. Now, does that mean he's just waiting for destruction, or am I looking at it all wrong?"

"You never look at anything all wrong, Marge," he said. "I couldn't possibly give you a complete psychoanalysis of a man I've never even met, let alone studied, if that's what you're after, but I have thought about him. How could I help it? No question he's a clever politician, but what fascinates me is that he doesn't appear to have any defined ideology and he doesn't seem to even attempt to lead his people toward any ideology, religious or secular. He isn't aligned with any religious doctrine, although, as I understand, he was raised Muslim, yet he professes to receive visions directly from God, who tells him what to do, and he does it, and I'm convinced he really believes that that is what happens. In other words, I don't think he puts on a show of that for anyone's benefit."

"Why do you say that?" she said.

He shrugged his shoulders. "Call it instinct, I guess, or experience, or whatever. I just don't think it is."

"Then you're saying he's just psychotic," she said.

"Whatever that means," he said. "It's just that, if a person were really doing something like that in a coldly logical way, some sort of logic would appear, but if it's there, I certainly can't see it."

"Nor can I," she said. "Although what he's doing now has a painfully direct logic to it."

"In a way," he said. "Matulo is a strange one. From what I understand, he lives an almost totally secluded life. He rarely leaves his residence. He runs the country through people who live with him in the palace, and over the telephone. There doesn't seem to be any personality cult. He's never been noted as a charismatic figure. Sometimes he talks like a socialist, sometimes like a confirmed capitalist, yet the Togandans must like him. After all, he's managed to stay in power for, what is it, about seven years?"

"About that," she said.

"I don't know," he said. "Maybe he rules by default. Maybe nobody else wants the damn country."

They both broke out laughing. "Really," he said. "The country shows virtually no growth, although I'd guess the average Togandan worker probably has a car of some sort and a television set. And there is another thing. From what I've read, there have been rumors of mass killings and suspicious deaths of political opponents, but the impression I get is that the people just aren't that concerned about it."

"That's the impression I get," she said and nodded her head.

"All I can figure is that he has some uncanny ability to spot just the right source of trouble and kill it before it erupts into something dangerous," he said. "Maybe that indicates he really does get these supernatural visions. Maybe that's what the visions are and maybe that's how he stays in power. I imagine it's possible. I don't know. A country does need some kind of leadership, though, and I suppose if nothing else can get organized, people just settle for what there is."

She looked at him admiringly. "I'm impressed."

"But I haven't started the analysis yet," he said.

"I mean about the facts," she said, "but you're telling me some things, too. I think what really concerns me, though, is whether or not he would sacrifice himself, lose everything, for the good of his country, or maybe the world, for that matter."

"Who knows, really," he said. "If he had come to power at the head of a truly popular movement, or if he were a dedicated Communist or something like that, it would be a lot easier to say yes, but he isn't any of those, at least not as far as I can tell."

"Then could he simply be suicidal?" she said.

"It's possible," he said. "A lot of things are possible. Maybe he's a magician and something magical is going to happen, or at least maybe he believes he is."

"But would you say he wants to live just as much as we do?" she said. "Does he want to enjoy the physical realities of power, or does that just not matter to him?"

He looked closely into her eyes, at how serious her expression was. "Marge, I don't believe the things you're asking," he said. "How could I possibly know the answers to those questions?"

"Sorry," she said. "I didn't expect you to tell me what to do, how to handle the man, or how to handle my negotiations with him."

"Your negotiations?" he said.

"Yes," she said, taken aback. "I guess I didn't tell you. I'll be going to Toganda tomorrow to meet with Matulo."

"I see," he said.

"But I just can't understand what's going on," she said. "I can't pin the man down and I can't remember ever being this confused."

"I can," he said.

"I mean professionally," she said. "It just doesn't make any sense. I can see it generating a profound, dramatic change in the world, but the details just don't fit together. How'd Matulo get the missiles, why Matulo, what does he get out of it, and what the hell do I say to him when I meet him face to face? We'd like our missile back, no hard feelings?"

"I think I see the dilemma," he said. "But I don't see why you're so obsessed with knowing every little detail."

"Because it's important," she said.

"Important how?" he said. "I thought you were the world's greatest exponent of minimal information theory. Isn't that what you call it?"

"Yes, but not now," she said.

He felt like saying to hell with politics. "Maybe you're getting too complicated. What's the most obvious way for Matulo to get out of this? Offer to give the missile back, say it was all a joke, do penance?" He chuckled. "Maybe that's all there is to it."

She shook her head. "No," she said. "There's really

only one way I can think that Matulo could get out of all this whole, with all his power intact as well as his skin."

"What's that?" he said.

"If enough countries, small ones like Toganda, had that missile or its equivalent, they could form an alliance," she said. "Fraternal terror with strategic capability and there wouldn't be a damn thing anybody could do about it."

"I suppose it's possible," he said. "But how are they going to get the missiles? Toganda is surrounded, literally."

"How did Matulo get them in the first place?" she said. "If he could get them, there's no reason anyone else couldn't. That's why it's so important that I understand this, where the missiles came from, what Matulo is planning."

"You really think this alliance is going to form," he said.

"I feel like it's a certainty," she said, "and it scares me. How are we going to handle it, how are we going to control it?"

He rubbed his chin and waited. "I think I'm starting to see what you're getting at," he said. "I think I'm even starting to see why this sense of urgency."

"Henderson sees it, too," she said, "but he seems to prefer getting himself interiorized in petty political crap."

"You don't think Matulo stole the missiles on his own, do you?" he said.

"If Matulo got those missiles on his own," she said, "I'll eat your desk. He hasn't got the money, he hasn't got the organization. He just hasn't got what it takes. I'm sure of that, and that's why it's driving me so crazy."

"How about who would stand to gain the most from this alliance you mentioned," he said.

"I've thought about it," she said, "and it's gotten me nowhere. Maybe if I had a few hows, or wheres, or whats, I might be able to come up with something."

"Maybe it's some private organization," he said.

"What?" she said.

"A private organization," he said. "A corporation, a clandestine group of evil people."

"That's out of Ian Fleming," she said, "not reality."

"Then what kind of a country would give something like that to Matulo?" he said.

"I don't know," she said, sounding even more confused and frustrated. "It doesn't make sense. If I ruled a country and had the resources to get that missile, I certainly wouldn't hand it over to someone like Matulo."

"Then Henderson must be right," he said.

"About what?" she said.

"Matulo must have built them himself," he said.

She shook her head vigorously, destroying what little was left of the set in her hair. "No," she said. "I refuse to believe that."

"Then you're insane," he said coolly. Her eyes opened wide. "All you're left with is God handing them to him."

She rubbed her face in her hands. "I don't know," she said, and arched her head back. "I just can't think straight."

"Hey," he said. "I hope you didn't just come here to be depressed."

She smiled and shook her head. "No," she said. "That wasn't my intention."

"Good," he said, half jokingly. "I had enough of that last time."

"I know," she said with a touch of regret.

"There was something else you wanted to talk about," he said.

She nodded her head and, for a moment, looked as though she were about to cry. "Did I tell you I just talked to Henderson?"

"No," he said. "Why?"

She hesitated. "He's getting ready to get rid of me."

"He is?" he said. "Why? I thought you two got along exceptionally well and this meeting with Matulo . . ."

"My attitude's wrong," she said.

"Your what?" he said.

"My attitude," she said.

"But your meeting with Matulo," he said. "That could be a real breakthrough."

She shook her head. "I'd be very surprised if it produced anything at all. I'm still not even really sure why he wants it."

"What did Henderson say?" he said.

"He didn't tell me outright that he was getting rid of me, if that's what you mean," she said.

"Then what makes you so sure?" he said.

"Ever heard of a man named James Hawkins?" she said.

He thought about it and then shook his head slowly. "Can't place the name."

"He almost had my job," she said. "He's sharp. A lot of people like him, and I ran into him on the way out of Henderson's office."

"And that's why you think Henderson's getting ready to get rid of you?" he said, slightly incredulous.

Her voice rose defensively. "Call it paranoia, call it jumping to conclusions or whatever, I know enough about Henderson and what he's up against that unless I produce a miracle with Matulo I'm going to be out."

"But why?" he said.

"Because the pressure is on and Henderson has to look like he's doing something," she said.

"And replacing you with this guy Hawkins is going to do that," he said.

"Exactly," she said.

"That's stupid," he said.

"It's realistic," she said.

"But you've been doing such a good job," he said.

"I've been doing Henderson's job," she said. "Let's face it, every problem that's come up in foreign relations during Henderson's term has taken care of itself. Oil, South Africa—just about anybody could have handled my job."

"But I thought Henderson admired you," he said.

"He does," she said. "Theoretically, we're eye to eye all the way. We've discussed more initiatives than I can remember, but between a hostile Senate and domestic problems, nothing's ever happened, and now that an issue has been forced on us, I've become a liability."

"You're jumping to conclusions," he said.

"Look at the total picture and you'll understand it," she said. She reached her thumb and middle finger to the bridge of her nose and leaned forward slightly. "Damn," she said softly, "it really pisses me off."

"I still think you're getting carried away for no reason," he said.

She brought her hand down from her face. "Maybe," she said, "but I really don't think so. I just don't think I'm that naive. No matter how much Henderson might like me or respect me personally, the pressure on him is just too great. He wants to survive and this one incident could destroy everything he's wanted to accomplish that I agree with. I can't even make myself criticize the man for that. I respect him too much."

"Then the hell with it," he said. "You wanted to be Secretary of State and you made it in spite of being a woman. You know what's really going on. What the hell difference does it make?"

"But don't you see?" she said, leaning forward, almost pleading with him. "That's all I achieved—the position. I never really did anything. This is the first chance I've had and when it started I was so sure I'd see it through, that I would see right through it, go to the heart of the matter, achieve something, affect history, and instead I'm going to be the incompetent who had to be dismissed. What the hell good was it?"

"What do you want?"

She leaned back in her chair. "Jesus," she said softly and slowly shook her head, "you're just as fucking dense as you ever were."

"And you're just as manic depressive as you ever were," he said. "You come here looking for some goddamn miracle and when you don't find it, you want to blame someone else."

"I guess I should have known better," she said.

He pulled a pipe from a rack on his desk and started to fill it from a wooden humidor.

"I'm sorry," she said.

"So am I," he said. He closed the humidor and held the pipe by the bowl. "I think I understand."

"I think you do, too," she said.

"It isn't fair," he said, "but it hasn't happened yet and you still might get your miracle."

"Maybe," she said, and smiled. "I guess I better get going."

He put the pipe down and stood up. "When'll I see you again?"

She stood up and brushed a strand of hair from her face. "I'll call you when I get back."

He stepped around the desk and reached his hand out to her. "I've missed you," he said.

"I've been busy," she said and took his right hand in her left.

"You're always busy," he said.

"I know," she said.

He pulled her toward him, touched her lips with his slowly, and lingered. Her right hand reached his shoulder and stayed there, lightly, until he pulled away.

"Don't forget to call," he said.

"I won't," she said.

He leaned back against his desk.

"I'm glad I came," she said and lifted her purse to her shoulder."

"So am I," he said.

She smiled invitingly. "Good-bye," she said and turned for the door.

"Good-bye," he said.

Reynolds's luck was holding. Matulo had given General Mwelo, Commander of the Palace Guards, an order to increase the strength of that elite corps. Reynolds was taken, along with three others, from the camp he was in to the palace grounds. He was given the coveted deep-blue uniform of the Guards and spent the day getting oriented to his new surroundings. He was issued an M-18 from one of the first shipments to arrive via the DC-10's that were moving regularly between Balingo and the United States. Reynolds demonstrated an exceptional aptitude in learning how to handle the new weapon.

While General Amdida Matulo lacked the ideological muscle of a Communist or the economic persuasiveness of an oligarch, he managed to support his divine taste for power through an ad hoc combination of terrorism, religious drive, and a facility for dividing and driving his own people into a sense of helplessness. His predecessors had attempted to foster a sense of nationalism to bring people of diverse cultural backgrounds and desires together to cooperate in thrusting a backward country into the mainstream of technologically advanced civilization, but the effort had died stillborn. There was too great a gap between the majority of the population and the concentrated capital with its small technocratic elite that controlled it and were trying to assimilate the more advanced technologies of the developed countries. The result was a two-layered society of rich and poor, and the rich couldn't see that they were really only middle class in terms of the rest of the world. Before

this privileged minority of this small African country
discovered what they had really achieved, they found
themselves trapped into a dependence on foreign capital and connections which left the majority of them
just as vulnerable, individually, to the politics and decisions of major multinational corporations as their
counterparts in the developed countries. Their su-
perior status was just an illusion and they resented it
but were helpless in the face of it unless they wanted
to give up their cars and their television sets. The
days where a few privileged countries could wield
their natural resources -as economic and political
weapons were virtually at an end. Only a few oil-ex-
porting countries still had a semblance of that kind of
power. The resulting sense of insecurity on the part
of these individuals carried over to their respective
governments, which, in turn, had to walk on the
knife edge of insecurity. Matulo's predecessor had
managed to form the semblance of a democratic,
quasi-parliamentary form of government, but Matulo
had been the result. As Matulo saw it, it was an inevitable result.

Matulo's power was the result of a unique cult of
personality that nobody could quite put his finger on.
He induced in his subjects a cacophonic set of
feelings of fear, hatred, awe, and esteem with an occasional touch of love and devotion, and his acts
seemed entirely arbitrary. At one moment he would
order the imprisonment of a wealthy industrialist and
the impounding of his funds, and the next, order the
suppression of a demonstration for better working
conditions. He would force the early retirement of a
high-ranking officer in the Togandan Army for misap-
propriating minor sums, then suppress a major scandal in the National Police. But beneath it all, the
steady hand of Amdida Matulo divided and conquered his own people, and guided them with his
own unique logic and heavenly inspiration. It was a
combination that worked.

This was why, after arranging his meeting with Marjorie Timkins, a pure, quintessential inspired change in his original plans, he went to the bedroom of his wife, Casethe. She had an oval face with an even dark-chocolate complexion, full lips, and dark eyes that frightened Matulo. He thought of her as divine. She saw through him and knew the limits of her power. Her beauty was wasted on Matulo the man. She was his succubus, picked to play that role which she did so well by instinct. The direct ancestress of an African king, he knew that she contained a magical power that had passed into her blood and he partook of it like a vampire. He had gone to great lengths to ensure her presence, even to threatening her with the destruction of her entire family if she wouldn't consent to being his wife. He assured her that the relationship would be purely political, since he didn't care to waste his energy through physical sex. She agreed and bore her position patiently. Gradually she changed and adapted and slowly even understood a little of what her role meant. She accepted it. She was convinced that it was only temporary and that one day Matulo would be gone and she would remain—winner.

She was asleep. He stood by her bed, watching the light cover across her chest rise and fall, slowly, rhythmically. He bent and held the corner of the cover. He concentrated on the quickening of his breath, a tightness in his stomach. Slowly he straightened his body, lifting the corner of the cover above her, revealing her nakedness. His eyes focused on the fullness of her breasts, sagging away from each other. His left hand began to knead itself, his breaths came deeper. He tossed the cover back. Her legs were spread apart slightly. Only her left foot was left covered. She moved. A soft sound came from her throat as she turned onto her left side, away from him, just as he had hoped. He watched her breasts jiggle out of his sight, then followed the gentle curve of her back to the mound of hip. He closed his eyes for a second, then turned back to the door. Outside, he stood erect, the door safely closed behind him. His breathing returned to normal. He reached into a back pocket, withdrew a handkerchief, and calmly wiped the palms of his hands and his forehead, while safely behind the wooden barrier his wife, eyes open, fully conscious, was pulling a cover back over her chilled body.

Iti Mlulo walked sullenly into his apartment. His brother was sitting on the couch reading a thin, paperback book. His wife was watching a foggy picture on their television. They turned their faces to Iti and the door swung shut.

"How'd it go?" Anti said.

Iti slid into his favorite upholstered chair and several score threads came a nanometer closer to breaking. "All right," he said.

Anti nodded his head; Iti's wife stood up.

"I stood in line for three hours," Iti said.

His wife headed for the kitchen. "I'll get something to eat," she said.

"Was it worth it?" Anti said.

Iti shrugged and cocked his head. "Lesi could use a new sewing machine."

"Think you'll get one?" Anti said.

"We've got the same chance as anyone else," Iti said.

"How many were there?" Anti said.

"Machines?" Iti said. "I don't know."

"How many people?" Anti said.

"More," Iti said. "A lot more."

"And you still think you'll get one," Anti said.

"What the hell is your problem?" Iti said, louder. "If we don't get that, tomorrow there's a chance at a television. What's the difference? We'll get our share. There's more to come."

"You're sure of that," Anti said.

Iti turned his head to the side. "Isn't that ready yet?"

"In a minute," his wife said.

"The rent's going up ten percent the first of the month," Anti said.

Iti turned back to his brother. "Where'd you hear that?"

"The landlord," Anti said. "He came by today."

"That bastard," Iti said. "Isn't he gouging enough out of us already?"

"What's the matter?" Anti said. "You're about to be a rich man. What's ten percent?"

"Ten percent is ten percent," Iti said. "That's what it is."

"Oh, well," Anti said and leaned back deeper into the couch. "It's just the beginning."

"Beginning of what?" Iti said.

"Speculation," Anti said. "Inflation. Money's getting easy, everyone's going to be rich, like all you construction people. The landlord just wants to make sure he gets his fair share."

"Fair share of what?" Iti said.

"You know," Anti said, seeming to ignore his brother's comment, "I really hadn't thought of it until the landlord came by, but it's really the only logical thing."

"What is?" Iti said.

"The way prices are going up," Anti said. "If I had more of a business mind, I would have seen it earlier. Obviously, Togandan businessmen are just as smart as any."

"Then I wish you'd explain it to a dummy like myself," Iti said.

Anti turned to his brother, looked at him intently, and spoke enthusiastically. "It's simple," he said. "A lot of money is coming into this country, and more is on the way. That means people can afford more, so why not raise prices a little, extend a little extra

credit since the money is going to be there, and cash
in right now."

"But the lottery," Iti said. "Everybody'll get their
chance."

"Who wants to be a good, patient citizen like you?"
Anti said. "And what about your raise?"

"It's nothing," Iti said.

"What about all those people who are being
hired?" Anti said.

"So?" Iti said.

"So it's basic," Anti said, getting impatient with his
brother. "It's a classic inflationary situation and all I
can think is that Matulo never expected people to get
so anxious about protecting their own interests. It's
beautiful."

Iti gave him a quizzical, confused look. "What's
beautiful about it?" he said. "If that's what's happening, this is all going to be for nothing."

"Exactly," Anti said triumphantly. "Except for one
thing. You and people like you are finally going to
wake up and do something about the idiot we've got
for a president."

"Your dinner's ready," Iti's wife said from the
kitchen.

Iti seemed to have lost his appetite. He waited quietly in his chair, thoughtful, while Anti watched him,
until his wife came out of the kitchen and asked him
directly to his face when he was going to come and eat.

Clarence Bishop felt he was the happiest man in
the world. One of the members of the Sons of Patrick
Henry had reported that he had a cousin who was an
engineer working on a hydroelectric project in Arizona which the Togandans were scheduled to inspect.
This same cousin, while not a member of the Sons,
felt that Togandans had become fair game and was in
a position to know when and by what route any inspection parties might come to look at the project.
He also agreed to help in any way he could.

Sixth Day

The palace grounds were an immense roughly circular park that had been personally designed by the English colonial governor who had preceded the first democratically elected government of the country. The Presidential Palace sat in the middle of the grounds, and immediately surrounding the Presidential Palace itself were several acres of carefully tended lawn with an occasional oak, birch, or maple tree. A hundred meters from the palace were several barracks, relatively new structures that had been built in the same architectural style as the palace. They housed approximately a thousand of the Palace Guards and adjacent to the barracks was an armory. Beyond the clearing was a man-made forest that contained electronic surveillance equipment and several additional scattered barracks. Edging the forest was an electrified fence, five meters high, and beyond that was another clearing a hundred meters deep which was regularly patrolled, and beyond that was a natural forest.

The only people who lived within the grounds, besides the Guards, were Matulo, his wife, a score of servants, cooks, chauffeurs, secretaries, and their families, and Matulo's translators. Matulo and his wife occupied nine of the palace's eighty rooms. The remainder of the rooms, as well as the apartments above the seven-car garage, were inhabited by its employees, Matulo's ministers, and others who Matulo felt should be close to the real center of Government, such as General Mgombwe who lived in a residential section opposite the main gate. The Legislative Assembly, which formally passed the laws of the land, was in Balingo, ten kilometers away.

Reynolds was part of a patrol near the main gate when the men he was with were suddenly ordered to come to attention. They were lined up along the drive that connected the main gate with the palace. After several minutes had passed, Reynolds spotted, from the corner of his eye, a car approaching from the left. The massive steel gates to the grounds opened and three limousines drove through. In the middle limousine Reynolds spotted a woman with light brown hair seated between two men and the brief glimpse he caught of the woman's face told him that it was Marjorie Timkins. He found it hard to believe. He suspected that something was wrong.

"At ease!"

Reynolds took longer than any of the others to respond to the order.

Matulo waited in his office for Marjorie to be escorted to him. He had a faint smile on his face, and when she was let in, he remained seated and silently motioned with his hand toward the padded chair in front of his desk.

The two soldiers who escorted Marjorie in waited by the double doors while the Secret Service men who had accompanied her to Toganda waited outside in the cars. She took her seat.

"You can go now," Matulo said to the guards.

They quietly turned and left the room while Marjorie's attention was drawn to the glitter of Matulo's custom-tailored uniform. She was amused and disgusted.

"Would you care for something to drink?" Matulo said. "A cigarette?" He held an elaborately worked gold cigarette case toward her.

"No, thank you," she said with a short shake of her head.

He reached into the case and removed a cigarette

for himself. "I'm quite pleased you were able to come so quickly," he said.

"I want to thank you for offering to meet with me, General," she said.

"Of course," he said and lit his cigarette, a filtered Balkan Sobranie.

"Could I ask why you requested a meeting at this time?" she said.

He blinked at the smoke that curled from his lips. "I understand your General Macklin would like to invade Toganda."

"It's true there are a few people in our country who feel that way," she said.

"They think I'm bluffing," he said.

"Yes," she said.

"Do you?" he said.

"No," she said.

"Why?" he said.

"Everything you've done indicates to me an almost certain probability that you're not," she said.

Matulo nodded his head slowly, approvingly. "Good," he said. "I do have it. Do you believe I'd launch it?"

"Yes," she said. "If provoked."

"Good," he said.

"What I don't understand is how you intend to end this threat," she said.

He looked above her head, blankly.

"You must realize that it has to come to an end soon," she said.

His eyes returned to her, focused. "Yes, of course," he said. "Isn't that why you came to this meeting?"

She hesitated. "To discuss ending it, yes," she said.

"Yes," he said.

She waited. "Does this mean you're ready to negotiate a conclusion at this time?"

"I thought I'd already made it clear when my threat will cease," he said.

"Yes, you have," she said, "but raising the standard

of living of the average Togandan to that of the average American is going to take billions and billions of
dollars. There's no way we can afford that. It would
be disastrous to our economy."

He shrugged. "I'd say that's a matter of opinion."

She waited, still patient. "Is that all you're really
after?"

"Yes," he said. "Yes, of course. Isn't that what I've
said?"

"Officially," she said.

"That's right," he said.

"I just thought that possibly there was something
you were looking for personally, something that you
didn't want to announce publicly, that you wanted to
discuss with me unofficially," she said.

He leaned back in his chair and laughed, a high-
pitched childish giggle that put Marjorie even more
on edge. "You think I'm after some personal money,
power . . ." He leaned forward. "Possibly women."

Marjorie waited as Matulo carefully positioned his
elbows on his desk. "I think you want prosperity and
economic and political autonomy for your people," she
said.

"Do you think I'm ready to give my life for Toganda?" he fired at her.

"I don't know," she said.

"Are you incapable of recognizing an idealist when
you see one?" he said. "A martyr, a national hero?"

"I have to consider every possibility," she said.

He slapped the top of his desk hard with his left
hand and put his cigarette out with his right. "You
don't want to understand anything," he said. He
reached for a pile of papers to his right. "You think
I'm some petty dictator looking out for himself with
delusions of grandeur or some such psychological
nonsense." He pulled out several sheets of paper. "I
have here," he said solemnly, "a recent editorial from
a Chilean newspaper. You'll excuse me if you've already read it." He cleared his throat. " 'It has become

very apparent that the Togandan missile threat is on the verge of becoming a major international political success for a man who may turn out to be one of the most enlightened and misunderstood political leaders of our time. While he has consistently maintained that he will launch the advanced cruise missile in his possession at any heavily populated area of the world, including, presumably, a city such as Santiago, it has become obvious to us that his threat is aimed directly and mercilessly at the wealthy countries of the world. Because of this, it is imperative that the Chilean people and the Chilean Government address themselves to some very pointed questions.

" 'How did General Matulo acquire the Thor S-27? The United States has said that no missile was stolen from them, and the preposterous theory that the United States has engineered the entire incident with the Togandans is not even worth considering. That leaves either the possibility that some country other than Toganda somehow built the missile and gave it to the Togandans or that the Togandans, themselves, somehow managed to build it. Since President Matulo has not made any statement concerning the origin of his missiles, one can only speculate.' Let me skip a few lines here. 'Dr. Martin Cavalho, a consultant to the Government, recently stated that it is perfectly possible for the Togandans to have built such a missile. The required technology in the form of plans, blueprints, and certain specific components could very well have been stolen from various U.S. military-industrial sources and a pair of Thor MPCM's could have been manufactured at a cost of no more than sixty million U.S. dollars.' I'll skip a few more lines here. 'If this is the case, it is time for the Republic of Chile to actively pursue the acquisition of a Multi-Purpose Cruise Missile of the type the Togandans possess.' "

"We're also working on an effective defense against the S-27," Marjorie said.

Matulo put down the sheet of paper and looked up. "What good is that going to do at this point?"

"Is that your goal, then?" she said. "You want every country in the world to have an arsenal of MPCM's?"

"Why shouldn't others have the same benefits?" he said.

"Do you intend supplying them?" she said.

He motioned to the papers he'd just put down. "I think it would be obvious that that won't be necessary," he said. "I couldn't ship a missile out of this country right now, anyway, unless all my neighbors decided to expel the U.S. military presence there."

"I suppose they don't have the courage," she said.

"Possibly," he said.

"Are you ready for what that would mean?" she said.

"The question is whether you're ready for it," he said. He looked off into space. "I'm simply the tip of an iceberg. What defense is there against a bullet? Anybody can buy one, along with a gun to fire it. Unless you want to live your life in a bulletproof case, you simply have to live with the reality."

"The analogy is hardly appropriate," she said.

He fixed his eyes on her and looked genuinely surprised. "Why not?"

"What is it going to accomplish?" she said. "Is that supposed to make the world a better place to live where any country in the world can annihilate any other one anytime it wants?"

"What it will do," he said, "is give the people of this country a feeling of independence, and the same thing will happen all over the world. Of course, my country comes first and I'll even admit that my demands will be reduced. I know I can't take everything the United States has. That would be absurd. This country is too small."

"But you're still talking billions and billions of dollars," she said. "And what happens when the next country gets the missile, as you seem to be so sure they will. Are they going to let you get everything you want first, and wait their turn?"

"Of course not," he said. "Arrangements will have to be worked out. You have to realize that basically I'm a very reasonable man, but I want what's due me for being the first, for having the courage, the vision."

"And what happens when we have an adequate defense and the S-27 is neutralized?" she said.

"It's too late," he said. "You had your chance with my demonstration."

Henderson's offer ran through her mind. She debated and suddenly the words were coming out of her mouth. "Give us the missile and the United States will take no action against you personally or the Togandan people. Your people can retain everything that has already been shipped. It'll all be considered a gift, but you will have to agree to leave the country. We'll ensure your safety anywhere you want to go, if it's within our power, of course, and we'll give you and your wife several million dollars for your own use."

He hung his head and laughed. "I expected much better than that."

Marjorie felt her face flushing and she wanted to leave as quickly as possible. "Why did you want this meeting?" she said.

"To keep the lines of communication open," he said.

She hesitated and tried to relax. "You'd launch the other missile, wouldn't you?"

"Yes," he said.

"Even if it meant your certain destruction," she said.

"Yes," he said.

"Even if no other country came to your aid," she said.

"I don't expect any help," he said.

"And in the process kill thousands of people, innocent people," she said.

"Nobody alive is innocent," he said.

"Why?" she said.

"There's no other way," he said.

"How can it be worth it to you?" she said.

"You should know the answer to that," he said.

"Is that all, then?" she said.

"No," he said. "It pains me to see you failing so miserably."

She stood up. "I think it's time for me to go," she said.

"Good-bye," he said with a taunting smile.

"Good-bye," she said and turned toward the double doors. The guards who had escorted her in were waiting outside to escort her back to her limousine.

Matulo reached for another cigarette, relaxed and self-confident. He lit the cigarette and drew on it slowly, his elbows resting on the desk and his eyes on the portrait of Napoleon directly before him, next to the double doors. He concentrated on the portrait with a distant look in his eyes as he brought his cigarette to and away from his mouth in a slow, steady rhythm. When the cigarette was half-consumed, he abruptly turned his eyes away from the portrait and pressed a button on his intercom. In a few moments Matulo's press aide was walking into the office as Matulo was once again drawing pensively on his cigarette.

"Anyone engaged in any type of illegal buying or selling of any type of foreign merchandise shall be punished with death," Matulo said. The press aide quickly jotted down the words on a small pad of paper. "That's all."

The press aide stood a moment, made a few strokes with his pencil, turned around, and left.

Marjorie was taken directly to Henderson. She had hoped to formulate a definite recommendation to the President during her trip home but hadn't quite been able to put enough bits and pieces together, and then she met Hawkins on his way out of the President's office.

"Mr. Hawkins," she said coldly.

"Ms. Timkins," he said, smiling cordially. "How was your trip?"

She hesitated. "It's classified."

"I understand," he said and reached out his hand, a little stiffly. She shook it. "Maybe we'll get a chance to talk about it."

"Maybe," she said, letting go. He passed on and she opened the door.

Henderson seemed a little more relaxed, his face seemed a little clearer. "Marge," he said, standing up. "How'd it go?"

She shrugged and found a seat. "At least I think I know what his strategy really is, finally."

"What's that?" Henderson said, sitting down.

"He's waiting for more countries to acquire an S-27," she said.

"What's that supposed to do for him?" he said.

"Defend him, I guess," she said.

Henderson nodded. "Did you make him the offer?"

"Yes," she said.

"What did he say?"

"He laughed," she said.

Henderson half-grinned. "Figures."

"That's the first time I've ever been embarrassed in an official capacity," she said. "Let's face it, Wendell, the man is on a crusade, he's got the upper hand right now, and there's no reason for him to deal."

"Then why the meeting?" he said.

"To test our reaction," she said. "Information . . . I'm not completely sure. Maybe nothing. Maybe it was just another of his stupid inspirations."

Henderson grabbed his bony chin in his hand and rubbed it thoughtfully. "Then I guess we keep paying."

"He also read me part of an editorial from a

Chilean newspaper that was incredibly outspoken. Have you seen it?"

He nodded. "I was just discussing it with Jim."

She felt a little more defeated. "What do you think?"

"Marquez is about to appear with an S-27," he said.

"What did Hawkins think about it?" she said.

"The same," he said.

"What do you think should be done about it?" she said.

"What can we do?" he said.

She turned her head aside and closed her eyes for a moment, then turned back to look at Henderson. "My God, is that all you can say?"

"What do you think we should do?" he said. "Invade Chile?"

She pressed her lips together. "What does Hawkins think we should do?"

"Give Toganda an ultimatum," he said. "Stop payments immediately. Refuse to deliver any more merchandise."

"He's changed," she said.

"Not really," he said. "He's reading Matulo's meeting with you as a sign of weakness on Matulo's part."

"Maybe he's right," she said.

"You think so?" he said.

She took a long breath. "Damn it, Wendell, don't you think it's time you made a decision?"

"What decision do you want me to make?" he said. "You talk about the impact this incident is about to have on our entire foreign policy, but you don't seem to want to accept the fact that our domestic policy is going to be affected as well, and dramatically at that."

"Of course I do," she said.

"Then you give me the right decision," he said.

"I don't have it," she said. "Maybe we should get together and start working it out, though."

"We don't have enough facts to do any more than what we're doing right now," he said.

"How many more facts do you want?" she said. "Let's start doing something before it's too late."

"Look, Marge," he said. "I'm ready to take the most far-reaching foreign policy initiatives we've ever discussed, and I know that's what you're looking for, except for one thing—the people of this country are going to have to be told that they're going to have to give up a few luxuries, luxuries which they consider necessities, to satisfy the demands of countries like Toganda."

"Then tell them," she said. "You're their leader—lead."

"Are you crazy?" he said. "You think I could say something like that right now? That would be suicide. It would lead to chaos. That's something nobody wants to buy. Everyone is willing to give up a little surplus, but there never is enough surplus, because the fact is that people have to give up something they think is necessary even though it really isn't. In a way we're probably lucky that Matulo is forcing the issue for us, but we have to let that sink in."

She felt a little more tired and defeated. "Then we're not going to do anything."

"No," he said. "We're doing something right now, but there's only so much available for us to do."

She suddenly found herself relaxing. "Maybe I haven't really understood you, Wendell."

"I'm not sure I know what you mean by that," he said, "but I do think we're basically agreed on what has to be done. In a sense, Matulo's already won. He's forced an issue that has been avoided much too long and the Togandan people are eventually going to be better off for it. I'm convinced of that. Yet at the same time, neither of us wants to see someone like Matulo get away with it. That makes it even more frustrating, but right now all we can do is let him get away with it."

She nodded her head slowly and thoughtfully.

"Have you heard anything from that man, Reynolds?"

He shook his head. "Nothing."

"Too bad," she said. "I was hoping . . ."

"Marge," he said, "I don't think I've ever felt this frustrated. I don't even want to hope. All I'm doing is getting by one minute at a time, by instinct, and I suggest you resign yourself to the same thing."

"You're probably right," she said. She sensed that it was time to leave and stood up.

"Are you going?" he said.

"Yes," she said.

"What about the meeting?" he said.

"I told you," she said.

"That was it?" he said.

"That was it," she said. He looked only a little disappointed.

"Well, you did your job," he said. "What are you going to do right now?"

"I'm not sure," she said. "There are some things I should look over, clear my head, try to take a fresh look."

"Relax," he said. "Like me."

"Is it natural or induced?" she said.

He laughed in a sincere and friendly way she remembered.

"You've done a great job, Marge," he said.

"Done?" she said.

He tightened up. "I'll talk to you later," he said.

"Later," she said and turned to leave. She wondered why she didn't feel like kicking down the door in front of her.

Seventh Day

Reynolds was with a company being drilled in the vicinity of the barracks nearest the palace when General Matulo decided to take his daily walk. Reynolds's company was brought to attention for one of the General's informal inspections. Matulo walked in front of the men, smiling, and evidently quite pleased with what he saw. "Very nice," he said as he approached Reynolds, but when he reached Reynolds he stopped his leisurely pace and their eyes met. Reynolds could smell the stale tobacco on the General's breath. Matulo stopped smiling for only a second and then continued his inspection as though nothing unexpected had happened. When he was finished with the inspection, he walked up to the company commander, Colonel Lubwa. They talked briefly and Matulo headed back toward the palace.

Marjorie Timkins awoke refreshed and ready to begin a hard day's work. She lingered in her shower, thinking about the dinner she'd had the night before with Henrik. They'd gone to a friendly Washington restaurant that concentrated on simple, home-cooked meals. They'd had chicken and dumplings and a light white wine, and her most pronounced memory of their dinner was how surprised they were to find the bottle empty. They had gone to a show where the actors' enthusiasm more than compensated for the playwright's shortcomings. They'd discussed finishing the evening at his place but somehow found themselves reluctant. Her justification was fatigue; his, caution. As she stepped out of the shower, she completed convincing herself that her reluctance had been a mistake.

As she dressed she was interrupted by a call from a presidential aide informing her that Henderson wanted her to be present at a meeting later that day. She attached no special significance to it and finished dressing, still thinking about Henrik.

As she was driven into the capital she half-listened to the radio, until she realized that there was a commentary on the Togandan situation. " . . . that sixty-three percent of the people polled think that President Henderson is not doing enough to resolve the situation. At the same time, thirty-two percent are still undecided on the use of direct military force to recover the Togandan missile. It is quite clear that something has to be done, but no consensus on what that should be. Possibly the most disturbing news about this entire affair is recent reports from Chile that that country is very actively seeking to build their own equivalent of the S-27. While the Russians have been actively engaged in developing their own counterpart to the S-27, and are suspected of being very close to a working prototype, Chile is the first non-major power to publicly announce that they intend to do whatever is within their means to build the equivalent of the S-27. There are also rumors of a similar attitude in a number of other countries who have never been considered part of any arms race.

"The attitude of these countries is that if the Togandans can do it, so can we, and those countries who have stated that they have no intention of engaging in any such mini-arms race are discouragingly few in number. Notable among them are Japan, Canada, and Mexico, but it might be only a matter of time before even these countries begin to feel a necessity for having a low-cost, strategic capability. Where this will all lead is a very good question. Is it inevitable that every country in the world will soon have a global strategic capability?

"Another disturbing issue revolves around defensive capability. The Joint Chiefs of Staff issued a statement yesterday saying that there is now an adequate defensive capability against the S-27. While this may or may not be true, the fact is that nobody will know unless the Togandan missile is actually launched. If it is true, then one might be able to assume that the world will return to its former status, but if it isn't, a bad situation may grow even worse. Can our Government risk the failure of that defensive capability? Does it, in fact, have the right to take such a risk?

"In the opinion of this commentator, the Government does not have the right to risk life and property needlessly when the people of this, the wealthiest country in the world, are only being asked to send a relatively small amount of money to one of the poorer countries of the world. It may be galling to see someone like General Matulo, an unsavory leader if there ever was one, holding the United States for ransom, but that is just a matter of personal and national pride. False pride, if it leads to the deaths of innocent people.

"The Togandan situation cannot continue forever. Even General Matulo has announced that there is an upper limit to the sums he wants and even if, as seems all too likely, other countries begin appearing with the equivalent of the S-27, no sane political leader would want to see the economic destruction of the United States or any other wealthy country in the world, and nobody wants to see total, global destruction. Accommodations will be made, just as they have been in the past, to this new political reality."

"In compliance with federal and state regulation . . ." Marjorie stopped listening as the announcer began speaking. The short commentary had lifted her spirits a little higher. She felt herself relaxing and gaining confidence in the good sense of the American people.

She was still feeling that way when she entered the

President's office. Blaine was there, sunk into his chair with a smoldering cigar in his hand. Marjorie had a great deal of respect for the man who managed to survive election after election and had risen to his position by an ability to doggedly see that the legislation the party wanted passed, actually did. That he used as few words as possible in the process was decidedly to his credit; that he retained his own mind and definite views beneath his party loyalty was even more to his credit. Sitting next to him was Westbrook, who watched Marjorie as though she were his prey. Hawkins was also present, and apparently in a very good mood as he laughed privately with Westbrook and gave Marjorie the most cordial welcome of the group. She found her own seat.

"This is an unusual gathering," she said as she settled down.

"There were supposed to be some others present but they couldn't make it," Henderson said.

"We wanted to personally discuss your meeting with General Matulo," Blaine said.

"Didn't the President tell you what I told him?" she said.

"Yes," Westbrook said, "but we're concerned about the way you handled yourself there."

"What?" she said, turning to the senator. "I don't understand. The General told me what his intentions were; I made an offer which the President and I had discussed; Matulo considered it a joke. That was all there was to it. It was a very short meeting."

"Yes, we understand that," Westbrook said, "but did you let him know that we have no intention of allowing this blackmail to continue?"

"Of course I did," she said, "but even if I hadn't, that's obvious. The General's not an idiot."

"I didn't say he was," Westbrook said, "but I'm worried that our public image has been giving the impression that we're ready to wait him out and that we're perfectly willing to continue paying."

"I don't see that," she said, "and I don't think Matulo sees it that way. He knows he can only keep this up so long and then he's going to have to come to terms with us."

"I'm afraid I can't see it that way, and neither do a lot of people," Westbrook said. "In many ways I have to agree with the approach that's been taken so far, at least what's been revealed publicly. But on a private negotiating level, such as you had with Matulo, we had an opportunity and an obligation to present our real intentions more forcefully, and whether you're aware of it or not, I'm speaking for a great many people and I know Wendell is aware of that."

"Yes," she said, "I'm aware of that also, but I can't see what your point is. I just heard on the radio a recent poll which said that over a third of the people in this country are against the use of direct military force at this time. What did you want me to do? Make an empty threat?"

"No," Westbrook said, "that's not it at all. All I'm saying is that there are a great many people who think we should be more definite with Matulo. That same poll, I think, showed almost two-thirds of the people out of favor with what the Government is doing about Toganda. That's what I'm concerned about, as well as the international prestige that we've already lost."

"I wish you'd come right out and say what you're really getting at, Senator," she said. "Are you saying that I didn't handle that meeting with Matulo properly?"

"I'm questioning it," he said.

"I don't want to be insulting," she said, "but how can you make a judgment about that? Matulo and I were the only people present."

"I'm only trying to uncover the facts," Westbrook said. "I'm fully aware that there was no one else at that meeting, but since I'm putting together a complete investigation into this Togandan matter, I have to look into every element to the fullest extent that I can. I think it's become common knowledge that I'm very disturbed at the way this entire situation has been handled from the very beginning and how it's being allowed to develop."

"What concerns me more," Blaine said, "and what is really concerning the entire Congress, is what is going to be done now."

"Of course," Westbrook said defensively.

"The simple fact is that the majority of people in the country are not happy with the way things are being handled," Blaine said.

She turned to Blaine. "That may be," she said, "but I can't see that what we've done, or what we're doing, is anything other than what we have to do or are able to do."

"That could be," Blaine said, "but part of the question is not just what is being done, but how it's being done."

She thought for a moment, her enthusiasm from that morning already gone. "I get the feeling this is all leading up to something."

"The point, Marjorie," Henderson said, "is that the initial appropriation for the Togandans is just about spent. Kantho and his buyers are already making commitments above the two hundred million mark and it's accelerating, and unless we want to get into a situation where I have to throw up my hands and tell Matulo, 'Sorry, there's no more money,' I'm going to have to do something, we're going to have to do something, and one of the possibilities that's been presented to me is appointing Jim the new Secretary of State."

"But," she started, "I thought . . ."

"I know I haven't mentioned it before," he said. "I really didn't think it would come to this. I thought it would be enough to simply use him as a consultant. I think we've worked together exceptionally well over the last few years, but last night I was informed that I had lost my majority in the House over my welfare bill and wouldn't get it back until I did something about Toganda. This was presented as a workable compromise."

"Then I'm out," she said softly.

"I'm afraid so," he said.

She could tell he was genuinely sorry. She had known it was coming and she thought she was ready for it, but still she felt betrayed.

"I realize this is somewhat of an unusual way of breaking this kind of news," he said, "but I thought it best."

She nodded her head.

"I wanted the Senator and the Congressman here to talk to you first," he said. "I thought that maybe after questioning you about your meeting with Matulo they might change their minds, but I can tell they've already made them up." He turned to Westbrook. "Am I right?"

Westbrook quickly nodded his head.

"And Mr. Hawkins?" she said, turning to look at him.

"I thought he should be here and have a chance to ask questions," Henderson said. Hawkins's smile was gone and he looked ill at ease.

"I see," she said. She moved her attention away from Hawkins to Henderson. "I thought this was going to happen. From the moment I took this office, I always suspected in the back of my head that if something really critical ever occurred, I would be out. I was a popular appointment as long as my position wasn't that important." She turned to Westbrook. "I understand what you were getting at now, Senator. A woman can't really deal with a foreign head of state, can she? She really can't be forceful or persuasive enough, especially when she's up against a man, isn't that it?"

Westbrook looked a little embarrassed, pursed his lips, and didn't say anything.

"What about Simmons?" she said. "Or, for that

matter, the heads of all our intelligence or investigative agencies? Why aren't you going after one of them? Isn't that really the source of the problem?"

"My committee will be looking into that," Westbrook said, "but that's beside the issue now. What's done is done. The question now is finding a solution."

"A solution to what?" she said, and let her anger get out of control. "What does getting rid of me solve? That's just a political mirage and you know it. The fact is that there's only one place where there's even a choice and that's how to get rid of Matulo, because something like the S-27 shouldn't be in the hands of a capricious lunatic, and that's it."

"I think you're oversimplifying the matter," Westbrook said.

She turned back to Henderson. "Is that what you think?" she said. "Am I oversimplifying?"

"That's not the point," Henderson said. He drew a deep breath. "I hoped you would understand."

"But I do," she said. "I understand perfectly. That's the problem."

"This is getting nowhere," Westbrook said.

She turned to him. "That's the point. There's nowhere to get."

There was an awkward silence.

"I think this was a mistake," Henderson said. "Why don't you take the rest of the day off, Marjorie. Jim can debrief you about the meeting tomorrow if he wants."

"Okay," she said and stood up. "I'll talk to you later about what I should say to the press."

"Fine," Henderson said.

She turned and left and felt relieved.

"Think she'll do anything out of line?" Westbrook said when the door had closed behind her.

Henderson shook his head. "She's too professional. Let her cool off. Like I said, I think this was a mistake."

"Maybe," Westbrook said. He stood up. "I have to get going."

Blaine stood up and started to follow him out of the office and Hawkins started to follow after. "Jim," Henderson said. "I want to talk to you." He turned around and returned to his seat.

Hawkins had been openly critical of Henderson's choice of Marjorie Timkins as Secretary of State from the moment Henderson had announced his choice. He felt that he was more qualified for the job, but was willing to reluctantly accept Henderson's reasoning. Marjorie's appointment had been very popular, much more popular than his own would have been. He could accept that, and he could also accept that, for the most part, Marjorie had been right in the Togandan situation.

"Jim," Henderson said, "I just want to make sure we start on the right foot. I want to make sure we understand each other. Up till now I've been listening to what you've had to say, but now I want you to listen."

"Okay," Hawkins said.

"There's not going to be any invasion of Toganda," Henderson said.

Hawkins simply nodded his head and said, "I know."

"No extra pressure, either," Henderson said.

"All right."

"We're going to continue the same approach that Marorie and I were using. We're going to wait for more information."

"Fine."

Henderson looked at Hawkins closely.

"What's the matter?" Hawkins said.

"What's the matter?" Henderson said. "I should be asking you what's the matter."

"Surprised?" Hawkins said.

"A bit," Henderson said.

"Wendell, it's obvious you're shocked, but you shouldn't be," Hawkins said. "I know I've recommended pushing Matulo a little harder, but I'm not ready to see him drop his missile someplace. I know what's going on here. I know I'm just a part of some political maneuvering."

Henderson looked him over more intently. "Don't be too clever, Jim."

"I don't intend to be," Hawkins said. "Basically, I've agreed with what you and Marjorie have been doing, and I agree with continuing that policy at this time. I agree that we need more information before doing anything more. I know Westbrook is out for your job and he's just using this Togandan mess for his own ends. Don't get me wrong, though. I still think we should move toward a harder line, but before that I think we'd better know whether Matulo actually has that other missile. What really concerns me more, right now, is what the Chileans are doing. They're acting too militant about getting their own missile."

"What do you suggest?" Henderson said.

"A meeting with Marquez," Hawkins said. "As soon as possible."

"Toward what goal?"

"Letting him know that we're not about to put up with any proliferation of the Thor-type cruise missile."

Henderson thought a moment. "Maybe."

"What do you mean?"

"You intend to threaten Marquez with something?"

"Nothing specific."

"But something implicit, though."

"Yes."

"Such as?"

"Military intervention. Economic pressure."

"And you think he'll buy it?"

"Yes," Hawkins said, "if we approach it correctly."

"Christ, man, wake up."

"Do you want to see the S-27 handed to every country in the world on a platter?"

"I don't want to fight the inevitable," Henderson said.

"Then do you really think it's inevitable that the

world is going to become totally destabilized because of the S-27?"

"I didn't say that."

"That's what you're implying."

"Not necessarily."

"What else can it mean?"

"We can deal with it."

"What do you think I'm talking about?"

"But not with threats of violence."

"I didn't say that."

"Implied, explicit, economic, whatever," Henderson said. "In this context they're all the same as far as I'm concerned."

"Then what do we do?" Hawkins said. "Sit back and wait to be dictated to?"

"I didn't say that either," Henderson said.

"Then what are you saying?" Hawkins said, exasperated.

"I say we talk reasonably to the Chileans. We let them know we understand their situation. We let them know that we know that it's only a matter of time before they get their own S-27."

"Are you talking about handing them one of those missiles?" Hawkins said, incredulous.

"No," Henderson said and shook his head. "Look at the facts. We don't know where Matulo got his missile. We don't know how many missiles he has left. Maybe he doesn't have any, but maybe he has two, or three, or four, and we don't know how many more he can get if he wants them. We don't know whether for a fact the Chileans can get one of those missiles from the Togandans or not or whether they can get one from the same source Matulo used. We don't know any of that and you're talking like we should act as though we have everything under control when it's obvious we don't. In the eyes of the world we look like a bunch of fools, and I don't intend continuing that way."

Hawkins looked away, then back to Henderson. "I'll have to think about that."

Henderson assumed an almost paternalistic air. "Jim," he said, "it's the only way, believe me, and no matter what anyone else is expecting out of you, if we don't work together we're just going to have a hell of a mess."

"I know," Hawkins said, "but believe me, I'm basically a very reasonable person."

"Good" Henderson said. "Now, I'll see you back at one. That'll give you enough time to think about what I've said. But if you decide you don't want to do things my way, I'll just take it to the People. I'd rather not at this point, but if I'm forced into it, I will."

"I understand," Hawkins said, and stood up. He reached his hand across the desk to Henderson and Henderson took it. Hawkins smiled reassuringly. "I'll see you at one."

Henrik ran his finger around the rim of his glass and studied the olive in his martini. "I guess you were right."

"Ah, well," she said. "It really doesn't matter anyway."

"I wonder what Henderson is going to do with the women's vote next election," he said.

"As well as the last would be my guess," she said.

"Seriously," he said.

"Why shouldn't he?" she said.

He lifted the glass to his lips. "You're starting to get me depressed."

"Sorry," she said. "I didn't think I was that contagious."

"You knew it was coming," he said.

"I know," she said. She leaned her right elbow on the table and started massaging her forehead between her thumb and fingers.

"So what are you going to do?" he said after an edgy silence.

"I don't know," she said. "I was working on an idea . . ."

He waited as patiently as he could. "What idea?"

"Just something," she said. "Something you said once."

He waited again. "You think you can finish this idea before dinner?"

She finished her martini, double, extra dry. "Remember what you said about some secret organization out to take over the world?"

"I don't remember putting it in quite those terms," he said.

"Well, anyway," she said, "while I was in my office yesterday, I noticed a request for help from the State Department for some big electronics company. They were having trouble with the Indonesian Government and it started me thinking about how involved U.S. multinationals have become with the Government. I mean, it's always been there and I've been aware of it, but the reality of it just struck me, and that got me thinking about multinationals in general and what the results of this Togandan mess could mean to them." She held her glass out to a passing waitress. "Another." The waitress took it and turned to Henrik. Henrik nodded his head.

"The same," he said and turned back to Marjorie. "So what did you come up with?"

"I'm not completely sure," she said, "but I think it should generate more competition."

"Why is that?" he said.

"Because the multinationals have become so involved with their host governments," she said. "There was a time, not too many years ago, when it looked like it would go the other way, but it didn't. They need that host-government support because they're such a major part of the economy of every country and without that support they'd be much too vulnerable. Of course, in return for that support, they have to be ready to reciprocate, and as a rule they're very happy to. What's happened, and it's been such a gradual process that it's hardly been noticed, is that, while at one time these same multinationals had to be very careful about how they conducted their business abroad and their host governments were more sensitive about what they did, they don't have to worry about how they operate as much anymore. There was a time when we had to worry about the Russians moving into a country after an American company had left a bad image behind them, but the politics, and the economics, are different now. We don't have to worry about the Communists the same way we did because they, in effect, have their own multinationals conducting business in those same countries in substantially the same way ours do."

"I don't see what you're getting at," he said with a shake of his head. "How does that relate to competitiveness?"

"You have to focus on what the goal of a multinational is and the fact that they've become so involved in national foreign policy," she said with the first hint of enthusiasm she'd shown since meeting him at the bar. "On the surface it would appear that there should be a tremendous amount of competition for penetrating the auto market or building a factory in Malaysia between this company and that—with the backing of their respective governments—with the concomitant benefits going to this underdeveloped country, but the reality is that it doesn't work that way. That market in that underdeveloped country is too small for that kind of competition. These economies can't support the size of operation that these companies need to work at, so what has developed is a sort of global market fixing. You get Malaysia and I'll take Singapore and thus the foremost goal of the multinational is achieved—maximization of return on their capital and technology."

"That sounds a little far out," he said.

The waitress returned with their refills. Marjorie waited for her to leave before continuing.

"It's not that blatant," she said, "and this is what really started hitting me. It's a very subtle process and there seems to be a sort of unwritten agreement. You see, right now there are a lot of countries coming to a point where the marjority of the population could be said to be rising to a level of middle-classdom that was achieved in this country maybe fifty years ago. Their demands have become too insistent. Their governments have to supply the people's desires, and the multinationals have the capital but, more importantly, the know-how to make it happen. They're in a seller's market, and they can count on their respective governments to support them and, likewise, other multinationals which aren't going to step on their toes and create an unprofitable precedent, so they can operate as they want, pretty much. I mean, there are limits, but there was a time when certain countries could exercise some political autonomy because of natural resources. With the escape from fossil-fuel dependence and undersea mining, that leverage has virtually disappeared. In the host countries, glaring inequalities are the result, but yet per capita income keeps rising, and everyone hopes things will work out eventually. The result is a screwed-up situation where things seem to be improving quite nicely economically, but where the social and political situation is incredibly frustrating. Now, if they could do what Toganda is doing, they could express a certain political autonomy and the whole picture could change virtually overnight."

"You mean, if country X didn't like the way GM was running their business, country X's leader could threaten to blow up Chicago if they didn't straighten up," he said.

She shook her head. "No," she said. "Well, yes, in a way I suppose you could put it that way. What they could really do, and what Toganda is doing at this moment, is force the wealthier countries to simply supply the needed capital and other resources. They could develop their economies the way they wanted to without having to let DuPont or whoever come into their country if they're not completely happy about the terms. In many ways it's almost more psychological than anything else, but that's important. It's really just a question of good old freedom."

"I'm getting lost," he said. "How does this relate to tracing the source of the missile? If the effect of the missile is to make multinationals more competitive and to make them give the countries they operate in a better deal, then they would have to be going with those missiles, unless they were stupid enough to simply want a little short-term profit off of selling it."

"I know," she said. "That's exactly what's been running through my mind. It really doesn't seem to make any sense, but then it was a sharp capitalist who financed Lenin and his revolution."

He chuckled, glad to see Marjorie back in form. "Good point."

"But I did come up with an idea that might make sense," she said. "It could be in the interest of an extranational corporation that was truly not supported by any host government. For that kind of a corporation, this new type of competition could be a great thing."

"But I got the impression from what you were saying that there wouldn't be any incentive for a corporation like that to even exist," he said. "It would be locked out."

"That's true," she said. "But maybe there's one that's planning to go extranational, one that's willing to sever its national political ties and go on its own because it sees better prospects."

"I see what you're getting at," he said. "Now, my question is, how do you propose to track down something like that?"

"My guess is that it would be a smaller multinational," she said. "One with assets, say, between one and two billion dollars and one that's had some problems with its host government, say, where the government wouldn't intervene on its behalf, one that had lost a big contract, or something like that, because of some political expedient—most probably, one that's had that happen a number of times."

"Interesting," he said. "Did you mention this to Henderson?"

"I didn't get a chance," she said. She took a drink. "There were a lot of things I wanted to mention to Henderson that I didn't."

"Don't you think you ought to say something?" he said.

She shrugged. "I suppose," she said. "Oh, I guess I will, but not now. Right now, I just feel tired."

"You want to go?" he said.

"What about your drink?" she said.

"I've had enough," he said.

She reached her hand across the bare oak table, squeezed his hand, and managed a smile. "Let's get out of here."

Reynolds was lying on his bunk, relaxing in his barracks after a filling dinner, when he was approached by Colonel Lubwa. "Umlika."

Reynolds sprang up and to attention. "Yes, sir."

"Come with me," Lubwa said.

"Yes, sir."

Reynolds followed Lubwa out of the barracks and toward the Presidential Palace.

"General Matulo wants to see you," Lubwa said.

Reynolds relaxed. It was common practice for Matulo to personally meet each of the guards at some point in his career.

"Go ahead," Lubwa said as they approached Matulo's office. Reynolds stepped past the Colonel and between the two guards flanking the double doors to Matulo's office. As he entered the office, Matulo was sitting behind his desk. The General fixed his eyes on Reynolds the moment he passed through the double doors and kept them fixed on him as he walked up to the chair before Matulo's desk. The double doors swung shut and Reynolds sat down without being asked.

Matulo took his eyes off Reynolds to open the gold cigarette case sitting on the desk. "Cigarette?"

"Thank you," Reynolds said. He took a cigarette and placed it in his mouth, then reached for the lighter sitting next to the case.

"I wasn't expecting you," Matulo said cooly and distantly as Reynolds lit his cigarette. "I didn't expect to see you at all until all this was over."

"I know," Reynolds said and replaced the lighter.

They studied each other for a few moments.

"Why?" Matulo said.

"I wanted to make sure everything was going all right," Reynolds said.

"You betrayed me," Matulo said.

Reynolds felt a sinking in his stomach. His mouth started drying up. "What . . ."

"You know what I mean," Matulo said sharply. "The missile is mine now and I should have you killed on the spot."

"I was afraid something might happen to you," Reynolds said quickly.

"You were afraid I might win," Matulo said.

"I want you to win," Reynolds said.

"You're lying," Matulo said.

"Then kill me," Reynolds said.

"No," Matulo said. He reached for the cigarette case. His fingers trembled slightly as he went to open it. "I'm going to let you live—here."

"In the palace?" Reynolds said.

"In the barracks," Matulo said.

"Why?" Reynolds said.

"Because you're a divine instrument," Matulo said. "You betrayed me once—that was a test. One must always be the most cautious when things are going the smoothest. You reminded me of that."

"As I intended to," Reynolds said.

Matulo nodded his head in a smooth and rapid rhythm. "But if you betray me again, then I'll know you've changed sides. You'll be with the devil and I'll have to kill you."

"But you're winning," Reynolds said. "I want you to win and I've helped you. I fixed the missile for exactly the reason you mentioned. Now you're transforming the world, you're transforming Toganda. You cannot lose and I've seen to it. Never forget that."

"God has given me my mission," Matulo said, "as he has given you yours. That is all I know. If you betray me again, I shall have you killed."

"I understand," Reynolds said. He felt the tension throughout his body. "The United States Secretary of State," he said. "She was here."

"Yes," Matulo said.

"What happened?" Reynolds said.

"We talked," Matulo said.

"Did you come to an agreement?" Reynolds said.

"Yes," Matulo said.

"What was it?" Reynolds said.

"Our meeting is over," Matulo said.

Reynolds stood up and quickly let his eyes run along the wall behind Matulo, the large, uncurtained windows, the picture of Matulo's wife and Matulo himself.

"You may go now," Matulo said.

Reynolds nodded his head once briskly, and turned. His eye caught a large picture, a landscape, and he had a feeling about it. He kept walking, through the double doors and out into the hall.

It was a clear night with a crescent moon. As Reynolds made his way back to his barracks, alone, he stopped behind a tree to shield himself from the sentry who was working his way around the palace. Reynolds considered the situation and decided this was as good a time as any. The possibility that Matulo might continue to talk with Umlika, the recruit, for hours would be reasonable to Colonel Lubwa. He left the shelter of the tree and headed away from the barracks, toward the perimeter of the grounds.

As he entered the woods, he tried to orient himself to some of the more distinctive trees he'd committed to memory during his short stay. He walked slowly, straining to remember the locations of the few infrared cameras that regularly scanned this section and hoping he was walking where they weren't aimed. When he reached the fence he sat on his knees and breathed slowly and evenly to steady himself. When he felt relaxed enough, he started pulling away the twigs and leaves that covered a slight depression in the ground beneath the electrified fence. When he'd cleared the space, he checked for the sentry. The sentry passed by without noticing the slightly disturbed ground at his feet. When he was gone from sight, Reynolds rolled onto his back and squirmed under the fence.

Once through, he rolled over onto his stomach and sprinted the hundred meters to the forest ahead of him. As he passed between two trees, he went to his knees, turned around, and looked for the sentry. The sentry was passing the spot Reynolds had crawled through but didn't break his stride. Reynolds turned around and headed into the forest. He passed three trees he'd marked in his head and came to the base of a small hill. He spent the next ten minutes looking for the camouflaged entrance to a cave. He rolled the stone aside that was covering its mouth and crawled in. Once he was in, the cave opened up and he was able to stand but he went to his knees and once again concentrated on his breathing. His heart was pounding and his mouth was dry and hot.

Everything had been planned so perfectly. Marjorie Timkins had unexpectedly shown up for an interview with Matulo, but that really didn't matter. What mattered was that Matulo now had absolute control of

the missile—probably. The only element Reynolds
had really worried about was not going according to
plan and he couldn't get it out of his mind. He
concentrated on his breathing. He started to relax
and his thoughts returned to the immediate task. He
reached to his right and pulled a heavy canvas bag
toward himself. He opened it, glanced inside for a
quick check, closed it back up, and dragged it outside.
He slung the bag over his shoulder and headed back
toward the palace grounds.

He waited at the edge of the clearing for the sentry
to pass, then sprinted back to the fence with the canvas bag still over his shoulder. He pushed the bag in
ahead of himself and crawled back under the fence
on his back. Again, he crouched and waited for the
sentry. When the sentry had passed, he turned and
started to make his way through the forest toward the
main gate.

Men were inside, joking but not drinking, while
Reynolds placed his first charge beneath a pile of
wood stacked against the guardhouse. He slipped
back into the woods and headed toward the Presidential Palace. He placed his second charge by the garage where Matulo's bulletproof limousines were
kept. He waited in a shadow for two soldiers to pass
and then sprinted across the narrow clearing to the
barracks he'd been living in. He placed his third
charge, along with the carefully folded canvas bag,
behind the air-conditioning unit which sat on a slab
of concrete at the rear of the building. He then
worked his way around the building to the entrance,
where he was stopped by a sentry.

"Who goes there?"

"Umlika," Reynolds said. "Returning from an audience with General Matulo." Reynolds started to
move forward.

"Hold it there," the guard said. He held his gun
leveled at Reynold's stomach less than two meters
away. "Colonel Lubwa wants to talk to you." Rey-

nolds stopped. "Colonel Lubwa," the guard called out. Reynolds steadied his breathing and waited. "Colonel Lubwa!" The sentry turned his head to the side and for an instant had his attention off Reynolds.

Reynolds stepped forward with his right foot, caught the rifle with his left hand, spun to his left in a circle on the ball of his right foot, then spun again on the ball of his left foot. The guard went sprawling and Reynolds had his gun in hand. He heard footsteps and, from the corner of his eye, saw two men running toward him. He ran for the nearest tree, then he spun around to take in the scene. He could see five men and two rifles already aimed in his direction. Puffs of dirt formed a pattern in front of him and *krangs* of rifle fire reached his ears. He turned and ran into the forest. When he reached the spot at the fence, he flattened. He pushed the rifle through and crawled after it on his back. Suddenly there was blinding light in his eyes. He covered his face with his arm, but he was already through. He grabbed the rifle, crouched, and spotted the sentry aiming his rifle. Reynolds rolled, ended in a crouch, aimed, and fired a single round into the sentry. Before the sentry's body hit the ground, Reynolds was up and churning his legs toward the safety of the forest. He felt his leg scratched just before he dived behind a tree. He rolled and reached his hand to his leg. His fingers touched wetness and pulled away. He listened to the rifle shots for a moment, then pushed himself up and started running again.

When he reached his cave, he threw the rifle in before him and went to work rolling the stone back over the mouth of the cave. It stuck. He cursed. It came free. It was done. He laid on his back. His chest heaved up and down as he gasped for air. It was only after his breathing started to quiet that he wondered if he'd left a trail of blood to the cave. He dismissed the thought, closed his eyes, and concentrated on relaxing and clearing his mind.

Eighth Day

Marjorie Timkins went to her office at the State Department to clean out her personal belongings. She was staring at the open briefcase on her desk when she heard a knock at the door. She looked up. "Come in."

Hawkins stepped into the room, smiling, but not in quite the self-satisfied way Marjorie expected. "I was told I'd find you here," he said.

"How are you?" she said.

"Fine," he said. He softly closed the door and looked for a place to sit.

"Did you want to talk about Matulo?" she said.

He nodded his head.

"He's got it, he'll launch it, leave him alone, give him the money, wait for someone else to say they've got the missile, and see what happens," she said.

He let out an involuntary chuckle.

"You think I'm kidding," she said seriously. "Matulo's won and the sooner you and everyone else realizes it, the better."

"You don't think we can get it away from him?" he said.

"You referring to Simmons's man?" she said.

"Well, yes," he said. "That's one possibility."

"That's bullshit," she said. "It doesn't make a damn bit of difference what that guy does."

"So you think it's hopeless," he said.

"No," she said. "I didn't say that."

"There's just nothing we can do about it," he said.

"No," she said. "There's plenty you can do about it."

"You're getting too esoteric for me," he said.

"It's simple," she said. She walked to one of the walls and lifted up a framed diploma. "You can start preparing the public for it, you can talk to Marquez—he's probably the next one to have it—you might try waking up some congressmen."

He let out another chuckle. "In other words, you think we should do exactly what we're planning to do."

She stopped with the diploma in her hand. "What's that?"

"What you're saying is basically the way Wendell feels," he said.

"And you're going along with it?" she said.

"Yes," he said.

"You mean there's no get-tough, call-in-the-Marines, cut-off-the-money?" she said, just faintly surprised.

"No," he said.

"Hmm," she said with a half smile and tossed the diploma into her briefcase.

"I don't blame you," he said.

"For what?" she said.

"For feeling the way you do," he said.

"How do I feel?" she said.

He shrugged his shoulders. "Bitter, angry, hurt," he said.

"That's how it goes," she said.

"I guess," he said.

She waited a moment, then snapped her briefcase shut.

"If I were you, I think I'd be ready to kill," he said.

"Maybe I am," she said. She smiled at Hawkins and reached for the briefcase.

Hawkins shifted in his chair uncomfortably. "There was something else I wanted to ask you about."

"What's that?" she said.

"Where do you think Matulo got the missiles?" he said.

"I don't know," she said.

"I know that," he said. "I mean, where do you *think* he got them?"

A bemused look came over her face. "I've got a theory," she said. "Just an idea."

"What is it?" he said.

"I haven't worked out the details yet," she said.

"Well, then, what have you got?" he said.

"Ever read *Man With The Golden Gun?*" she said.

"James Bond?" he said.

"Yes," she said. "It's not exactly the same thing, but in the same area."

"I never read it," he said.

"Neither did I," she said with a chuckle. "I only saw the movie."

He shook his head and looked slightly disgusted. "Are you going to tell me or not?"

"It has to do with extranationals," she said.

"Extranationals?" he said.

"Extranational corporations," she said. "Ones that can't rely on some national government to support their interests."

"I didn't think there was such a thing," he said.

"There may not be," she said.

"Then what's the point?" he said.

"What if there were?" she said.

He shrugged. "I don't know," he said. "What if there were?"

She pulled the briefcase to her side. "I'm sorry, Mr. Hawkins, but I really have to get going. I've fiddled around here too long as it is. Like I said, it's just an idea and I haven't gone through the details yet. For all I know, it might just be a wild-goose chase, but if you think about it, maybe you'll see something there." She stepped around the desk.

He stood up. "Thanks for the thoughts," he said.

"No trouble," she said.

"Maybe we could discuss some things in more depth at another time," he said.

"You can reach me at home," she said.

"I'll be in touch," he said.

"Good-bye, now," she said. "Nice meeting you again."

"Good-bye," he said.

She jaunted out the door, feeling lighthearted and swinging her case at her side.

Reynolds awoke to the sound of water rushing. He raised his head and felt his muscles aching at the base of his neck. He reached into his pocket, pulled out his lighter, and turned it on. His surroundings became more real and he made his way to the chest sitting against one wall. His body ached from his neck to his feet but he ignored it. He flipped the top of the chest open and reached in. He pulled out an Aladdin lamp, set it on the musty floor of the cave, and lit it. He stood up and shook his hands by his sides to get his blood flowing and the stiffness out. He breathed the damp, stale air of the cave deeply and felt himself relaxing and warming up, then stooped down and put his head close to the rock that covered the cave's entrance. He could hear the rain dripping, the source of the rushing water he was hearing from somewhere in the bowels of the cave. He felt his luck returning and he turned back to the chest. He removed the shortwave radio from its clear plastic cover and set it against the chest. He then pulled out a can of his favorite baked beans, a can opener, a pan and a fork, and a Coleman stove and began fixing his meal. While the beans heated in the pan, he removed the plastic cover from the radio and considered the report he was about to make. He adjusted the dials.

"This is Stingray. Come in. Come in," he said.

He waited. He repeated his words and waited again. After several attempts, a scratchy voice said, "This is Shark."

"Prey alive, location later. Over."

"Over and out."

Reynolds turned the set off and went to his beans. They were bubbling invitingly as he took the pan off the fire. He leaned back against the chest with the corners of his mouth turned up slightly.

"At least we know now that he's got it." Henderson was still elated over the small scrap of information he'd received from the CIA.

Hawkins couldn't help being somewhat amused at Henderson's excitement. "Where is it, though?"

"It's coming," Henderson said enthusiastically. "I think Simmons got the right man this time."

"It's taken him long enough," Hawkins said.

Henderson shrugged. "It may not be much, but at least it's something. Something solid."

"Granted," Hawkins said. "What about Marquez, though?"

"What about him?" Henderson said.

"Shouldn't we adjust our approach?" Hawkins said.

"Why?" Henderson said. "Just because of this?"

"I think so," Hawkins said. "We've found the missile and there's a possibility it'll be disarmed before too long. I'd say that changes things considerably."

"I agree," Henderson said. "It takes a lot of pressure off."

"Then you're willing to get a little tougher," Hawkins said.

"What?" Henderson said. He looked at Hawkins in disbelief.

"We can get a little tougher," Hawkins said, surprised at Henderson's reaction. "Isn't that what this is telling you? We have a chance to neutralize Matulo's missile, meaning we can put a damper on Marquez."

"What for?" Henderson said, with a look of disbelief still on his face.

Hawkins looked aside and back to Henderson. "If we can neutralize Matulo's missile, we can neutralize

Marquez's missile if he gets one. It's going to make these countries think twice."

"So?" Henderson said.

Hawkins's voice rose. "So it puts us back in control."

"Is that why you think I'm so happy about this report?" Henderson said.

Hawkins looked aside and shook his head. "I thought it was, but I guess I must have missed something."

"I'm happy because I know he has it," Henderson said. "Because I can show this report to all these idiot congressmen who can't make up their minds."

Hawkins got out of his seat, thrust his hands in his pants pockets, and started pacing in front of Henderson's desk.

"Somewhere I've missed something," he said.

"I guess you have," Henderson said.

Hawkins kept pacing for several moments, then turned and faced Henderson. "What is it you're after?"

Henderson looked at Hawkins like a patient professor at a struggling student. "A little rationality," he said, "and thank God Matulo really has that missile, because maybe now, finally, is the time to do something, maybe the perfect time or even the only time to do something I've wanted to do for years that I've never really had the opportunity to do."

"What's that?" Hawkins said softly.

"Initiate some real, positive action to equalize the distribution of wealth and economic power on this planet," he said. "Every country with a strategic nuclear capability. I feel like I've seen it coming in the back to my head, and now Matulo has forced the issue, and it's real. It's really real and that's what it takes to get something real started."

Hawkins shook his head and sat down. "I can't see it," he said. "Yes, Matulo has done something very dramatic, yes, it looks like a strong possibility of some rapid proliferation, and yes, something has to be done about it, but to say it's suddenly going to turn everything upside down—that's a little too much for me to accept."

"You're missing the psychological impact," Henderson said.

"But who besides someone like Matulo would ever launch that thing?"

"Why is there a Matulo?" Henderson said.

"There are always Matulos," Hawkins said.

"When their subjects have too much to lose?" Henderson said.

Hawkins was silent. "Nothing changes that fast," he said. "I'll agree this is going to create a stir, some things will be done, committees and study groups will be created, but that'll die down. An effective defense against the S-27 will be developed and we'll return to the same balance-of-power situation, basically, that we have today, and that is exactly the reason why we have to put some restraint on Marquez right now. We have to assert our authority or else it's going to slip through our fingers."

Henderson shook his head. "That's exactly why we have to encourage Marquez now so we can take the lead."

Hawkins's eyes started wandering as he tried to find the right words to say. "What if that scrap of paper doesn't convince everybody the way you think it will?"

Henderson picked up the piece of paper that contained the memorandum about Reynolds's report and looked at it. "There's no question if Matulo were to actually launch that second missile it would help things considerably but even just considering that makes me sick to my stomach."

"If that happened," Hawkins said, "I think I could see the psychological impact you're talking about."

Henderson looked at the memorandum for a few more moments, then put it down and looked up. "I'm betting this paper is enough," he said, and his expression changed and Hawkins suddenly felt his heart beating a little faster. "It's enough for me. Enough for me to go as far as I can, no matter what happens. I want that meeting with Marquez and I want it as soon as possible. If I have to, I'll leave here tomorrow and go myself, if that tells you something. I want this. Matulo has given me the key and I'm going to use it."

Henderson's face was electric. Hawkins felt a rush of mixed emotions and was lost for words.

General Matulo was taking the news of Reynolds's desertion quite calmly.

"We also found an explosive charge behind the barracks," Lubwa said.

Matulo remained impassive. "Have you searched for others?"

"Yes," Lubwa said. "Without result so far, but we're continuing the search."

"What about Umlika?"

"The dogs lost his scent in the rain," Lubwa said. "He could be anywhere out there. There must be a thousand caves in a square kilometer in that area."

"Very good, Colonel," Matulo said. "Continue your search. When you find him, kill him."

Colonel Lubwa briskly saluted, turned on his heel, and left the General's office. When the double doors had swung shut, Matulo smelled the burning filter in his ashtray and realized he'd forgotten the cigarette he'd been smoking and it had burned itself out. He reached into his cigarette case for another. His hands trembled ever so slightly. He took a deep draw, let his breath out, and turned back to the report he'd been reading about a food riot in Balingo which had had to be suppressed. There were one dead, thirteen wounded—a bad omen, he thought to himself—and two profiteers arrested.

*   *   *

Word that a delegation of Togandans was about to visit a hydroelectric project in Arizona had come to Clarence Bishop like a shot of cool breeze on a hot, sweaty face. The rest was mechanical. The first bullet hit one of the Togandans sitting in the backseat of the State Department car. The second bullet shattered the windshield and hit the driver in the shoulder. The car went out of control, ran off the road, turned over, and came to a shuddering stop. The fourth, fifth, and sixth bullets harmlessly pierced the car's body. The seventh bullet hit the gas tank and the surviving passengers burned to death.

Several hours later, UPI was carrying an announcement from the Sons of Patrick Henry that they were responsible for the Arizona incident and would continue in their patriotic fight against the Togandan menace even if the President of the United States wouldn't.

Dr. Julio Marquez publicly announced that he had received statements from seventeen countries expressing their interest in meeting in Geneva to discuss the special implications of the Togandan situation to the less developed countries of the world. This announcement was released before Marquez was contacted by the United States. The Foreign Minister presented the communiqué to Marquez, who was sitting in his office with a yellowed meerschaum gripped between his teeth.

"I never expected this," Marquez said, taking the pipe from his mouth.

"What do you make of it?" Anquierro said.

"They're worried," Marquez said. "I like Henderson, though. The man has good intentions."

"Could he be ready to make a commitment?" Anquierro said.

"It's hard to say," Marquez said. "They must be taking us seriously."

"Hawkins has a very conservative reputation," Anquierro said. "It worries me that someone like Henderson would change secretaries so abruptly in the midst of a crisis like this and bring in such a person."

"And then send this," Marquez said. "I know what you mean." He thoughtfully chewed on the end of his pipe. "If he's coming here to make threats, that'll go badly for them."

"Will they see it that way?" Anquierro said.

"Henderson must," Marquez said. "That has to be the only safe conclusion." He read over the communiqué once more and then looked up. "How long, do you think, would it take an expert to tell whether our missile is the real thing?"

"But we know it is," Anquierro said, a little surprised. "Our people have been checking it from the beginning."

"That's not what I mean," Marquez said. "How long would it take an outsider to determine that our missile is, in fact, equivalent to the S-27?"

"Offhand I wouldn't know," Anquierro said. "Why? What do you have in mind?"

"I'm just thinking," Marquez said with a vague smile on his face. "An effective way of beginning this meeting might be for someone from the United States to confirm that we have the missile."

Anquierro raised his eyebrows and nodded his head. "Interesting," he said. "Cavalho would probably know. Do you want to get in touch with him or shall I?"

"I think I will," Marquez said. He had a distant look in his eyes as he tapped the stem of his pipe on his lower lip. "I like this very much. I like the way things are going."

"How close is the missile to being completed, then?" Anquierro said.

Marquez returned his attention to his minister. "Very close," he said. "Surprisingly close. These people are extremely thorough and well prepared. It's only a matter of days before they'll be through delivering the parts and we'll have it assembled and operational."

Anquierro pursed his lips and nodded. "Have you learned anything more about the organization that's supplying it?"

"Nothing," Marquez said. "I've tried to have them traced through all sorts of connections, but there's nothing. They're incredibly well organized."

Reynolds was sitting cross-legged on the floor of the cave with a cup of coffee to his right. He finished putting his .375 Magnum back together and slipped it into the holster strapped to his back. He was wearing civilian clothes. His Guard uniform and M-18 were already wrapped in cheesecloth and stored in the chest. He checked his watch, took a last sip of coffee, and tossed what was left in the cup onto the floor of the cave. He stood up and covered the few paces to the stone that covered the mouth of the cave and slid it a few centimeters to the side. He felt refreshed by the cool, clean air that filtered through the tiny opening he'd made. He looked out the hole to see if any of Matulo's men were about, and when he was satisfied there weren't any, he pushed the stone completely away.

He crawled through the opening and stood up. He stretched his arms out and wished he didn't need the canvas jacket he was wearing to conceal his gun and money belt. He pushed the stone back in place and headed toward Balingo, always keeping an eye out for signs of Matulo's men.

Marjorie answered the door wearing blue jeans and a shapeless sweatshirt. Henrik looked shocked. She looked at his dinner jacket for a few moments and the same shocked look appeared on her face.

"I forgot," she said meekly.

He stepped through the doorway. "What happened?"

"I got busy," she said, closing the door behind him.

"Doing what?" he said.

"I'll show you," she said and stepped past him headed for her study. He followed her, out of the short hallway, down a pair of carpeted steps, through her living room. The French doors to the study were open and he noticed the chaotic stacks of paper before they were halfway there.

"What's all that?" he said.

"Research," she said as she entered the study. She went to her desk. "Have a seat."

He looked around, trying to find a clear space to sit, and decided to lift a stack of *Congressional Records* off the chair beside Marjorie's desk. She smiled as he stood, holding the stack, trying to find a place to put them.

"Use the floor," she said.

He turned around, plopped the stack next to the chair, and sat down. "What is this?" he said.

"Research," she said.

"I mean, about what?" he said.

"The extranational," she said.

"You're really hooked on that idea, aren't you?" he said.

"It's the only thing that makes sense unless Matulo did it himself," she said.

He pulled a *Time* magazine, several years old, sitting on the desk, toward himself. "What about dinner?"

She put her hand on his. "I'm sorry," she said. "I guess I just got carried away. I'm not that hungry anyway." She pushed her chair back and started to get up. "Why don't I get something here?"

He shook his head. "That's all right," he said. "I'd rather hear about what you've come up with."

She pulled her chair back in and her enthusiasm of a moment before disappeared. "Well," she said. "To put it very simply—nothing."

"Nothing at all?" he said.

"As good as nothing," she said. "The problem is that every multinational has had its share of problems and the trade-offs are so complex it's virtually impossible to know who's getting stuck. I should know. I've been involved in a few of these deals myself. So I decided to narrow the candidates down. I figured it would probably have to be some company that was highly liquid and controlled by a single individual, someone who would be in a position where they could do pretty much as they pleased without having to answer to stockholders or bankers."

"Sounds reasonable," he said.

"I thought so too," she said. "That narrowed it down to maybe forty or fifty, that I know of. Who knows how many privately owned corporations there are in the world with enough assets to carry this off, and then I started thinking maybe it isn't a specific company after all but a revolutionary group, a strictly idealistic organization. So I started checking to see what known groups might have the capital and the organization."

"And what did you come up with there?" he said.

"One," she said. "An offshoot of the Palestine Liberation Organization called the White Army Group. There were some top leaders who left the PLO and it's suspected they carried away a big chunk of oil money when they did. Where it is, nobody knows."

"Haven't they been suspected from the beginning?" he said.

"Of course," she said, "but no connections have been made. No connections at all have been made. That's what's so maddening about it."

"Then what are *you* going to do about it?" he said.

She looked about to lose her patience. "I just thought I might have another angle on them, that's all."

"Okay," he said, backing off.

She picked up a magazine and tossed it at the corner of her desk. "So that leaves me just about where I started," she said.

"Have you told Henderson about your idea yet?" he said.

"In a way," she said. "I talked to Hawkins. It really doesn't matter to Henderson at this point, though. The only reality for him is that Matulo almost certainly has the missile and the Chileans are hot to get their own, as well as any number of other countries who haven't been as open about it. All he can do is wait to see if Matulo really has the missile and try to get as many people as he can ready to confront that reality."

"What about all those people who might get killed?" he said.

"What about them?" she said.

"You never say anything about them," he said. "Aren't they real to you?"

"Of course they're real," she said.

"Then why don't you discuss your theory with Henderson?" he said. "Maybe he can find that extranational you're talking about."

"And do what?" she said.

"Talk to them," he said. "Find out what's really going on. Make sure the missile can't do any harm."

She turned her head aside and looked toward one of the glass-covered bookshelves, rubbed the back of her neck, and turned back to Henrik. "I'm going to tell Henderson—all right? When I've got the time, because I can tell you right now what it's going to mean to him—nothing. Maybe a week, maybe a month, maybe a year from now it'll mean something, but not now."

"Then what are you so obsessed about?" he said. "If it's so unimportant, what are you doing driving yourself crazy trying to deduce the most likely candidate for this gambit?"

She looked down at her desk and played with a

manila folder. "Because it means something to me," she said softly. "It means a lot to me."

"What does?" he said.

She looked up at him. "Who did all this," she said.

He looked at her askance. "I don't get it."

"Look, Henrik," she said. "I devoted my life to getting the position I had."

Her words evoked frustrating memories for him. "I know," he said.

"And what the hell good was it?" she said.

He looked at her, confused.

"I never did anything," she said. "It was always Henderson. Henderson was the expert on foreign policy. He took all the initiatives, what few there were. Anyone could have done what I did. The man in the moon could have done what I did. And then Toganda came along. It portended something big, and the more I thought about it, the bigger it looked. It's the biggest thing I'll see in my life, and what am I—the incompetent who had to be dismissed."

"I think you're getting a little carried away," he said.

"No," she said, shaking her head. "I'm not. I'm telling it like it is. All my consciously striving adult life all I wanted was to occupy a position where I could do something, where I could affect people's destinies, the world's destiny, even, and I knew I could do it. I knew I had the brains and the guts to do it and what the hell did it get me?"

"I'd say it got you quite a bit," he said.

"Maybe in your terms," she said. "Maybe in other people's terms, but not in my terms."

He waited. "That still doesn't explain why you're so obsessed with this search you're on."

She brushed a lock of brown hair with a slender silver streak in it back from her face. "When Henderson let me know I was out, a funny thing happened. I knew it was coming. I'd even prepared for it. I'd imagined how it would happen, what he would say, what I would say, but aside from a little depression last night, I wasn't upset about it. Actually, I was relieved. I was glad it was over, done, finished.

"This morning I felt great. I even felt a little sorry for Hawkins, and then I started the research. At first I was casual, like sitting down to write a letter to a friend, and then I found myself getting carried away with it and I started thinking: Who is that person behind the Togandan missile? What's that person like? Did that person see all the consequences that I'm seeing now? Was it a conscious, deliberate, far-seeing act to change the world? Did that person really know what he or she was doing? Then I started thinking about Henderson and what he's done. What did he control, really? Those few incidents in the Middle East and Africa he handled—was he really in control or was he really just as much a spectator as I was? And I went on and on and the more I thought about all these things, the more I had to discover who that person was, because I knew I had to meet that person. I had to find out, I had to know what that person was like. Can you see what I'm saying?"

"In a way," he said, "but I can't see what difference it makes. I can see where it would be interesting, like having an interview with Napoleon, but what's it going to prove? That you're a failure? That you missed the boat? That your life took the wrong direction?"

"That's not the point," she said emphatically. "This is different. This isn't just another terrorist act. This goes beyond that."

"Sure," he said. "Someone's risking a lot of lives to make a few more bucks."

"Maybe," she said. "Maybe that's all there is to it. Maybe it is just some tycoon who came up with a clever way of making a little more money."

"Sick way," he said.

"Okay," she said, "but that's what I want to know. I just want to know. For me, personally, because I was a part of it. That's all."

He waited for her. "So where do you go from here?"

"I don't know," she said. "Keep digging, I guess. Try to come up with a way of narrowing the candidates down a little more. I know I'll come up with something. It's just a matter of time."

He started loosening his tie. "Well," he said, "I guess this means I wait again. Do you prefer to work on your own or would you like company?"

She looked at him, startled and a little embarrassed. "Sometimes I wonder why you put up with me," she said.

"Have you ever considered love?" he said.

Julius Senghor was sound asleep, dreaming he was dancing around a blazing campfire, faster and faster, the insistent beat of a drum working him into a frenzy. He woke with a start. There was an insistent knocking on the door to his apartment. He swung his feet out of bed, grabbed a robe, and pulled it around his shoulders as he made his way in early-morning grayness to the door.

"Who is it?" he called out.

"Reynolds," was the muffled reply.

Julius quickly threw the bolt locks, opened the door a crack, and peered out. "Reynolds," he said, and hesitated. "Come on in." He pulled the door open wider and turned on the lights. Reynolds stepped in and threw himself into the nearest chair. Julius gently pushed the door shut and turned around. "What are you doing here?" he said, still only half-awake.

"I'm here to spend the night," Reynolds said with a strained smile. "What's left of it, anyway." He yawned and grabbed his jaw to keep from dislocating it, then shook his head. "Have you got anything to eat?"

Ninth Day

She was rubbing his shoulder, gently, back and forth, making his body sway. He let his head fall back, ecstatic, with his eyes closed, but he had to open his eyes. He had to see her face once again. He strained and at last his eyelids responded. "Julius."

"Are you going to sleep all day?" Julius said.

Reynolds slowly pushed himself up to a sitting position on the sofa, rubbed his eyes, and stretched. "No." He was still wearing his clothes. "What time is it?"

"Ten," Julius said. "I didn't think you'd want me to let you sleep too late."

"Good." He noticed a half-eaten slice of bread sitting on the table in front of him. "That's right." He picked up the slice of bread, left from the night before, and bit into it. "Lot of things to do," he said with his mouth full.

"Did you bring the money?" Julius said.

Reynolds leaned his head back and swung it in a circular motion to loosen his neck. "Yes," he said. "It's in my belt."

"How much?" Julius said.

"Fifty thousand," Reynolds said. He exhaled sharply. "There's more if we need it, but I don't think we will."

"What about the guns?"

"That's all arranged," he said. "Have you got some coffee?"

Julius turned and headed out of the room. "What's the plan now?" he called from the kitchen. "What are you going to be doing? What have you been doing?"

"Get me that coffee and I'll explain it all," Reynolds said.

Julius appeared with a steaming mug in his hand and placed it on the table in front of Reynolds, then sat down on the edge of a chair to Reynolds's right. Reynolds picked up the cup and took a gingerly sip. He wrinkled his face. "Wow. That's strong. What'd you put in there?"

"Sorry," Julius said. "It's left from yesterday. Everything's gotten so expensive, I hate to waste anything."

"So soon?" Reynolds said.

"Where've you been?" Julius said. "Matulo's been giving out free food, free housing. There's rampant speculation and black marketeering. The city is filling up with people from the country."

Reynolds spent a thoughtful moment looking at his coffee. "I didn't think Matulo would get that carried away. Not that much cash and merchandise could have entered the country already."

"It hasn't," Julius said. "It's all speculation, and a good thing, too. I thought this missile thing was going to ruin everything, but fortunately it's not."

Reynolds smiled. "Didn't I tell you to trust me?" he said. "I wanted you to hold off before because you weren't really ready, but now there's nothing Matulo can do to improve his situation and you're the only group that has any organization, except the Guards."

"But the missile . . ." Julius started.

"Is a product of Matulo's desperation," Reynolds said. "Just like the giveaways. I knew he'd get carried away with it, I just didn't think he'd go quite this fast. No matter, though."

Julius gave him a suspicious look. "Sometimes I think you know too much."

Reynolds chuckled lightly. "Don't worry. I'm on your side." He reached under his jacket and unbuckled his belt. "Here's the money," he said as he placed the belt on the table.

"Where have you been?" Julius said.

Reynolds twisted his head to look at Julius. "I was at the palace. I thought I told you."

"You know Matulo?"

"In a way," Reynolds said with an amused tight grin.

Julius lost his patience. "What the hell kind of game are you playing, anyway?" he said. "I ask you straight questions and you give me cryptic answers like you're some kind of holy man. Why can't you just talk straight, like you used to? Or did you? I'm starting to wonder."

"Julius," he said. "Didn't I tell you the last time I saw you that this is for keeps, this is the real thing, this is it?"

"What the hell is that supposed to mean?" Julius said.

"It means it's easy to talk straight when you're just talking," Reynolds said, "but now it's time for action and things aren't so clear-cut."

"Not with you, anyway," Julius said.

"I'm putting the finishing touches together, that's all," Reynolds said. "It's delicate."

"What is?" Julius said. "What is it you're finishing, that's what I'd like to know."

Reynolds held his cup in both hands and slowly sipped at his coffee. He shook his head slowly and put the cup down. "I'll explain everything as it's necessary," he said, and turned to Julius. "Right now, all you have to know is that I've had to go through a lot of complex maneuvering in order to guarantee a successful coup for you, and I'm here to make sure that nothing goes wrong. For instance, you don't even realize that, in reality, what Matulo is doing right now is going against you."

Julius turned his head aside, disgusted. "What are you trying to give me?" he said. "If he hadn't gotten so carried away with this missile power and just let the money slowly roll in, he'd be stronger than ever and then we really would have been in trouble. I've been bluffing my people about the whole situation, telling them it was going to go against Matulo from the beginning and not believing a word of it, just hoping for a sign of weakness. Fortunately it came and I was off the hook, but I was worried. Listening to you almost cost me everything."

Reynolds bowed his head and shook it slowly. When at last he turned to Julius, he had the look of a patient teacher trying to help his over-eager student who'd missed the entire point of the lesson. "The benefits of the missile could only be an illusion. At first, people would be anticipating their bounty, and then when it didn't happen the way they wanted, they would have slowly realized that it wasn't really what they wanted after all. The inflation would have started, but gradually. There would have been a month or more before the real points of friction would have started appearing. That was the way it should have progressed. The fact that it's happening so fast is extremely dangerous for your position. If what you describe as going on is correct, there should be some demonstrating and Matulo should be using the army."

"That is what's happening," Julius said.

Reynolds nodded his head. "I've spent the last few days in the army, including the Palace Guards. The Guards are the key to what I'm talking about. General Mwelo knows what's going on and he's got people like Lubwa to back him up. Matulo thinks they're loyal, but he's kidding himself. They have the discipline and they have the position. Given the right opportunity, they'll move and you'll be out in the cold, and what's going on right now may be just what they need." Julius looked at him skeptically. "Think about it," Reynolds said, and waited for him to speak. "Think what you want, that's the way it is. It means we're going to have to move faster than I thought. Now, there should be a barge coming into Balingo with a load of Japanese motorcycles. Some of the cases have the guns. They have a special marking, a

. . . Get me a paper and pencil and I'll draw it. That'll be easier."

Julius continued staring at Reynolds and showed no signs of getting ready to get out of his chair.

"You want me to hold your hand?" Reynolds said. "Get me a paper and pencil, damn it. Get with it."

Julius slowly got out of his seat and started searching his tiny living room for a paper and pencil.

"I want to set up a mass rally for the Freedom Party in two days," Reynolds said.

Julius stopped where he was and spun around. "Two days."

"It can't be helped," Reynolds said. "We don't have time. At least I don't want to take any chances. Can't you find a simple paper and pencil?"

Julius looked to his side. "Here," he said. He picked a pen off a book and a newspaper off a chair. He slowly walked back to Reynolds and handed them to him, then sat back in his chair. He arched his fingers together and pointed them at his chin with his elbows resting on the arms of the chair. Reynolds was concentrating on the diagram he was drawing.

"I'm getting out," Julius said softly.

Reynolds felt his heart start to pump harder and blood rush to his head. He wanted to burst out in rage but instead slammed the pen down on the table and turned his head to the side. He glared at Julius with so much anger in his eyes that the young revolutionary had to turn his head aside.

"I don't trust you, Reynolds," Julius said. "I don't know what it is, man, but you're doing things that I don't know about, that I don't understand. Either you level with me or I'm getting out, and it's obvious you don't want that. Talk straight now, or forget it."

Reynolds stood up and started anxiously pacing about the room. He was shocked and embarrassed at the way he was acting, the way he was letting his emotions get out of control. He realized he was doubting himself, something he hadn't done in a long time, and he didn't like it. He couldn't tell if Julius was being stupid, obstinate, or just getting more intelligent. He wondered if it was just the strain of the past few days. He pulled a cigarette pack out of his jacket pocket and pulled a cigarette out of it with his lips. Julius nervously shifted his weight in his chair while Reynolds lit his cigarette. Julius was about to say something when Reynolds stopped pacing and lightly sat back down on the couch.

"All right," Reynolds said. "I'll give you the entire plan, straight from beginning to end."

"All right," Julius said.

Reynolds looked straight at him. "I gave Matulo the missiles," he said.

"You what!"

"That's right," Reynolds said evenly. "I arranged to have the plans stolen and the missiles built. One was delivered to Matulo's yacht and the other is in Toganda."

"But you nearly . . ."

"Nearly what?" Reynolds snapped. "Nearly ruined your plans?" He stopped and focused on Julius's eyes. "When I asked you to back off, you weren't anywhere near ready. The reality was that Matulo could have had General Mwelo round up every last one of you and that would have been the last anyone would ever have heard from you again."

"How does that justify . . . ?"

"I'm not justifying anything," Reynolds said. "I'm just telling you the way it is. I haven't ruined anything. You're ready now and I'm here to make sure you win. I've always said I would, and I will, and if you want to hear what I have to say, you can stop interrupting."

Julius shrank into his chair from the intensity of Reynolds's glare and closed his mouth.

"I picked Matulo because I thought he was the best candidate for the missile threat," Reynolds said. "I'd thought of several others—Marquez, for one—but I was afraid they would try to get too involved in it and try to use it with their own personal diplomatic maneuvering. I wanted a simple dramatic demonstration, and with Matulo I got it."

"Why . . . ?" Julius started.

"If you'll give me a chance, I'll explain," Reynolds said. "I contacted Matulo shortly before I persuaded you to put some restraints on the Freedom Party. I did it in a way that I knew would capture his imagination and permit him one of his religious inspirations, and it worked. He agreed to take the missiles and pose his threat just as he's done. I agreed to get more of the missiles into the hands of other countries which could form an alliance with him, but he would be the leader. In exchange, I told him I wanted certain economic concessions, which we would arrange at that time. That was all I asked in return and he accepted it."

"But why . . .?" Julius said.

"The missile crisis is part of a total game plan I devised to avert the imminent global disaster I saw developing," Reynolds said. "What's happening now is something I've seen as an ultimate necessity for some time and I chose to make it happen now. You should know what I'm talking about. We've discussed it enough."

"The fundamental conflict between the haves and the have-nots," Julius said.

"Exactly," Reynolds said. "Every country with its own strategic capability and before it's too late, before a real global conflict erupts. It's the only solution."

"And to do it, you've put an S-27 with a nuclear warhead in the hands of a maniac."

"Precisely."

Julius had calmed down and, for an instant, wondered how it was that he could talk in such cold, impersonal words so easily. "You know, Reynolds, this is really interesting. You talk like you're so concerned about people, yet you're willing to risk the lives of thousands of innocent people just to prove a theory, and it really makes me wonder about something. Who's crazier, you or Matulo? He could be launching that second missile right now and I hate to think where it would land."

"I know," Reynolds said, "but I'm sure he isn't and he won't unless he's pushed too far."

"How can you know that?" Julius said. "How do you know how far 'too far' is?"

"I can't, a hundred percent," Reynolds said. "I know I'm taking a calculated risk, but if things keep going smoothly, there shouldn't be any problem."

"But what if he does launch it?"

"I've considered that," Reynolds said, "and I have a contingency plan."

"What's that?"

"The remaining missile has been fitted with a device which will allow me to redirect it once it's been launched."

"And you're sure it'll work."

"Reasonably."

"What does that mean?"

Reynolds took a deep sigh. "It means Matulo may have had someone check the missile over and found my device. He has people capable of doing it, and if he has, then I won't have any control over it. It'll go wherever Matulo wants it to."

"And if he has and he launches it unexpectedly?"

"Damn it!" Reynolds exploded. "Nothing's perfect. There's always a risk. Life's a risk. I can't be perfect. I'm only human."

"You don't act like it."

Reynolds stood up. He stepped around the table, keeping his eyes on Julius. Julius looked back at him, unintimidated, looking ready to offer a new challenge.

"If you would stop to think for just one minute about what I'm saying and what I've done, you'd realize it's for everyone's good," Reynolds said. "I'm making something happen that might not have happened for years without me, if at all. The Chileans are going to announce that they have an S-27 within a matter of days. The proliferation could be worldwide within a year and Henderson should already be starting to take the lead in handling that new reality. In other words, my plan is working."

"Then why do you need me so badly?" Julius said. "You seem to be doing quite well by yourself."

Reynolds shook his head. "Do I have to spell it all out? Matulo is unstable. There's a chance that I may not be able to control that second missile. Toganda's part in my drama is just about over. All that's left is to get rid of him and leave the control of that last missile in the hands of someone stable, like yourself, and you're the leader of the only organized opposition group other than the Guards, and I'd rather not see General Mwelo get his hands on it."

"But you said you had control of it," Julius said.

"I should have," Reynolds said.

Julius got out of his chair and walked to the other side of the room from Reynolds and turned around. "You're incredible," he said. "What kind of a crazy game are you playing? You risk the lives of people you've never even met like they're pieces on a chessboard. You double-cross Matulo, you double-cross the CIA, you double-cross your own government. Who else are you getting ready to turn on? Me? What's the next step in your plan? How do I know what you're telling me is the truth? How do I know I'm not just walking into a trap?"

Reynolds held his arms out. "Julius," he said, pleading with him. "Just listen to what I'm telling you and you'll see that I'm being perfectly consistent. Liars can't do that and everything I'm telling you fits together. Look at the way you're reacting right now. Could I have told you all this a year ago when I was setting it all up? You think you would have believed

me more then? You think you would have been able
to tolerate me handing Matulo two of the most technologically advanced weapons in the world while in
the back of your mind you kept thinking, 'Maybe he's
wrong, maybe this whole plan is going to backfire?'
Of course not."

"Maybe, maybe not," Julius said.

"All right, maybe not," Reynolds said, "but the fact
of the matter is that what's done is done and the reasoning is consistent and logical if you take the time to
think about it."

Julius slowly made his way back to his seat, turned
on his heel, and let himself sink into the padding.
"Where'd you get the money to do all this?" he said.
"Stavropoulos?"

Reynolds nodded.

"If I replace Matulo, what'll I owe him?" Julius
said.

"Nothing," Reynolds said.

"Nothing," Julius said. "I don't believe that."

"Nothing that won't be to your, and Toganda's,
benefit," Reynolds said. "All Stavropoulos sees in
this is an opportunity for more room to deal."

"He must know that if that missile drops on the
wrong heads, he's going to get hurt when the truth
gets out."

Reynolds returned to the couch and dropped into
it. "He might."

"I guess he doesn't think there's any chance of a
mistake," Julius said.

"He put a great deal of faith in me," Reynolds
said.

"Someone that shrewd doesn't put that much faith
in anyone," Julius said. "You must have convinced
him there was no way that missile could go where you
didn't want it to."

"All right," Reynolds said. "I'll admit I did convince him of that. That was one of his conditions for
backing the plan."

"So who are you conning now?" Julius said. "Me or him?"

Reynolds seethed inside. "Him," he said coolly.

"So you're double-crossing Stavropoulos as well."

"If you want to put it that way."

"Damn it, Reynolds, how else am I supposed to put it?" Julius said. "God, I just don't understand it. We always seemed to get along so well. I liked you. I figured you for a tough, worldly, realistic, intelligent human being, and basically a nice guy, but what you're saying now makes me feel like I never knew a thing about you, really. Who are you? What are you after?"

Reynolds hesitated. For a moment, he thought of being glib, but discarded that. "Have you ever heard of the three ways of winning?"

"What's that?"

"An old Japanese saying," Reynolds said. "There's winning by fighting, there's winning before fighting, and there's winning without fighting. Winning by fighting was never to my taste. Maybe it was because I was never good enough at any one thing to ever excel in comparison to other people. Winning without fighting I never really could understand. It's like a contradiction in terms. To me, it's the same as not winning. Winning before fighting means to have a situation so arranged that once a battle begins, everything moves in its natural way to an inevitable conclusion. That I can understand and appreciate. It has an aesthetic quality to it. To me, it's a challenge, and that's what I'm doing to achieve a worthwhile end."

Julius looked confused. "That's it?" he said. "That's all this is to you, just a game that gives you an aesthetic satisfaction, a thrill like an orgasm?"

"What else is there?" Reynolds said. "Really?"

Julius was stopped. He looked at Reynolds, trying with all his intellectual might to find the right words.

"But everything isn't going exactly the way you wanted it," he said.

"How does someone know a plan is perfect until the plan has been tested?" Reynolds said. "How could I know that every little detail would work out perfectly without ever having done it? But even so, everything is very close to going exactly as I planned it."

"Except for me," Julius said.

"Except for you and a few details," Reynolds said. "But it can still work. If you believe me, we can make the last step work. It's in your self-interest. That's the trick. Each player must satisfy his or her own self-interest. That's the hardest part."

"And when I have the missile?" Julius said.

"I don't understand," Reynolds said.

"Is that it?" Julius said. "Is that the checkmate?"

"Yes," Reynolds said, looking genuinely surprised.

The seconds passed, heavily.

"We're going to have to take the palace by force," Julius said.

"That's right," Reynolds said. "That's what the guns are for."

"Isn't it possible, even likely, that that is exactly the thing that could make Matulo launch the missile that might or might not be under your control?"

"It's possible." Reynolds felt a surge of confidence. "Except for one thing. Assuming Matulo is driven into launching the missile in one last panic-induced fit of insanity by your attack on the palace, it will take a minimum of twenty minutes for him to get it ready and launched from the control panel in his office. If he begins getting the missile ready the moment you attack the main gate, there should be enough time to get to him."

"What makes you so sure of that?" Julius said.

"I've planted several strategic explosives on the grounds," Reynolds said. "One at the main gate as well as one at the barracks nearest the palace and one by his garage so he won't be able to get away. That should create enough confusion, along with a surprise attack, to carry the fight in your favor. The Guards are disciplined, but they've never been confronted by anything like what you'll be doing. You shouldn't have any trouble."

"You're sure they'll go off at the right time," Julius said.

"Completely," Reynolds said.

Julius reached his hands to his face and rubbed his eyes. For a moment Reynolds thought his protégé looked older and wiser than when they'd started their talk.

"I'll do it," Julius said, as though he were agreeing to take out the garbage or sweep the floor.

Reynolds felt another surge of confidence.

Hawkins couldn't keep his hands still. He nervously played with his pen and scribbled on a sheet of paper next to his right hand. Henderson was calm and steady, the steadiest he'd been since the first announcement from Toganda. The mounting pressure and the seemingly steadily worsening situation were presenting more clearly defined challenges, and as the decisions he had to make became more clearly defined, the problems more concrete, the alternatives more focused, one clear-cut plan of action formed in his mind.

"I arranged the expert through Macklin," Hawkins said. "You should have seen him."

"Who?" Henderson said. "Macklin?"

"Yes," Hawkins said, and snorted. "Aside from the four-letter words, he made it quite clear that he was ready to repopulate South America or turn it into a cinder, whichever you wanted."

Henderson grinned, amused. "What happened to him?"

"Toganda," Hawkins said.

"I guess," Henderson said.

Hawkins made a few scribbles with his pen. "I don't mind saying I feel at a real loss for what to do right now."

"Why's that?" Henderson said. "I thought we'd already decided."

"But he's got the damn missile already," Hawkins said.

Henderson leaned back in his chair and folded his arms across his chest. "So?" he said. "What's the difference?"

Hawkins stood up and started pacing around the room. He stopped and turned to face the President. "I don't understand how you can be so calm. You saw what happened when they brought in that guy, what's his name . . . ?"

"Bishop," Henderson said.

"We're lucky there wasn't a full-scale riot," Hawkins said.

"It was staged," Henderson said.

"Maybe," Hawkins said. "But what if it was more than that? And what about that missile confirmation?"

"What about it?" Henderson said.

"It didn't exactly work the way you expected," Hawkins said.

"I know," Henderson said.

Hawkins stood facing the President, his arms folded across his chest. "What are you going to do?"

"What I *have* been doing," Henderson said.

"And you think that's what the People want?" Hawkins said.

"What people?" Henderson said.

Hawkins shook his head in disgust and frustration and dropped his arms to his sides.

"Jim," Henderson said, "I realize you got this post at an awkward time under unusual circumstances, but if you don't calm down, you'll be worthless. If you'd just relax and think about it, you'd realize it's not really as bad as you're trying to make it out to be."

"It's not?" Hawkins said.

"No," Henderson said. "It's not."

Hawkins stepped back to his chair and sat down.

"Have you set a time with Marquez?" Henderson said.

"Two days," Hawkins said.

"Good," Henderson said. "That'll give us time to work on the summit."

"And in two more days Westbrook might have your hands tied completely," Hawkins said.

"He can try," Henderson said. "He's riding a crest right now, but confirmation of the Chilean missile isn't public yet."

"I wish I had your confidence," Hawkins said.

"Nobody's going to cut those Togandan payments off on me," Henderson said. "Not yet, anyway, and when that announcement comes out, nobody'll be stupid enough to. We spend more for one bomber than we've sent Toganda at this point—a lot more—and when people start to get their emotions under control, they'll start thinking like that."

"What about Matulo, though?" Hawkins said.

"What about him?" Henderson said.

"Are we just going to let him get away with it, then?" Hawkins said. "Let the world be run by a madman because everyone's too scared to do anything about it?"

"I don't know why you say that," Henderson said.

"Because it's the truth," Hawkins said. "Every country in the world is so scared shitless, besides us, that the missile is going to land on them, have been from the beginning. You can almost feel the world shudder every time the subject of cutting off payments comes up. At least Marquez is stable."

"You're forgetting about the profiteering," Henderson said, "the black marketeering and the overcrowding in Balingo. The few reports that are leaking out of there are saying one thing—Matulo is letting the situation get out of hand. Nobody can survive very long under that kind of pressure."

"But there's no opposition party," Hawkins said.

"There's always the army," Henderson said.

"What does that change?" Hawkins said.

"It gets the missile out of the hands of a lunatic," Henderson said.

"It could trigger the launch," Hawkins said.

"Maybe," Henderson said.

"Or put it into the hands of a real general," Hawkins said. "Is that really any better?"

Henderson was genuinely surprised. "A lot, I'd say," he said. "At least we'll be able to deal with someone a little more rational and reasonable."

"Who wants to build the best-equipped army in Africa, or something like that," Hawkins said.

"Maybe," Henderson said.

"More like likely," Hawkins said and leaned back into his chair. He shook his head and squeezed his lips together. "Christ, it seems hopeless."

Marjorie had the telephone receiver firmly planted against her ear. "Yes," she said, and looked into the living room where Henrik was sitting with a book in his lap, watching her. She motioned to him and he stood up. "His guest?" she said, and watched Henrik coming toward the study. "What about?" Henrik stopped in front of her desk and she raised her eyes to him. "I see," she said. I don't know." She looked perplexed. "I'll have to think about it. Is there a number I could call . . . All right, I'll be here . . . Okay. Oh, wait. Can I bring somebody with me? . . . Just a friend. . . . No, he's not." Henrik started to open his mouth and she raised her free hand up with opened palm to stop him. "Fine, I'll be here," she said and put down the receiver. She looked up at Henrik with the same perplexed look on her face but with a touch of anticipation in it.

"What was that?" he said.

"Stavropoulos," she said.

"Who?" he said.

"Andros Stavropoulos," she said. "He wants to meet me."

"The billionaire?" he said.

"Yes," she said.

He stepped around the desk and sat down in the chair that was waiting there. "Why does he want to see you?"

"He wants to talk to me," she said. "Two tickets to Greece will be delivered here in about an hour and he's going to call back to confirm."

"Are you going?" he said.

"I don't know," she said. "I'm not sure what to make of it."

"Maybe he's your extranational," he said.

Marjorie thoughtfully cocked her head. "I don't know," she said. "He could be a candidate, but if he is, why would he want to see me?"

"To see if his plan is working?" he said.

"Maybe," she said. "What do you think? You're invited, too."

"I think you've already made up your mind," he said.

Tenth Day

Reynolds's eyes snapped open and he raised his head. Julius was standing in front of the front door, which had just banged shut. "I must have dozed off," Reynolds said groggily. Julius walked toward the kitchen. "Did you get the guns?"

There was a click of a refrigerator being opened, a soft clanking, a slam, and a pop while Reynolds got to a sitting position. Julius reappeared from the kitchen with a beer can in his hand.

"Did you get the guns all right?" Reynolds said.

Julius nodded and belched.

"Any trouble?" Reynolds said.

Julius shook his head.

"Hair up your ass?" Reynolds said.

Julius snorted and went to a chair while Reynolds rubbed his eyes.

"Still not satisfied?" Reynolds said.

Julius took another swallow of his beer. "I didn't think that was relevant."

"It isn't." Reynolds was waking up. He wiped perspiration off his forehead and breathed the dusty air of the small apartment deeply.

Julius rested his arms outstretched on the arms of the chair. "If you want to know what's really getting me," he said, "it's your damn attitude since that discussion we had yesterday. You act like it's all over."

"Basically it is," he said. The early-afternoon sun was beating into the apartment. He nodded toward the beer can. "Is there another one of those?"

"Yes," Julius said.

Reynolds got up and walked into the kitchen. "It's

over for me, anyway," he said as he opened the refrigerator. "For you, it's just beginning." He pulled
out the beer can and closed the door. "There's really
very little for me to do right now. Either everything is
set up or it isn't."

"Aren't you even worried about the way things are
going?"

"If you mean, have I been thinking about it," he
said as he popped open the can, "of course I have,
but the die is cast." He ambled back into the living
room. "You're in the right frame of mind so you'll do
what has to be done. You want the presidency. You'll
do what's necessary. If the Freedom Party is organized
well enough, you'll be successful. If not, you won't.
There's nothing I can do about that now." He sat
down and took a long swallow. "I think you'll make
it, though, and when Matulo's out of the way my
plan will be complete. The loose ends will get
wrapped up and it'll be over. I'll win, you'll win.
What's the point in worrying about it?"

"I wish I could be that cool about it," Julius said.
There was a knock on the door. "Wonder who that
could be." He put his can down on the floor and
walked to the door.

A terrified Anti burst in and quickly shut the door
behind himself. "We've got trouble," he said breath-
lessly.

"What's the problem?" Julius said.

"Police," Anti said. "They're rounding people up."

"Who?" Julius said.

"Kele, for one," Anti said.

"What!" Julius said. "Why the hell is all this happening?"

"A spontaneous demonstration started at that big
housing project," Anti said. "The one you were working on."

"How did that happen?" Julius said.

"I don't know," Anti said. "It just started and
they're going after everybody. They were even wait-

ing for me at my brother's apartment, but his wife signaled me. If I were you, I'd get out of here—fast."

"Damn," Julius said. He walked back to his chair, picked the beer can off the floor, and finished it off. He turned to Reynolds. "So everything's set up. What the hell do we do now?"

"Get out of here," Reynolds said and put his beer can down. "You must have someplace to go."

Julius turned around and looked inquiringly at Anti. "What about the warehouse?"

"I don't know," Anti said. "It might be safe."

"Then let's go." Reynolds got up and pulled his jacket off the back of the sofa.

Julius took a step toward the door, and stopped. "Just to be safe." He turned around and went to the window. With his head by the window frame he said, "They're here."

There was a knock on the door. "Open up. Police."

Reynolds reached down for his gun sitting on the floor next to the sofa.

"They couldn't have followed me," Anti said.

Julius went to the table next to his chair and jerked its drawer open. He pulled out a gun and turned to Reynolds. "What now?"

Reynolds's eyes shot back and forth between the door and Julius. His mouth tasted bitter and his stomach was turning into a knot. "Give up."

The banging on the door became louder and more insistent. Julius looked at Reynolds and Reynolds could feel the hate in his eyes. Julius lifted his gun, aimed it at the door, and fired three fast rounds into it. There was a groan. Reynolds dropped to the floor. Bullets came crashing through wood and Reynolds pumped three rounds into the door.

"What now?" Reynolds said.

A bullet crashed through the window to their backs. Reynolds pulled his feet under him and ran in a crouch to the side of the living room out of line of the one window. Anti was against the opposite wall with his arms up and spread wide, a terrified look in his eyes. There was another series of rounds through the door. Julius was on the floor beneath the window, partially covered by the sofa.

"The bedroom," Julius said and fired two more rounds into the door.

Reynolds walked in his crouch to the bedroom door and looked up to the ceiling. There was a scuttle in the middle of it. There was a groan from behind him.

"Anti!" Julius said.

Reynolds turned around. Anti was writhing and moaning on the floor and there were spots of red on his clothes.

"I'm going to close the curtain in the bedroom," Reynolds said. "When I give the word, get your ass over here."

Without waiting for an acknowledgment, Reynolds turned back around and entered the bedroom. He ran in his crouch the length of the room to the window, pulled the cord, and cut out the sun.

"Now!"

He could hear Julius's footsteps coming toward him and then glass shattered above his head. When he opened his eyes, Julius was crouched in the doorway.

"Well, get it open, damn it," Reynolds said.

Julius nudged a chair into the middle of the floor and a shower of bullets from an automatic rifle crashed through the window. Julius cringed and waited. There was a lull. He jumped onto the chair and pushed up the scuttle. He stood on the chair for a moment with the sun coming through the ceiling and jumped. As his feet slowly disappeared, Reynolds crawled to the chair. As a crash from the living room mingled with Anti's moans. Reynolds shoved his gun into his belt, hopped on the chair, and jumped for the edge of the roof. For a second he was blinded by the sun. He heard footsteps in the apartment and shots, and he was on the roof. He shoved the scuttle shut and turned in a crouch. Julius was up against a false front.

"Where to?" Reynolds said.

Julius pointed to his right. "That way."

Reynolds turned and started running toward the edge of the building. There was a small gap and a drop to the next roof. He stopped and turned around. The scuttle was rising. He pulled out his gun and fired two rounds at it. It fell back down. There was a thud. He turned. Julius was already on the next roof. Reynolds jumped and they ran.

Stavropoulos was reaching out a bare, muscular, deeply tanned arm to help Marjorie up the last step to the deck of his yacht. His smile revealed a mosaic of gold and enamel. "Ms. Timkins," he said.

She took his hand and hopped onto the deck. "Mr. Stavropoulos?" she said. She was struck by his height. Never having met him before, she had assumed he would be at least as tall as herself, but she felt that she was towering over him in her deck shoes, and it unsettled her.

"Can I get through?" Marjorie realized she was blocking the ladder and stepped aside for Henrik to get by.

"Mr. Loomis," Stavropoulos said, extending his hand.

Henrik took it. "This way, please," Stavropoulos said as he let go. He turned around and started walking toward the bow of the ship.

They followed him to a small wrought-iron table and tried to ignore the two heavyset bodyguards who had been escorting them from the airport.

Stavropoulos sat down and gestured to the two remaining chairs. "Please," he said.

They sat down and Stavropoulos motioned for the two guards to leave. Marjorie looked about, feeling the gentle rolling of the ship and smelling the fresh sea air. Henrik had his attention fixed on their host.

A young man with olive skin appeared by Stavropoulos's side.

"Would you care for something to drink?" Stavropoulos said.

"No," Marjorie said. "Thank you."

Stavropoulos turned to Henrik. Henrik shook his head. "Bitters," Stavropoulos said, and the waiter left.

"I want to thank you again for coming," Stavropoulos said to Marjorie.

"I must confess," she said. "I couldn't resist."

Stavropoulos smiled and laughed easily. "I've watched your career for a long time," he said.

"Really?" Marjorie said and felt herself starting to flush.

"You're a very intelligent woman, Ms. Timkins," he said. "I hope your friend appreciates it." He turned to Henrik.

Henrik smiled. "I think I do."

Stavropoulos turned to Marjorie, then Henrik, then back to Marjorie. He seemed unsure of how to proceed and they began to feel uncomfortable. "How would you like to work for me?" Stavropoulos said.

She looked to Henrik, startled, and back to Stavropoulos. "I . . ." she started, "I don't know."

"That was probably unfair," Stavropoulos said, "but then, that's the way I am."

"It's certainly direct," she said.

"Yes," Stavropoulos said. "If you go to work for me, you'll find me very direct."

"I don't know," she said. "I'll have to think about it. I never expected . . ."

"I know," Stavropoulos said. "You're welcome to spend a few days here, both of you, and decide."

The waiter reappeared and placed Stavropoulos's drink next to his employer's right hand.

"I'm afraid I couldn't accept," she said.

The waiter left.

"Don't be so hasty," Stavropoulos said.

"I meant the invitation to stay," she said.

"Why not?" Stavropoulos said.

"There's something I'm working on right now," she said. "Something I have to finish."

Stavropoulos sipped at his drink. "I thought you'd resigned."

"I did," she said. "This is something else, something personal having to do with the Togandan crisis."

Stavropoulos's interest was piqued. "Really?" he said. "What would that be?"

Marjorie hesitated, wondering if she was talking to the object of her search. "I have a theory," she said. She could feel Stavropoulos's cold gray eyes on her and it made her uncomfortable. "About who is really behind the Togandan missiles."

"You mean it's not Matulo?" Stavropoulos said.

"I'm sure it's not Matulo," she said.

Stavropoulos pursed his lips. "Who then?"

"I don't know," she said. "Yet. My theory concerns who that person is."

"This sounds intriguing," Stavropoulos said. "Please go on."

"My theory is that there is a multinational, such as yourself, that wants more freedom in which to operate," she said. "One that feels that the current system of apportioning markets to multinational corporations is too restrictive and unfair."

"And I take it this multinational you're referring to supplied Matulo with his missiles in order to accomplish that," Stavropoulos said.

"Yes," she said.

Stavropoulos rubbed his chin thoughtfully. "Very intriguing," he said. "Go on."

Marjorie felt a lightness in her body as she looked into Stavropoulos's deeply tanned face. "Are you the one?" she said.

A smile broke on Stavropoulos's face instantly. He

took his hand from his face and reached for his glass. He looked aside and his smile disappeared as he turned back to Marjorie. "Yes," he said.

Marjorie felt frozen, floating through space. She swallowed.

"You see, Ms. Timkins," Stavropoulos said, "I don't have much of a government to stand behind me like a General Motors or an IBM and I don't like to be frustrated. I don't like to have to go through complex and sophisticated machinations to run my business. I prefer to be direct and to the point. With the MPCM's, that problem should disappear."

"But Matulo," she said.

"Reynolds's choice," Stavropoulos said, "but a good one."

Marjorie looked at him a moment, stunned, then leaned her head back. "Son of a bitch," she said. "How stupid could I be." She lowered her head and looked at Stavropoulos.

"There was no reason for you to make any connection," Stavropoulos said. "Reynolds has worked for me, many people have worked for me, some of them in your own government."

"Was it Reynolds or you who worked it all out?" she asked hesitantly.

"Reynolds," Stavropoulos said.

"Is he still in Toganda?" she said.

"As far as I know," Stavropoulos said.

"You're sick," Henrik said.

Marjorie and Stavropoulos turned to him.

"Henrik!" Marjorie said.

"It's all right, Ms. Timkins," Stavropoulos said. "Why do you say that, Mr. Loomis?"

Henrik was startled. "You and this man Reynolds are risking the lives of thousands, maybe millions of people, simply in order to improve your business. You've put the most deadly weapon in existence in the hands of a psychotic. If that isn't sick, I don't know what is."

"Mr. Loomis," Stavropoulos said patiently, "I'm genuinely surprised that such a close friend of Ms. Timkins, as I'm sure you are, would see things in such simplistic terms. All I have done is help accelerate an inevitable process. What did you think was going to happen to those missiles once they were developed? Did you really think they were going to remain the exclusive property of the United States for some indefinite length of time?"

"No," Henrik said. "Of course not."

"Oh," Stavropoulos said. "Then who should have been the next country to get them?"

Henrik shrugged and shook his head. "How should I know?"

"I see," Stavropoulos said.

"But it shouldn't have been a madman like Matulo," Henrik said. "Not someone who is totally unpredictable. Would you hand a loaded gun to someone you knew was psychotic?"

"I suppose by your definition I already have," Stavropoulos said. "But I would have to ask you, what's insane?"

"I think you're too intelligent to start playing semantic games," Henrik said. "Insane is insane and you know very well what Matulo is."

"I'm not trying to play semantic games," Stavropoulos said. "I'm quite aware of what Matuto is. Reynolds picked him because he could be counted on to act in the proper manner, nothing else. The point I am trying to make is that I don't see anything inherently more insane in Matulo having those missiles than in the United States having them. What do you think they were developed for—expensive bookends?"

"The United States isn't about to drop an S-27 on some unsuspecting population just to get its own way."

"No," Stavropoulos said. "That's quite true, but isn't the implied threat just as effective and even more insidious in the long run? Is the sanctity of

General Motors more important than the aspirations of a small African country?"

"Who are you to sit in judgment?" Henrik said.

"Just a businessman," Stavropoulos said, "and I'm not judging anyone. I'm only trying to put things in perspective." He leaned back in his chair. "Besides, the innocent people you're referring to aren't in any danger anyway."

"What does that mean?" Henrik said.

"It means the remaining MPCM can be remotely controlled," Stavropoulos said. "Even if Matulo were to launch his missile at some major city, it wouldn't go there."

"You're sure of that," Marjorie said.

Stavropoulos turned to her. "Of course," he said. "What do you think would happen to my prospects if people, when they discovered the truth, blamed me for thousands of deaths? Believe me, I'm a realist first."

"What about Reynolds?" she said. "You said this was his plan. What's he getting out of it? Was it just for the money?"

Stavropoulos shook his head. "Reynolds is basically an idealist," he said. "You should read some of the things he's written. The man's brilliant. He can think and he can do. That's rare. You know, he even predicted your resignation. For him, this will improve the world and it will also give him a very personal victory. He's that simple."

"I don't think I'd call someone like that simple," she said.

"No," he said. "Of course not. I didn't want to give that impression. Obviously, he's a very complex individual. A genius when it comes to international politics, but a genius in a certain sense, though. He sees reality as it is and he wants to control it, but on a vast scale, an ever larger scale. Each project he's worked on for me has been that way. Each one had more far-reaching consequences than the previous one. That's all he's interested in, and there's no middle ground for him. Once he's conceived a project, it has to be completed just the way he wants it. It has to be perfect and he can't be controlled. He even scares me a little at times. The Togandan missile scares me a little, but I like the challenge. After all, I didn't get where I am by not taking any risks. Reynolds is his own man; he has his own goals. At the moment, his goals and mine coincide."

"I see," she said very thoughtfully. "Well, what happens now?"

"We wait," Stavropoulos said, "while the rest of the drama is played out."

"Which means?" she said.

"For me, actually, it's over," he said. "The Chileans will announce within the next few days that they have an S-27 of their own."

"The next few days!" she said.

"Yes," Stavropoulos said.

"And then who?" she said.

"Iran, Namibia, Turkey," he said. "Several others as well. They're all at various stages."

"You should make a small fortune," she said.

"Break even," he said. "That's really all I'm after. Call it public relations. The Togandan demonstration and getting the missile into the hands of a number of different countries is enough for me. That's all I was after from the beginning. Reynolds, however, is still involved in replacing Matulo."

"By whom?" she said.

"A more rational leader," Stavropoulos said. "His name is Senghor, if that means anything."

"It doesn't," she said.

"I didn't think it would," Stavropoulos said.

"What happens to us?" Henrik said.

Stavropoulos turned to him. "What do you mean?"

"We know your secret," Henrik said.

Stavropoulos looked confused for a moment, then burst out laughing in a deep bass rumble. "You think

I'm going to eliminate you or something equally as dramatic, don't you?''

"The thought had crossed my mind," Henrik said.

Stavropoulos shook his head with an amused look on his face. "Secrets aren't worth much these days," he said. "It's only a matter of time before everything will be revealed. What genuinely amazes me is how long Reynolds was able to keep his operations a secret. No, I'm afraid it won't be that long before it's all out."

"Then we're free to go," Marjorie said.

Stavropoulos turned serious and shook his head. "No, not yet. If word got back too quickly to Matulo that he didn't have control of that missile, it might upset Reynolds's plans. I wouldn't want that to happen, even though it really wouldn't affect my interests at this point. I am loyal to my own people, something you should keep in mind when you're considering my offer."

"Are you serious?" Henrik said.

Stavropoulos turned to him. "What?"

"You still think Marjorie would consider going to work for you after what you've just told us?" he said.

"Why not?" Stavropoulos said.

Henrik turned aside, lost for words.

Stavropoulos glanced at his watch. "Well," he said, "I'm afraid I'm going to have to leave you now." He smiled and nodded to Marjorie and Henrik in turn. "The steward will show you your cabin." He pushed his chair back and stood up. "We'll get together again later." He turned around and walked away in short, firm strides.

Julius sat down on the oily, gray concrete, closed his eyes, and leaned his head back against the steel wall of the warehouse. He rested his arm on a piece of wood running the length of a crate to his right. Reynolds was nervously pacing.

"I still want to know why you said 'give up.'" Julius said.

"Instinct," Reynolds said.

"Your instinct stinks," Julius said.

"My instinct would have kept Anti alive," Reynolds said.

"For a firing squad," Julius said.

"Maybe," Reynolds said.

"Admit it, Reynolds," Julius said. "You did it to save your own skin. You figured you'd be sent to Matulo."

Reynolds stopped pacing and faced Julius. "Okay," he said. "Okay, I was trying to save my skin and yes, I had a flash about Matulo. I saw myself talking to him, maybe working something out, maybe working something out for you, too, but that doesn't mean I was about to hand you two over for targets." He turned aside. "Anyway, it's over with."

"You're full of shit," Julius said.

Reynolds's voice rose. "So what have your heroics produced? Here we are. I've got a couple of rounds left, the police are after us, and your organization is shot. What am I supposed to do with that?"

"What makes you so sure I'm finished?" Julius said.

"Instinct," Reynolds said. "And if you think you've got something left to work with, you're crazier than Matulo."

"Maybe," Julius said, pounding his fist on the crate that was loaded with guns, "but I think I can do something with this, and I'm not about to run."

"Fine," Reynolds said. "Maybe I'll make it to your funeral."

Julius stood up. "Reynolds, you make me sick," he said, "but at least you've finally made me realize something. I am on my own. I have been from the beginning and it's about time I started acting like I was, so you can take your advice and shove it. Everyone was told it was going to be tomorrow and it's going to be tomorrow, whether you're with us or not."

"Fine," Reynolds said. "I won't be."

They stared at each other until Reynolds had to turn away.

Julius slowly rubbed the back of his neck. "Tell me something, Reynolds," he said. "What difference does it really make if I replace Matulo or General Mwelo does? Is your ego that sensitive? Does every little piece have to fit together that neatly? Are you that much of a perfectionist?"

Reynolds turned around to face him. "It doesn't make a damn bit of difference now," Reynolds said.

"All you want is to make sure the missile doesn't get launched," Julius said. "Right?"

"You got it," Reynolds said.

"You can lie, cheat, steal, betray your friends, your country, but you stop short at mass murder," Julius said.

"It wasn't part of the plan," Reynolds said.

"That's right," Julius said. "I'm sorry. It's the plan. Everything was supposed to be set up just so, but you blew it and you've got to set it right." He waited for Reynolds to respond. "Can you do it?" he said, taunting him. "Think you can make it, Reynolds?"

Reynolds looked away. "It wouldn't have been any trouble if I hadn't had to count on assholes," he said.

"I guess that's what I am, all right," Julius said.

Reynolds turned back around and they looked each other over, Reynolds with disgust and contempt, Julius with anger and a touch of regret.

"I'm going," Reynolds said. "Do whatever you want." He drew his gun and turned to the warehouse door.

Eleventh Day

Matulo opened the door to his wife's bedroom. His medals glistened in the sunlight from an opened window. She was lying in bed and rolled over at the sound of his approaching footsteps.

"What is it?" she said, sleepy-eyed.

He sat down on a chair next to the head of her bed, his eyes slightly glazed and brooding. She pushed herself up on her elbows and leaned back against the headboard.

"It's time to go," he said.

"Go?" she said. "Go where?"

"Wherever you want to go," he said, staring past her to a papered wall.

"What are you talking about?" she said, a trace of fear in her voice.

"It's over," he said.

She threw the covers back and sat on the edge of the bed looking directly into Matulo's eyes, but he didn't respond. "What's happening?" she said.

"I have no choice," he said. "They refuse to take me seriously. They talk and talk but they don't understand, not really. They just don't understand because they won't believe me, they won't take me seriously. That's why there's nothing else I can do."

"What?" she said.

"It's enough, though," he said. "There's only so much one man can do and I've done enough. I've touched the world, I've conquered the world, for Toganda, for myself, and that's the problem, because no man can conquer the world and hold it. It's never been done, it never will be done, and I

can't do it. I'm too much of a realist to believe I
could even have a chance. I conquered it, though,
and now I have to let it go. I've had my turn, now it's
someone else's."

"What are you talking about?" she said.

"I'm going to go beyond all my predecessors,
though," he said. "That's why I had to tell you this.
These will be some of my last words, and I want you
to remember them. I know you will because I know
you love me. I know you've had to endure a lot. I
couldn't give you what other men could. I hope you
understand. I couldn't. I was chosen and so were you.
It's the sacrifice we have to make."

Her arms and hands were trembling; her mouth,
dry.

"This is what I want you to remember," he said.
"This is what you have to tell people. I will not fight
to the bitter end. I've conquered the world but I
know I can't hold it, but I will make my final gesture,
my last statement in action, freely. I'm under
pressure, I know, but I could stay. I could stay for
years, even. I could hold the world, but I won't. I can
see what's happening and I have to make a change
that will be decisive, and once the decisive step has
been taken, then all is over for me. I know that. I'm
fully conscious of it and that is what puts me above
all the others—Napoleon, Hitler, Stalin, Caesar. I will
not be forced and I will not stay beyond my time. I
will make my statement and be gone."

"Please," she said. "Please tell me what you're saying."

A smile played across his lips. "I'm also going to
tell you what confirmed it. This is something else I
want you to remember. It was the key to my insight
but something that probably no one else in this entire
world would have, or could have, seen or understood.
To most it would be trivial, but to me it told an entire story. It spoke volumes more eloquently than
Jesus. Clarence Bishop. Clarence Bishop. His name is

fused to my brain. He was the catalyst that brought it all together."

"I don't understand," she said.

"I'm not surprised," he said. "Very few could. Maybe no one, no one but me. It may be a hundred years, a thousand years, before historians will understand this one small piece of information, how it connects to events that came before and after, how it affected the course of events for hundreds of years to come. It's so hard to say. History is so full of these seemingly minuscule bits and pieces, yet these same bits and pieces control our destinies." He lapsed into silence.

She waited, feeling chilled and frightened and confused. "But what about him?" she said. "What did he do?"

"He was let out on bail," Matulo said. "That was all. Such a small thing. I imagine there were very few who even thought twice about it. Of course, the bail was set quite high, over a million dollars, but that's not the important point. What is important is that it was allowed and that small fact has told me what I have to do. I have not been taken seriously; I have not been believed. I will be betrayed and I will be forced to act and that is why I will act first, calmly and rationally, before I'm forced." He stood up.

She hesitated, then looked up. "But what are you going to do?"

His eyes focused on her and opened wider in surprise. "I'm going to launch the missile, of course," he said.

Her body trembling from fear and uncertainty, she kept her eyes on his. "Where?" she said. "When?"

"I don't know where yet," he said. "I'm going to meditate first, but it will be today. I'll launch it today."

"And me?" she said.

"You can go," he said. "Go where you wish. Your chosen time is over here, as mine is." He turned abruptly and left the room in rapid, short strides.

She stood up, slowly, and touched the short, tight braids of her hair with her fingertips, gently, and turned to look into the mirror above her dresser and felt lost.

Henderson held a news conference in which he presented his five-point plan for initiating a massive redistribution of wealth throughout the world. He explained why it was necessary and why it couldn't be put off any longer. He announced that the Chileans were reported to have an S-27 and that there were unconfirmed reports of one being assembled in Pakistan. He was asked about Marjorie Timkins's resignation. He admitted that it had been a difficult decision for him to make, but both Marjorie and he had agreed that it was the best decision under the circumstances, taking all factors into consideration.

Clarence Bishop went with his friends to a mini-celebration of his victory over the Togandans. Dr. Julio Marquez authorized the delivery of ten million dollars worth of gold bullion to Fred Somerville. Kunthile Kantho went to the funeral of the Secret Service agents who had died with his associates. Sithele Mulele, after careful deliberation, put a bullet through his head in his New York apartment.

Amdida Matulo had completed his meditations and two massive concrete doors began their relentless movement outward to expose a man-made wound in the side of Mount Entike and a thousand-odd kiloton, indefensible pillar of death with a modified fan-jet at its tail—filled with enough electronic equipment to enable it to fly as low as forty meters above ground with the use of radar, laser scanning, triangulation from satellite signals, and inertial navigation and to land on any preprogrammed point with a radius of fifty meters, topped with a five-kiloton nuclear warhead—to the light of day.

* * *

Henrik pulled his windbreaker off and tossed it onto an antique walnut chair. "Stavropoulos is something else," he said.

Marjorie dropped onto the circular bed, interlocked her fingers behind her neck, and looked up to the planked ceiling. "I know," she said.

He walked over to the bed and lay down beside her, his head propped up on his hand. "You're really impressed, aren't you?" he said.

She turned her head to the side to look at him. "With what?"

"Stavropoulos," he said.

She turned back to looking at the ceiling. "Shouldn't I be?"

He rolled onto his back. "I don't know," he said. "He seems a little sick to me."

"We all have our neuroses," she said.

"More or less," he said.

"He's helped a lot of people," she said.

"He's also destroyed a lot of people," he said. "Maybe thousands in a single blow in the near future."

"Why do you say that?" she said.

"You really think that missile is a hundred percent fail-safe?" he said.

"Yes," she said.

"I don't believe you said that," he said.

"Why not?" she said.

He rolled back onto his side. "Wake up, Marge," he said. "You're the one who always insisted Matulo was smarter than people were willing to give him credit for. Do you really think he hasn't had that missile checked over from top to bottom? If you weren't so hypnotized by Stavropoulos, you'd accept that. Hell, Stavropoulos knows. I can see it in his eyes."

She rolled onto her side to face him. "I know that," she said. "You asked if the missile was fail-safe, and it is. Whether it goes or not, Stavropoulos has still won. That's what I see in his eyes."

He looked at her as though she were a stranger. "You want to work for him, don't you?"

She pushed herself up and off the bed, walked to the other side of the cabin, and dropped into a chair, facing Henrik. "Why shouldn't I?"

He sat up on the edge of the bed. "That's a good question."

"Reynolds did," she said.

"That's true," he said. "Jealous?"

"A little," she said. "I can't get him out of my mind. I keep picturing him, especially with Matulo. I keep seeing him chauffeuring Matulo when he made the proposal, the cap and the uniform, Matulo amazed, shocked, inspired, manipulated. It's incredible. The timing, the positioning, the planning, the phrasing. It was perfect."

"Nothing's perfect," Henrik said.

"Of course not," she said. "It was good enough, though. That's what matters."

"You wish it would have been you," he said.

"No," she said with a shake of her head. "I'm not black and I'm not a man."

"Something equivalent, anyway," he said.

She started examining her fingernails, one by one. "Am I a loser?" she said. "Is that it? Am I the kind of person who spends the better part of a lifetime preparing for that big chance and when it comes along blows it? I came here looking for a certain individual and I found him, not in the flesh, but I know who and where he is. I wanted to find that person because I wanted to gain control, and that was the first step, and now what do I have? I'm more helpless than ever. Hell, I would have been better off if I'd stayed with you."

"You know that's not ture," he said.

"Why?" she said.

"You wanted to pursue a career, a dream," he said,

"your own way. What else is life worth living for?"

"To end up like this?" she said. "Waiting out the biggest event of my lifetime totally helpless to affect it in any way?"

"Why can't you just accept it?" he said. "There was nothing you could do."

"How do I know that?" she said.

"You don't," he said.

"That's some comfort," she said.

"If you want comfort, you came to the wrong person," he said.

"I guess I did," she said, and stood up. She turned around, walked up to a small table set against the wall, and lifted a glass of water to her mouth.

"Why don't you find some other way to torture yourself," he said. "Something less depressing."

She put the glass down. "Why don't you go to hell!" She spun around. "Damn it," she said. "I could have done what Reynolds did. Not in the same way, but I could have forced the issue."

"You're not ruthless enough," he said

"Well, goddamnit," she said. "maybe it's about time I got a little ruthless."

"That's an idea," he said.

"That black bastard," she said. "I'm as smart as he is."

"I'm sure you are," he said.

"I can be just as gutsy as him," she said.

"I'm sure you could," he said. "What's your point, though?"

Her expression changed. "What do you mean?"

"Does this mean you've had your catharsis?" he said. "Where has all this gotten you?"

"I don't know yet," she said.

"Are you going to work for Stavropoulos?" he said.

"I haven't decided," she said.

"Then what?" he said.

"I don't know yet," she snapped. "All I know is that I'm going to do something."

"What?" he said.

"Something big," she said. "I don't know what."

"Like Reynolds," he said.

"Yes," she said. "Like Reynolds."

"And what will that get you?" he said.

She looked at him, uncomprehending and incredulous. "What are you getting at?" she said. "What do you mean, what'll that get me? Satisfaction, I imagine. What else is there?"

"You can get that in bed," he said.

She was amazed and disgusted. "Don't play games."

"I'm not," he said, and thought a moment. "Well, maybe I am in a way, but it just seems like history repeating itself."

"What does that mean?" she said.

"You sound just like you did when you got the appointment from Henderson," he said.

"I thought you just said you thought that was the right thing for me to do," she said.

"Then," he said. "I'm sorry, Marge, but I just can't see the sense in coming out of this the same way you were three years ago. Hasn't all this affected you at all?"

"Of course it has," she said. "It's shown me where I went wrong. I limited myself too much, while Reynolds didn't. That's why he's won, and I've lost—so far."

He shook his head slowly from side to side. "You've lost, all right," he said. "There was a time when I thought you were going to come out of this a real winner, but I guess it just couldn't work out that way."

"And you haven't changed a bit either," she said. "You still have to act like you know so damn much more than anyone else, like you know some great secrets that us lesser mortals can't comprehend. Well, screw it. You can take your crummy little practice and stuff it. Those people might feel like worshiping you, but I don't."

"I know," he said. "I didn't expect you to." He stood up. "I'll go see if Stavropoulos has another cabin for me."

"Okay," she said.

He walked over to the antique walnut chair and picked up his windbreaker.

"I didn't mean it," she said.

"What?" he said, turning around.

"About your practice," she said.

"I know," he said.

"It's not crummy," she said and hesitated. "I respect you, Henrik." She hesitated again. "I love you."

He looked at her, relaxed and thoughtful.

"It just doesn't work," she said. "I wish it could, but it won't."

He shrugged. "Maybe some day it will."

"And maybe not," she said, and smiled warmly.

"Maybe not," he said, and returned the smile.

She walked up to him and put her hands on his shoulders, lightly. "Why don't you stay?"

He tossed the windbreaker back behind himself toward the walnut chair. "Okay," he said, and chuckled lightly.

She reached her head up slightly and touched his lips with hers while his hands found her waist and her fingers touched his neck.

"Why do you have to admire Reynolds so much?" he said.

She pulled her head back. "What?"

"Why do you have to admire him so much?" he said.

"I don't," she said.

"You know you do," he said.

She let her arms fall to her sides and stepped back. "All right, damn it, I do."

"Why?" he said.

She took several steps toward the bed and turned around. "Because he took control, he made things happen in a way I've never been able to do. Can't you see that?"

"No," he said. "Not really. All I can see is someone who has gone to enormous lengths to take enormous risks to accomplish something that could have been accomplished in other, safer, saner ways."

"Maybe," she said. "But maybe what he's accomplishing couldn't have been done any other way."

"You're so hung up on how he did it, I can't see how you can even evaluate that," he said.

She turned away from him. He started to reach again for his jacket when she turned back around. "Damn it, what's the point, then? What am I supposed to do? Struggle to occupy a position for the prestige? What the hell good is that?"

"Can't you even imagine a middle ground?" he said.

"What middle ground?" she said.

"Sometimes you control, sometimes you're controlled," he said. "Why can't you just accept that?"

"Why do I have to?" she said.

"Because that's all there is," he said.

"No," she said. "That's not all there is. There's winning and there's losing and I intend to be a winner."

"Like Reynolds," he said.

"That's right," she said.

He took hold of his windbreaker. "You can have it," he said. He tossed the windbreaker over his shoulder and turned toward the door.

"Wait," she said.

He turned around. "What?" he said.

"Please," she said, and hesitated. "Stay."

"So we can fight it out?" he said.

"No," she said. "No. I don't want to fight with you."

"Then why do you try so hard?" he said.

"I don't," she said.

He smiled and chuckled. "But you do," he said.

"No," she said, and looked confused. "Damn it,

why do you always have to get off on some stupid tangent?"

"Because you insist on turning everything into a contest," he said. "I just don't feel like being a contestant."

"Make sense," she said.

"I am," he said.

She closed her eyes. "Would you please just stay?" she said softly.

He watched her, considering, till their silence was broken by the sounds of scuffling feet on the deck above them. "How can I say no?" he said.

She opened her eyes and smiled, relieved. The sounds of running feet became more insistent. She cocked her head to the side. "What's that?" she said.

"I don't know," he said. They waited. "Let's find out." He reached his hand to the doorknob and pulled the door open. A sailor was coming toward him. "What's going on?" The sailor looked at him blankly and shook his head. Marjorie touched his shoulder. "He must not speak English. Let's go on deck."

As soon as they reached the deck, they spotted Stavropoulos sitting at his wrought-iron table with a drink in his hand, squinting into the sky.

"What's going on?" Marjorie said as they approached him.

Stavropoulos turned to them with a concerned look on his face. "Matulo's launched it," he said coolly.

They stopped in front of the table. "He has?" Marjorie said. "Have you got control?"

Stavropoulos shook his head slowly. "We've already tried a course correction, and nothing happened. Matulo has control."

"But . . ." she said.

"There's nothing more I can do," Stavropoulos said. "Nothing anyone can do. It will go where he wants it to." He turned his eyes back to the sky. "There's a possibility it will fly over us."

Marjorie held Henrik's arm in her hands, tightly, and rested her cheek against his shoulder as they both looked up and squinted against the sun.

Reynolds leaned back against the trunk of a tree and leaned his rifle across his knees. He touched his false mustache to make sure it was still in place and then reached down to his side for the triggering mechanism of his explosive charges. It was a small green box with a toggle switch on its top. He placed it in his lap and turned his head to the side to watch across the clearing for the sentry. Several minutes passed before the Togandan soldier appeared. He walked slowly, his rifle slung over his shoulder. Reynolds picked his green box up in his hands and held it while the sentry slowly moved out of sight, then flipped the switch, tossed the box aside, grabbed his rifle, and jumped to his feet. He took one step toward the clearing and stopped, frozen. Nothing had happened. There had been no distracting explosions. Reynolds brought his feet together and stood, his rifle hanging at his side. He stared at the electrified fence through the concealing foliage of the forest's edge and breathed slowly and evenly, wondering what to do. Minutes passed. The sentry reappeared, going in the other direction. More minutes passed while Reynolds's mind raced through one plan after another. The sentry reappeared and when he was out of sight, Reynolds started walking forward, out of the forest's protection. He looked to his right for the sentry, saw no one, and sprinted toward the fence. The depression beneath the fence was still there. He pushed his rifle through and crawled after it on his back. Safely on the other side, he stood up and grabbed his rifle. As he turned toward the palace, he noticed an unexpected sound, and stopped. There were rifle shots and a soft rumbling from the direction of the main gate. Reynolds considered it for a few moments and then a broad smile broke on his face.

"All right," he said softly and started making his way through the forest.

As he neared the next clearing, he could see the guards running in the direction of the main gate and he knew he must have been right about the rumbling and the gunfire—Julius had managed to get his people together and had attacked after all. Reynolds stopped behind a tree by the edge of the clearing and watched the guards running toward the gate, their rifles in their hands.

"Stupid," Reynolds said softly.

The guards had disappeared from the clearing. Reynolds regripped his rifle and started running. He stopped behind one of the barracks and looked toward the palace. There were still four guards in front of the palace entrance. Reynolds paused behind the cover of the barracks to consider. He looked to his right, to his left, behind, and around, and still there was no one else in sight but the four guards by the palace entrance. Reynolds slung his rifle over his shoulder and walked out into the sight of the four Togandan soldiers. He walked directly toward them in strong, confident strides, giving the appearance of being involved in something important and official. His right hand rested on the butt of the Magnum holstered at his hip. The four guards each had their attention on Reynolds with quizzical expressions on their faces as he neared them. One of them took a step toward Reynolds and was about to speak when Reynolds drew his Magnum and fired four fast rounds, then sprinted through the moans and sprawled bodies toward the entrance, up the semicircular steps three at a time. One of the doors to the palace started to swing open. Reynolds crouched on the first landing and fired again. A Togandan body slumped out onto the next landing. Reynolds raced up the second flight of steps to it. He crouched, gun in hand, and peered into the entrance hall. A corner of a face appeared from behind a doorway and just as quickly disappeared. Reynolds glanced back behind himself, saw no one, and hopped over the slumped body into the hallway, wondering where the second guard to Matulo's office was. He walked forward, slowly, planting each step firmly and solidly on the inlaid floor, his gun in hand, his eyes darting from point to point over the walnut and ebony woodwork.

He reached Matulo's double doors with only the sound of his breathing and the muffled rumbles and cracks of the fighting outside in his ears. He felt more exposed than ever in his life. His stomach was a hard knot. He pushed open one of the doors, stepped in, to the side, went down to his knees, and raised his arms to Matulo's desk with his gun held in both hands. Matulo was alone in the room, sitting behind his desk, his eyes fixed on Reynolds. Reynolds glanced to where the large landscape should have been on the wall. It was gone and in its place was a control panel. Reynolds's breathing quickened and he fixed his eyes on Matulo.

"It's gone," Matulo said.

"When?" Reynolds said.

Matulo's popeyes gazed blankly at the wall above Reynolds. Reynolds stood up and ran to the control panel. He looked it over, trying to make sense of the various dials and their settings.

"It's airborne," Matulo said. "The controls are locked."

Reynolds swung around. Matulo had turned in his chair and was watching him.

"Where's the other guard?" Reynolds said.

Matulo shrugged.

"You son of a bitch," Reynolds said with his teeth clenched.

"I've played my part," Matulo said. "I've won my last battle. The missile will land where I've chosen and now I'm ready to die." He hesitated with his eyes fixed on Reynolds's. "You may have the honor."

"Where?" Reynolds said. "Where have you sent it?"

"Balingo," Matulo said.

Reynolds's mouth dropped open. "You what!"

"They betrayed me," Matulo said. "So many betrayed me—you, the United States. You all lied and wouldn't believe me, but my own people betrayed me the most of all. It wasn't easy. I meditated and prayed for hours, and I didn't want to believe it at first, I didn't want to accept it, but it was the only answer I could find. I love my people. That was why I did all this—for them. I wanted them to be prosperous and happy, but all they did was try to take advantage of it. They let their greed control them. They didn't deserve what I was bringing them, what I was bringing all people, everywhere. They, most of all, should have understood, but they didn't, and so it's only just that they should perish for their cupidity. It's unfortunate. It makes me very sad. You can never know how sad, but it had to be done. I had to do it, and now it's finished." There was a glistening in Matulo's eyes.

Reynolds felt a wave of relief. "But you didn't have control of it," he said. "You couldn't have, because if you had and had already launched it, Balingo would have been destroyed already. We would have heard it." Reynolds relaxed and smiled, satisfied with himself. "I've done it."

"The missile will go once around the world," Matulo said calmly, "to demonstrate beyond a doubt how vulnerable everyone really is."

Reynolds stared at him. Something in his stomach rose and he felt his head about to fly off his shoulders. "You bastard!" he shouted, lifted his gun, and pulled the trigger.

Matulo's head jerked back. Bits of brain and blood spattered on the oak windowsill. His body twisted and dropped to the beige carpet.

Reynolds's hands were trembling. He let his gun fall to the floor and reached for a wooden chair sitting next to the desk. He swung it around, above his head, with a moan like a small wounded animal, and crashed it into the control panel. There was a brief spatter of sparks. The chair splintered and collapsed and he let the remains drop to the floor. He took a step toward the wall and closed his eyes.

"*God!*" he screamed. "*Damn!*" and slammed his clenched fist into the plaster. He broke through to the wood lathing. Pain shot up his arm and through his body. He winced. There was a bang behind him. He spun around.

There was a man in civilian clothes standing in the open doorway to Matulo's office. He was holding a rifle already trained on Reynolds.

Reynolds raised his hand. "No!"

The first bullet passed through Reynolds's stomach and he doubled over. The second bullet entered his left temple, shattered his jaw, and splintered a strip of oak trim.

The man in civilian clothes lowered his rifle and looked around the office. He took a step forward and then turned around at the sound of approaching footsteps. Julius appeared in the doorway holding an automatic in his hand.

"What happened?" Julius said and stepped past the man with the rifle. He spotted Matulo's head behind the desk and the motionless Togandan soldier's body.

"I shot the soldier," the man said. "I thought he had a gun. Matulo was already dead."

Julius glanced again at Reynolds's body and stepped toward it. He stooped down, resting his arms on his knees, and examined the face wedged unnaturally against the floor. "Reynolds," he whispered.

"What was that?" the man said.

"Nothing," Julius said, and stood up. He turned to his follower. "Take them out."

Suddenly, light filled the office, so intense they had to close their eyes and cover their faces with their arms.